PENGUIN BOOKS

THE RAKEHELLS OF HEAVEN

John Boyd was born in 1919 and brought up in Atlanta, Georgia. He was commissioned into the U.S. Navy in 1940 and served in northern Russia, England, Japan, and the Philippines. He was the only junior officer mentioned in Samuel Eliot Morison's naval history of World War II. After Mr. Boyd's marriage in 1944 he received his degree in history and journalism at the University of Southern California. He is the author of nearly a dozen science-fiction novels, including *The Last Starship from Earth*, *The Pollinators of Eden* (both also published by Penguin Books), and, most recently, *The Girl with the Jade Green Eyes*. John Boyd lives with his wife in Los Angeles.

A Knight of ghosts and shadows
I summoned am to tourney
Ten leagues beyond the wide world's end.
Methinks, it is no journey.

—Tom o' Bedlam

THE
RAKEHELLS
OF
HEAVEN

by

JOHN
BOYD

PENGUIN BOOKS

Dedicated to Louise the Light Bender Baldwin

Penguin Books Ltd, Harmondsworth,
Middlesex, England
Penguin Books, 625 Madison Avenue,
New York, New York 10022, U.S.A.
Penguin Books Australia Ltd, Ringwood,
Victoria, Australia
Penguin Books Canada Limited, 2801 John Street,
Markham, Ontario, Canada L3R 1B4
Penguin Books (N.Z.) Ltd, 182–190 Wairau Road,
Auckland 10, New Zealand

First published in the United States of America by
Weybright and Talley, Inc., 1969
First published in Canada by Clarke,
Irwin & Company Limited 1969
Published in Penguin Books 1978

LIBRARY OF CONGRESS CATALOGING IN PUBLICATION DATA
Upchurch, Boyd.
  The rakehells of heaven.
  Reprint of the 1969 ed. published by Weybright and
Talley, New York, with new pref.
  I. Title.
[PZ4.U63Rak 1978]   [PS3571.P35]   813'.5'4   78–928
ISBN 0 14 00.4877 4

Printed in the United States of America by
Offset Paperback Mfrs., Inc., Dallas, Pennsylvania
Set in Caledonia

PREFACE TO THE PENGUIN EDITION

The following novel is one of a trilogy based on classic myths. Insofar as a writer plans for the marketing of his books, I chose mythic themes in hope of sounding echoes in the racial memory of readers. Such a scheme may sound a trifle grandiose, a form of Jungian commercialism, but it has a defensible rationale. As Carl Sagan implies, the eons-old reptilian complex of the human brain may retain neural patterns fixed on it by our terror of dinosaurs, our memory of dragons, which may well be the chthonic source of science fiction's bug-eyed monsters. Then, too, there was the realization that a story that survives for three thousand years must hold a permanent and compelling interest.

Such stories did for me, so I rewrote them in a futuristic setting, at times changing tragedy to comedy, and serious social comment to satire. Aficionados of science fiction know the pleasure of reading in the genre. There was also a great pleasure in writing these tales.

One of the problems in attempting to define science fiction is that the genre is too versatile, but its openness is a boon to writers. A free-form art in style and substance, the genre invites wanton wiles, requires little research, and is open to sly plagiarisms. Here, too, a writer may indulge his weakness for extravagant metaphors.

My interest in science fiction evolved from a boyhood spent reading pulp magazines after being given impetus in the direction of science fiction by Jack London's *The Star Rover*. The interest took a long time to incubate into action. I was forty-seven before I submitted a science-fiction story for publication, and the idea for the story had germinated for almost twenty years.

Rarely does a writer know the day or the hour when a story idea comes to him, but the idea for my first story came between two and three o'clock on a Friday afternoon in late April, 1946. I was sitting in a sociology class at the University of Southern California, listening to the involved, obfuscating, and nonsubstantive jargon of the professor, when it struck me that the language of sociologists was a fitting subject for satire. At that moment I knew I had the subject for the story, if not the form.

A short time later, a story appeared in *The Saturday Evening Post* dealing with a theme close to an English major's heart, the fictional re-creation of the life and art of a blind Homer of the spaceways. The tale was Robert Heinlein's unforgettable, unforgotten "The Cool Green Hills of Earth," and I had found the form for my satire—futuristic.

Hoping for a maximum of money for a minimum of effort, I wrote the idea in the form of a radio drama slanted for the then popular *Skippy Theater*. The drama described a young man, Haldane, on trial for impregnating a girl outside his own profession in an overpopulated world where human beings were bred to serve the needs of the state. The judge and jury were sociologists, and Haldane's lawyer was faced with the task of interpreting his client's lucid and straightforward testimony into the involved syntax of sociologists in order to make Haldane's motives understood to the judge and jury.

I thought the finished play was the most scintillating bit of social comedy since Sheridan. Surprisingly, the producer of the radio show did not callously disagree. He sent a letter with the returned manuscript, expressing his regret that the play did not fit his show's format and asking me to submit more of my work. But the play, then called *The Fairweather Syndrome*, constituted my entire oeuvre. With it, I shot my wad.

I threw the manuscript away but could not rid myself of the idea. After I left school and went about earning a living, I added mystic dimensions to the plot, further complications, more humor and sadness. Not writing the story, merely toying with it as the concern over the population explosion made the central idea more germane, I decided to write a science-fiction epic along Miltonian lines which, instead of justifying the ways of God to man, would justify the ways of a god to a man. It's easy to write an epic in the imagination; working it out on paper is more difficult.

This was a time-track novel, however. It occupied a time parallel to, and at points coinciding with, our own times, but different. The hero was still Haldane, but now he was a mathematician who grew interested in literature. The device allowed me to rewrite and to revise famous poems at my pleasure and to quote great works from my memory without having to check the source.

One of the delights in writing the narrative came in the creation of two original poems that the plot demanded. Derived from Yeats and Shelley, the poems, in my opinion, were well wrought, at least on a par with the middle works of Robert W. Service and Edgar Guest.

Finally, to rid myself of an incubus, I finished and typed

the novel. Looking around for a title—I did not wish to call it *The Fairweather Syndrome* because "syndrome" was not a word of general currency—I spotted *The Last Train from Atlanta* on my library shelf and considered it a good omen, since Atlanta is my native town. I called my book *The Last Starship from Earth*. It was a happy theft because it was a title in line with a paradox in the story: My last starship had lifted off from Earth some time around 34 A.D. or 1968, depending on the time track. Heinlein liked the work well enough to endorse it, to my knowledge the first time he ever endorsed a novel, and it was fitting that he should, since his story had helped foster the tale.

The mythic connotations of man's fall from grace seemed to work with the first novel, so in planning the second I unabashedly borrowed the myth of Phaedra. The heroine was named Freda, and her younger, illicit lover, Hippolina. I culled one of the tale's climactic speeches almost intact from Racine's *Phèdre*, and why not? He took the idea from Euripides.

Here again I attempted to infuse the narrative with the poetic shimmerings of "The Cool Green Hills of Earth," but it is harder to write a poetic novel than to write a poetic short story. Sustaining a unified style for *The Pollinators of Eden* was made even more difficult by the fact that the last book I read before beginning the novel was Oriana Fallaci's *When the Sun Dies*, and her stylistic tricks kept popping up from my subconscious like plums from Jack Horner's pudding. So I used them, too.

In the classic myth, Phaedra, remorseful over her incestuousness, strangles herself. In creating Freda, the thinking man's ideal woman who could quote Shakespeare while making love, I grew so charmed by her I could not submit her to strangulation. In fact, I destroyed Hippolina to keep him from getting to her, so reluctant was I to let her submit to the caresses of another man. She was mine. John Wyndham solved the problem. When Freda finally yielded, it was to a lesbian orchid on a planet of ambulatory plants.

I loved the paradox in the title *The Pollinators of Eden*. Logically there could have been no pollinators in Eden. Once Adam and Eve discovered the process of reproduction, there was no longer an Eden. They were ejected for their "sin."

If the books in this trilogy were characters from Shakespeare, *The Rakehells of Heaven* would have to be Edmund from *King Lear*. It was a whoreson of science fiction, but there was great sport in its making.

Initially the story was based on the myth of Prometheus, but my hero was to bring to men not fire but the truth of their origins, as XYY chromosome-bearers who were cast out of Heaven. Following the classical pattern, my Prometheus was to be torn by the Furies at the denouement, but strange things happened on the way to the denouement.

Two space scouts from Imperial Earth land on a planet that might have been the native home of mankind and the origin of man's concept of Heaven. The scouts, an atavistic Southern Baptist and an atavistic Irish Catholic, are appalled at the tolerance and permissiveness of the nearly human society they find on the planet and set out to institute a more rigid system of morality and ethics among the beings. Conflict develops between the Earth men over the form the "conversion" is to take.

The story was told from the viewpoint of the Southerner, a Junior Johnson of the spaceways, and in the vernacular of the "good old boy." As the plot developed and the characters emerged, my sympathies shifted from the Southerner to the Irish con artist, and I found the style, "Southern rhodomontade," a sheer delight. At times I would awaken my wife in the wee hours of the morning, chuckling over some riposte between the characters.

Gradually the mythic overtones of the story faded, and the Irishman won first place in my affections. He remains in Heaven—a self-convert to Judaism, apparently—while the Southerner, believing himself a murderer, is exiled back to Earth. Ramming his starship back through space, he attempts to exceed the speed of light, prove the Grandfather paradox, and abort the mission before it starts; and he fails, by a space of a few days, but it's a wild ride he takes.

Again on Earth, he is torn by inner Furies. No one will accept his revelations because it is obvious that he is a Jesus freak who has gone around the bend.

The ideal reader of The Rakehells of Heaven should have the mentality of a Southern stock-car racer, be a Baptist with a sense of detachment, have a well-developed sense of the absurd, and be fascinated with the quirks and accomplishments of the human animal. One ideal reader was the writer, who enjoyed every page of the manuscript.

J. B.
1978

CHAPTER
ONE

Astronauts hold few charms for psychiatrists.

With Their "Rogers" and their "Wilcos" and their "A-Okays," the eagle scouts of the Space Navy are all typical American boys who like girls and would rather go bowling than read a book. No matter if the astronaut comes from Basutoland, black and fuzzy-haired, he's still an all-American boy.

Malfunctions of the ego are as rare among the breed as roses on Mars, or so I thought when I came to Mandan. And so I continued to think until I debriefed Ensign John Adams after his unscheduled touchdown at the Mandan Pad. In John Adams, I found the psychiatric equivalent of an orchid blooming on Jupiter.

As a psychiatrist of Plato's school, I would have never volunteered for duty at the Mandan Naval Academy. Platonists are sculptors of the psyche who hold that sanity is innate in man's mind. Our tools are rhetoric, insight, empathy and, above all, the question, for wise interrogation is the better part of therapy. Our marble is mined from the loony bins of Earth. Yet, with Bellevue Hospital but a few blocks from where I was graduated, the bureaucracy ordered me to intern at the North Dakota space complex "to broaden my technical knowledge."

I got to Mandan in late September, a week before school opened, during the point of impact called autumn when winter kicks summer off the Northern Plains. I reported to Space Surgeon Commander Harkness, USN (MC), commandant of the infirmary staff. Doctor Harkness, or Commander, as he preferred to be called, was a neurosurgeon, which is a fancy name for a brain mechanic who uses laser drills and saws.

Harkness made no attempt to suppress his hostility toward interns in general and psychiatrists in particular. He

1

assigned me to interview incoming midshipmen who had
already been Rorschached from Johannesburg to Juneau.
It was salt-mine work. Any behavioral psychologist could
have handled it, but it implemented Harkness's policy of
making interns sweat.

In my first three weeks, I interviewed over two hundred
yearlings and found only one whose behavior was suspect,
an earlobe-puller from Shanghai. His ear-pulling suggested
a compulsion neurosis that can be dangerous in space—such
boys start counting stars when they should be tending the
helm. I offered my Chinese ear-puller to Harkness to demonstrate my application to duty. Harkness felt the lad's
earlobe, found a pimple which had irritated it and gave me
a dressing down. "One thing we don't do at Mandan,
Doctor, is stumble over facts to get at a theory."

Actually, Harkness's ridicule was my high point at Mandan until Adams touched down in late December. Curse me
for a masochist, but any emotion that colored that waste-
land of psychiatrists was welcome. I chewed my hostility
like a betel nut.

It was 5:45 P.M., Wednesday, December 28. I had the
medical watch in the infirmary when Harkness called. "Doctor, are you the only psychiatrist aboard?"

"Yes, sir," I answered, "and will be during the holidays."

"Then you'll have to do. . . . We've got a space scout,
Ensign John Adams, in orbit. His E.T.A. at the northwest
pad is 20:10. He's requested immediate debriefing in the
decontamination chamber beneath the landing pad, which
tells us something. He's the only man on a two-seater scouting craft, which tells us more. Moreover, he lifted off last
January with a running mate, Ensign Kevin O'Hara. Not
only is Adams coming back alone, he's better than a year
ahead of schedule. You're our question-and-answer expert,
Doctor, and you've been yearning for variety. Here's your
chance. Get cracking on the personnel files of Adams and
O'Hara, Probe 2813. Keep in mind, Doctor, the indices
point to stalker's fever."

"Aye, aye, sir."

"Another thing, Doctor: either Adams has aborted the
mission or he's coming out of a non-Galilean frame. In
either event, he's violating Navy Regulations."

"Yes, sir." I hung up, slightly addled.

Generally it took three days to prepare for the debriefing
of a returning probe. I knew this from department scuttle-

butt since there had been no debriefings during my tenure. Usually, the job was assigned to a senior psychiatrist, but I was more pleased than nervous. By sneering at me as a "question-and-answer expert," Harkness was subconsciously admitting that the debriefing of Adams was a task above and beyond the skills of a lobotomist, and Harkness would trepan a man for a headache.

I sprinted down the hall to the personnel-files locker, guarded by a midshipman, and took the psychological-profile cards of John Adams and Kevin O'Hara from the class of '27, last year's graduating class. On my way out, I paused long enough to ask the sentry, "What's a non-Galilean frame?"

He braced himself and looked straight ahead. "An inertial frame of reference, sir, in a constantly accelerating free fall, sir, which exceeds the speed of light at its apex velocity, sir."

"At ease, sailor," I said. "What does all that mean in plain language?"

"That is plain language, sir. Mathematically, it's stated like this, sir: if the square root of one, minus V squared, C squared . . ."

"Never mind," I said. "If light is a constant, how do you exceed the speed of light?"

"You don't, sir. Under the New Special Theory, sir, the speed of light is constant in reference to any inertial frame —that's the observer's point of view, sir—even when the frame is thinned to a Minkowski one-space, sir."

I nodded, "But how does the frame get thin?"

"The Lorentz-Fitzgerald Contraction, sir."

"Thank you," I said, and went back to the office to insert Adams' profile into the typewriter.

Reading the machine almost as fast as it converted the card into typewriting, I found what I expected in John Adams, the same well-adjusted, nontraumatized stimulus and response mechanism I would have gotten from any other card in the Academy files. Adams went a little above the norm in aggressiveness, an understandable deviation when related to the speed of his motor reflexes, which were also faster than the norm. He had probably won a lot of fistfights as a schoolboy—in Alabama, I noted.

Genealogically, too, there was nothing unusual in Adams' background except a great-grandmother who had been a female journeyman preacher, a traveling evangelist for one of those off-beat Protestant sects that still crop up in the South.

Before I read Keven O'Hara's card, I knew something about him from reading Adams's profile. It's Academy policy to match the personalities of running mates on space flight on a basis of compatible differences—the separate-but-equal theory—in order to diminish boredom on long flights by permitting an active interreaction of personalities without arousing antagonisms. Boredom mixed with antagonism gives a breeding ground for stalker's fever, that ailment indigenous to space flights wherein spacemen stalk each other through the confines of their ship as animals intent on their prey. It is a peculiar ailment; usually fatal, since the spaceman who suffers it least on a flight is the one most apt to succumb.

O'Hara, too, stood high on the chart for aggressiveness, but he was smaller than Adams and his reflexes were adjudged slower. His genealogy also offered an anomaly, a grandfather who had been a Catholic priest and an underground colonel in the Irish Republican Army who had been slain in the Rebellion of 2160. O'Hara was from County Meath, in Ireland.

First, I had to consider the possibility of murder based on the index of aggressiveness in the profiles of the two. Aggressiveness is hostility under restraint. Weaken the restraint and you have violence, a principle long ago recognized by the Law and Order Statutes of Imperial Earth. With two such men confined in a space shell, without law and custodians of their own order, a chance remark might have stirred old religious antagonisms into a flare of anger. Then, after a sudden blow, a corpse might be shoved through an airlock to tumble forever through infinity.

This theory was supported by the faster reflexes of Adams, who was also the larger man of the two.

On a hunch, I put Adams's index card back into the machine and punched "Student Infractions."

The platen ball whirred and I read, "Midshipman Adams placed on indefinite probation, spring semester, 2227, for assault with bodily harm intent on three-man Shore Patrol during altercation after raid on Madame Chacaud's, a Mandan pleasure parlor."

Kevin O'Hara's card turned up the same tidbit, with one significant difference: O'Hara had been punished for evading arrest.

To Harkness, my next act might have seemed a fanciful waste of time, but we Platonists are trained to ask questions. I inserted the indices of both men into a Mark VII computer and engaged them in a boxing match. Adams knocked out O'Hara in the third round, but it was a slugging match.

Adams beat O'Hara two chess games out of three, but O'Hara cleaned Adams out in a poker game. Adams had intelligence but O'Hara was shrewd.

This deduction prompted me to engage them again in a rough-and-tumble brawl specifying that the fight must end in a fatality.

O'Hara killed Adams.

I extended the period of conflict to three months and the result was the same, O'Hara killed Adams. After one year, a longer time than the actual voyage, O'Hara killed Adams.

What the machine was telling me was this: Since stalker's fever is indigenous to space ships and since these voyages are scheduled for six months outbound and six months for the return, there had been no stalker's fever aboard. There had been no galactic touchdown since all the time was taken up by the inflight period. Harkness to the contrary notwithstanding, if stalker's fever had broken out aboard, Ensign Kevin O'Hara would be up there orbiting Earth and not the probe commander, Ensign John Adams.

As a space facility, the Mandan Naval Academy ranks among the best-equipped in the world. Forty feet below the landing pad where Adams was touching down, the decontamination chamber is divided from the debriefing room and the witnesses' gallery above by a wall of resonant glass. The incoming spacemen arrive at decontamination by a sliding chute which extends from a snorkel nozzle that automatically clamps onto the exit lock of the ship above. Recording and medical monitoring equipment is as good as any in the world and no known microbe, terrestrial or extraterrestrial, can survive the light-irradiated atmosphere of the chamber.

In twenty-degree weather with three feet of snow on the ground, I took the underground dolly to the landing site, reading the Operations Data Card as I rode.

The Adams-O'Hara Probe had been sent to scout the 320-330-degree segment of a galaxy beyond the star Lynx. Object of the probe was to chart the area and explore it for habitable planets. Ten degrees of arc might seem a thin slice of galactic pie, but the area covers a large bite of parsecs even when measured along the perimeter of the circle.

However, I'm not paid to think along astronomical lines. My job, or so I thought at the moment, was to interview a returnee to determine his mental and physical condition and welcome him back to Earth on a human-to-human basis. We medical men are chosen to be the greeters not merely because of our professional qualifications but because of the mystique attached to us as healers.

In the old days, chaplains welcomed the star rovers home. But men of the cloth have an aura of funerals around them and some of the scouts, their senses wracked by time and warped with radiation, felt so strongly that they were about to receive extreme unction that their blood pressure soared.

Later, the cross or crescent became even less potent as a symbol because the traits that make a religious mind were weeded out of space men. An undue sense of awe can drive a man mad amid the naked glory of stars and once an astronaut succumbs to the raptures of the deep, his voyage is forever outward-bound.

UNASA wants stimulus-response mechanisms for those trips and stimulus-response experts to check them when they return, but UNASA is not faultless. Mendelian laws do not conform to precise patterns. Genes will out. Some ancestral tendency compressed beneath Adams' and O'Hara's behavior erupted like a volcano to alter forever the topography of their computer-matched personalities. Their fight in the Mandan house started a fall of dominoes which, after they had passed all selection boards and undergone their final analysis, triggered alterations in their psyches only vaguely apprehended by the two who strapped themselves into a starship cockpit.

Given power to look upon one moment in the past, I might well choose that January night, in 2228, when the Adams-O'Hara Mission lifted off the Mandan Pad. In the glow from their instrument panel, I would study and commit to memory the faces of the two astronauts, young, fearless and superbly skilled, who would guide the pulse of a laser beam through the voids and time. I would treasure as unique in history the moment when their starship, propelled by its thundering light, set course for a far galactic swirl bearing the first Southern evangelist and the first Irish rebel to sail the seas of space.

But this is the revery of hindsight. At the moment, I was rolling toward an interview with John Adams and a meeting, no less real, with the ghost of Red O'Hara.

Doctor Harkness was waiting at the debriefing desk before the decontamination chamber wearing an officious frown.

"Doctor, I'm sorry to impose on your inexperience in this matter, but this is an unscheduled touchdown and there's no senior psychiatrist aboard. I'll be observing from the gallery with Admiral Bradshaw and other officers, and I've prepared you a list of questions you can use as guidelines."

I took the sheet of paper, a little miffed by his gratuitous reference to my inexperience in the presence of the Academy superintendent.

"Adams is stern down and making his approach," Harkness advised me, despite the fact that earth around us was already shaking with the blasts from the retro-jets of the starship above us and the dial marker on the bulkhead behind him was recording the ship's position above the pad.

"Introduce yourself to Adams and keep your voice warm and relaxed. Don't put your lips too close to the glass. Get him into the telemetering jumper as soon as possible. Don't stare at him as if he were a specimen of wildlife. Usually they're unshaven and out of uniform when they land and they stagger a bit until they adjust to Earth's gravity. Welcome him, get him to relax and make him feel wanted. That's your specialty—making one feel wanted."

Above us the thunder of the ship's descent was dying to a rustle. I heard the click and wheeze of the decon nozzle as it unshipped itself from the base of the landing pad.

"Don't worry about taking notes," Harkness continued, "but keep your eyes and ears open for any aberrant behavior."

Harkness was carrying out the monologue to impress his superiors in the gallery above. I was perfectly willing for him to share the limelight from the decon chamber, but he was not giving me a chance to read the guidelines he had written out for me.

"Above all, keep him talking," Harkness said. "There may be a violation of Navy Regulations, here, more grave than aborting a mission—looks that way, in fact—and anything he says can be used against him."

On the bulkhead, the ship's altitude marker had fallen to zero. The starship was down.

"Usually, they're bursting to spill a gut, particularly if they build up hostilities on their voyage. Use your empathy on Adams. Get him to hang himself if he's gallows material."

Above, I heard the snorkel clunk onto the airlock of the vessel. In minutes, Adams would be sliding down the chute, but the imminent arrival of my patient concerned me now only peripherally. The intent behind Harkness' words stunned me.

"Remember Plato's injunction," the lobotomist had the gall to tell *me*, "that the better part of a prosecution rests on a faculty for wise interrogation, so get him to incriminate himself. One of his monitoring systems has been programmed with a copy of Navy Regulations, and it will be checking for violations as he talks. So, keep him talking, Doctor."

"Aye, aye, sir," I answered with a reflex action, as Harkness turned and vanished up the stairs to the gloom of the witnesses' balcony. All the delicate tools of my trade, insight, empathy, interrogation, were to be used on John Adams not to help him re-relate to a human environment but to entrap him for violation of Navy Regulations.

Through the exit tube across the chamber, I could hear the sough of an opening airlock as I glanced down at the guidelines Harkness had handed me.

1. Ask him why he aborted his mission.
2. Ask him where in hell is O'Hara.

Commander Harkness had been playing to the gallery when he handed me the note and I replied in kind as I heard the *swish-swish* of Adams spiraling down the chute. With a contemptuous smile, I crumpled the note and tossed it into a wastebasket. Then I turned to look through three inches of polarized glass as Adams shot from the chute, breech foremost, to land on a canvas mat.

"Nice landing, sailor," I called out, and to identify myself as a medical man, added, "a breech delivery."

Adams seemed to spring from the pad and stood upright for a moment, tottering. He was over six feet with long hair and the beginnings of a beard. He was barefoot and wore a sleeveless tunic embroidered over the left breast with a strange device. The tunic barely reached below his jockstrap and his skin was so pale it seemed whitewashed. His legs were as muscular as a ballet dancer's but his ankles were swollen and both of his arms bore identical purple welts above the elbows. Remembering his Alabama background, I compared him to a Confederate general aloud, "Ensign Adams, you look like General J. E. B. Stuart going drag."

Despite an expression of intense anxiety on his face, his mouth broke into a wide grin as he looked at me. It was almost a stage grin, but it had enough sincerity to indicate he had understood and appreciated my wit. Gingerly, he started toward me.

"I'd like to introduce myself, Adams," I began, but he ignored my remark.

"What day is it, Doctor?"

"Wednesday, December 28," I told him. He had recognized the caduceus on my lapel, which attested to the normalcy of his power of observation.

"Thank God!" The relief that flooded his features seemed to steady his walk. "Forget the debriefing, Doctor. Call Operations and tell them to scratch the Adams-O'Hara Probe."

He was pointing at a telephone on the bulkhead on my side of the glass and behaving in such a normal manner that I blurted out a normal rejoinder.

"You *are* the Adams-O'Hara Probe, or what's left of it."

"What year is it?" he asked.

"2228."

Adams reacted like a man struck in the stomach. His body crumpled backward and agony contorted his face. Dazed, he walked over and collapsed in the chair across the panel from me. His eyes focused on some private hell as he half-mumbled to himself, "It didn't work. It didn't work."

"What didn't work, Adams?" I asked, seating myself at the desk.

"I was trying to invert the dilatation factor and reverse my reference frame."

Whether his answer was rational or irrational, I couldn't tell. Spacemen operate in a relativistic universe and I use classical logic. But I remembered the midshipman's remarks outside Personnel Records.

"Are you referring to a non-Christian frame?"

"Non-Christian frame?" Adams looked at me in puzzlement, and then a broad smile covered his features, a manic-depressive reaction, I decided, in view of his depressed state. "I reckon you mean a non-Galilean frame," he drawled.

"Well, I'm only a psychiatrist," I said, "and the only Galilean I know is Christ."

"The name honors Galileo, Doctor," he chuckled, "but maybe you hit on the right answer for the wrong reason. Maybe I didn't pray hard enough."

Adams was not only sane but sharp. He had detected my confusion of the word "Galilean" with Christ, which indicated a much higher verbal facility than his profile had revealed. But he had forgotten me in some vast inner struggle. Horror and disbelief in his eyes were shifting to resignation. His features were so facile I could read emotions on his face.

Remembering Harkness, I asked, "Why did you abort your mission a year ahead of time, Adams?"

"I didn't, Doctor. I aborted it by three weeks, from necessity."

Counting his six-month voyage out, six months in, plus eleven months on the mission, his figures came to twenty-three months. "But you've only been gone eleven months," I pointed out.

"That's the story of my life, Doctor—too little and too late. I needed to get back two years and I couldn't gain but one."

Suddenly, I got a vague glimmering of what he was talking about. "Adams, are you telling me that you were trying to get back here before you left?"

"Reckon you can bring out your straitjacket, Doctor, but that's what I was trying. I know the theory says one solid can't occupy two places, but theories don't grow cotton. The Good Book says 'Ask and you shall receive.' Lord knows, I *asked*. I strewed prayers from Cassiopeia to Orion. After that, I was too busy gearing down that whaleboat, topside, to do much praying."

Here I wanted to take a breather myself but Harkness was observing from the shadows. I quoted my second guideline verbatim. "What in the hell happened to O'Hara?"

"He has joined the immortals," Adams intoned.

"How did he join them?"

"By the words that issued from my mouth, much as anything. I joshed a university dean who didn't have a sense of humor. It never pays, Doc, to joke with a man with a literal mind."

Psychiatrists weigh answers on all levels. Adams's answer confused me superficially and in depth. There were no known universities on any planet other than Earth, and his answer implied a distaste for a literal mind, the *sine qua non* of spacemen. Moreover, the laser jockey's concept of comedy is a double-take followed by a prat fall. Adams was an astronaut complaining about a university dean's lack of a sense of humor.

Stimuli were piling in so fast that my own response faltered, and I made an ambiguous statement. "Tell me about O'Hara."

"O'Hara? That old boy was the original kisser of the Blarney Stone. . . . No, I'll take that back. Whenever old Red kissed anything, he made love to it."

"I mean, how did he die?" I corrected myself.

"You might say he was trapped in a non-Galilean frame. . . . Your kind, not Galileo's. . . . If he'd just kept his hands off my woman. . . . He knew I was a forgiving person, but he knew I'd hit first and forgive later."

Adams was rambling, following a flow of ideas, and I remembered Harkness. "Before you tell me about O'Hara, would you take off your clothes and get into that jumpersuit?"

I pointed to the medical monitor suit hanging from the bulkhead on his side of the panel.

Adams almost leaped to his feet, and he grinned at his own reaction. "After hoisting 800 pounds," he said, "I feel like a bag full of helium."

After his initial leap to his feet, Adams moved freely, slipping out of his tunic and jockstrap with a down and up movement of his arms and wobbling only slightly as he walked over to the stretch jumper. An eleven-month tour of duty on a planet with four times the pull of Earth's gravity explained his swollen ankles but there was one condition of his body revealed by his nakedness which it did not explain: encompassing his torso above his navel was a livid welt that matched the bruises on his arms.

"Looks like you've been manhandled around your belly," I remarked.

"Little old girl hugged me," he said, and the sadness that came to his eyes told me that his relationship with the "little old girl" had not been as casual as his words suggested.

When he slipped into the suit and came over to resume his seat, I glanced down at the telemetering chart. Both lower ribs on each side of his ribcage were broken. On Earth, a contusion of such nature could only have been inflicted by the coils of an anaconda.

When I glanced up, the glaze was descending over his eyes. To draw him out of himself, I said, "You were saying O'Hara had the gift of gab."

Adams straightened. His voice came stronger, more resonant, and a strange light glittered in his eyes. "It was more than the gift of gab, Doctor—in the beginning there were words, and the words were O'Hara's, but O'Hara *was* the Word."

With that remark, he knocked my stimulus-response tactics awry with the joy that surpasses understanding by any save a psychiatrist at Mandan. I recognized the original of his paraphrase. Those words had been uttered 2,200 years ago by another John, Saint John the Apostle.

At that moment, I lost whatever interest I might have had in the entrapment of John Adams for alleged violations of Navy Regulations. Sex and religion are the two best-paved lanes to lunacy and Adams was driving in both lanes with a load of guilt. Inwardly I laid out my sculptor's implements, insight, empathy, interrogation, for the chunk of marble before me was pure Carrara—a loony who used Einstein's Revised General Theory as a tool of his trade.

"How did you meet old Red, John?" I let my voice snuggle close to him. "Tell me from the beginning."

CHAPTER TWO

In the Academy yearbook (Adams began), O'Hara's official nickname is King Con. He was the first man I met at Mandan, and within five minutes of our introduction I became the victim of his first confidence trick. I had tossed my bag on the lower bunk of the room assigned to me when an upperclassman ushered him in. "Midshipman Adams, your roommate, Midshipman O'Hara."

Right then I should have been wary, for O'Hara was carrying his gear in a carpet bag, but the calluses on his hand were as horny as mine and the smile that cracked his freckles beguiled me. "From your friendly face and honest eyes," he said, "I gather you're an American."

"Right," I answered.

"And from your accent—I have a fine ear for dialects—that most hospitable of all Americans, a Southerner."

"Jacksons Gap, Alabama," I said, astonished because I had spoken only one word.

His accent was neutral English, that hybrid of Midwestern U.S.A. and Oxonian which television actors affect, but all the rest of him was Irish, red hair, freckles, a nose pinched out of his face, protruding cheekbones and a cleft in his chin.

"I'm shanty Irish," he said, "from County Meath. We Irish are so poor and cramped on our little isle that we cannot afford the open-handed generosity of you Americans. . . . Ah, I see you have taken the lower bunk. No matter, the climbing will do me good."

"O'Hara," I said, "if you want the lower bunk, you're welcome to it."

"Now, doesn't that bear out all that I've said. . . . What is your first name."

"John. My friends generally call me Jack."

"Jack! A lovely, no-nonsense name. Kevin's mine, but I prefer Red. . . . No, Jack. I'll not take advantage of your generosity. Rather I'll risk my neck in a fall, for I'll confess: I imbibe a bit on Saturday nights."

"She's all yours, Red," I said. "I could never bear the death of a drinking man on my conscience."

Suiting action to words, I hoisted my bag to the top bunk when I noticed a Delta Airlines waybill dangling from the handle, stamped large with the code "Montgom-Mandex," meaning "Montgomery to Mandan."

O'Hara was as honest as his talents permitted. He spoke a fractional truth when he said he imbibed a "bit" on Saturday nights. In the following three and a half years, the only sober Saturday night we spent together was on our junior training cruise three parsecs out into the Milky Way, where he demonstrated that his skills as a space jockey were equal to his skills as a tippler. He could turn a starship in the solar

system and give you back Pluto and Uranus for change.
Ashore and aloft, he was fearless, for he truly believed in
the luck of the Irish. He wore green polka-dot drawers at
all times and dangled a green leprechaun from the abort
throttle of his cockpit. Now, I carried a rabbit's foot in my
pocket, but I didn't *depend* on it.

Our Saturday sorties into the wilds of Mandan sometimes
resembled forays. Red chose the "off-limit" houses guarded
by military police on the theory that such places catered to
officers who did not wish to be recognized by midshipmen.
He might have been right about Madame Chacaud's—Dirty
Mary's to the midshipmen. Her girls were refined enough
not to stick their gum behind their ears and she kept a bottle
of Jamiesons on tap for Red. Each girl had a television set
in her room and Red would lounge around on a Sunday
morning indulging in another of his passions—soap operas.

Until our senior year, Red and I came and went freely
because we kept civilian clothes in the bus-station locker and
the military police never questioned civilians.

One February night in our senior year, Red and I were
enjoying a few social drinks preliminary to the festivities at
Madame Chacaud's when Red took affront at a Swede who
preferred aquavit to Irish whisky. Red argued that his
travels in space qualified him as an expert on drinks. His
adversary pointed out that space travel did not qualify a man
to be a judge of whiskies. Red resented the intrusion of
logic into the argument and decided on other methods of
persuasion.

Unluckily, Red was too small and too drunk to persuade
the man who was about to sum up his case in defense of
aquavit when I interposed a few arguments in favor of
bourbon and branch water. Bourbon was about to be
crowned king of drinks in Mandan when the crash of furniture, the squeal of females and the quivering of the building drew the M.P.s in from outside.

My opponent pointed at O'Hara. "That space cadet
started it, and this dehorn jumped in."

"Space cadet?" The M.P. sergeant turned to O'Hara.
"Show me your I.D., mister."

"I was rolled, Major, so my wallet is missing, but that
gentleman," Red nodded toward me, "is a farmer from
Dubuque and I am his hired man. He will vouch for me."

The sergeant turned to me. "Show me your palms, mister."

As I extended my palms, I realized I had been tricked by

a soldier with only slightly less brains than brawn. In my three years as a midshipman, my calluses had navigated around my hands from my palms to my knuckles.

"You're a liar, too," the sergeant said.

"Are you letting that dogface call a midshipman a liar, Adams?" O'Hara bellowed in anger from between two restraining M.P.s.

Suddenly the honor of the Navy was mine to uphold and defend. When my fist slammed into the sergeant's belly, his "*whoof*" drew the attention of his comrades, who dropped O'Hara and turned on me.

Treason and betrayal!

Through a picket fence of billy clubs flailing before my eyes, I glimpsed my comrade slinking out of the door when he should have been attacking the exposed flank and rear. The red rat was deserting me. Anguish slowed my defenses and an M.P. slipped around me and cold-cocked me from the rear.

But justice triumphed. Too drunk to negotiate the icy steps, O'Hara slipped and fell to the sidewalk. When the M.P.s dragged me out, Red was asleep and snoring, in easy tossing distance of the arriving paddywagon.

Before noon Sunday I awakened in the section of the M.P.D. drunk tank reserved for military personnel and I staggered to my feet, hungover, battered and disgusted by the memory of O'Hara's cheap attempt to sacrifice me and escape. For once he was sleeping in the upper bunk, where his lighter weight had made it easier to toss him, with hardly a bruise showing beneath his freckles. Bending close to his ear, I whistled "The Battle of Boyne's Waters."

He snapped awake and swung to the edge of the bunk.

"You shanty Mick," I said. "You picked a fight between me and the M.P.s so you could save your own skin."

"Jack, lad, you do me a grave dishonor. I was attempting to escape to get a writ of *habeas corpus* for you."

"*Habeas corpus*? At a military hearing? . . . Come off the bunk. I'm going to *habeas* a piece of your *corpus*."

I'll say this for O'Hara: knowing right and might were on my side, he came down fighting. Before the turnkeys pulled us apart, our bruises were fairly balanced.

I relate this incident to show that O'Hara learned to respect my fists, and I truly believe that I had the only pair of fists on the continent that he did respect. But I also wished to demonstrate that his mind schemed in such a

manner that his most spontaneous plots left him lines of
retreat.

After justice was done, we sat on the lower bunk and held
the shortest strategy conference in naval history. We were
in custody, out of uniform and were lacerated and bruised.
We had been arrested in an "off-limits" area for disturbing
the peace. We had resisted arrest and I would be charged
with assaulting a policeman. By now, a full report of the
incident would be on the disciplinary officer's desk at the
Academy.

We decided to tell the truth, but Red seemed strangely
optimistic. "Just leave it to me, Jack."

At noon, the shore patrol hauled us back to the Academy
under house arrest. Monday morning, we went before the
mast, which was conducted by Commander Omubu, a
Ghanaian who used the regional English of Afro-Americans
as his status dialect. It took him twenty minutes merely to
read the M.P.s' report aloud, and then he leaned back, looking first at me and then at Red in disbelief, repugnance,
awe, or sadness.

"Gentlemen, it seems from this report that you both are
unfitted for this service. After you have been expelled,
Adams, I suggest you join the Harrier Corps. There your
fighting prowess would be welcomed. You, O'Hara, should
be a mattress-tester for the Department of Home Appli-
ances. . . . How say you both to these charges? Guilty or
not guilty?"

"Guilty," we answered.

"What say you to these charges?"

O'Hara stepped one pace forward. "Commander," he
sang out, "I'm just a dumb Irishman and my only excuse is
ignorance, but I would like to say a word in defense of
Midshipman Adams."

"At ease, O'Hara, and tell it like it was."

"Sir, as midshipmen of the United Space Navy, we are
expected to behave as officers and gentlemen. Before an
officer can be a gentleman, sir, he must first be a *man*. An
insult offered to one midshipman besmirches the honor of
the entire Navy, sir, your Navy and mine, sir, and that
honor was at stake when the M.P. called Midshipman
Adams a liar, sir."

"Unless Midshipman Adams lied," the Commander
pointed out.

"That's precisely the point, sir. *Ipso facto*, Midshipman Adams could not have lied, sir, since he uttered not one word to the M.P.s."

"Is that right, Adams?"

"Yes, sir. I didn't open my mouth, sir."

"Expel us if you must, sir," Red continued, "but do not expel us with dishonor, and particularly Midshipman Adams, who fought with valor against odds whilst I went to summon reinforcements. . . . With valor and against odds, sir, he fought to defend the honor of the USN, your honor and mine, sir."

"Midshipman O'Hara," the Commander said, "will you await the verdict in the anteroom while I recover from your speech?"

After Red left, Commander Omubu sadly shuffled the pages of the report into order and looked up. "At ease, Adams. Well, I can't give you a medal. There are five charges against you and four against O'Hara. On the other hand, I can't expel you. The transcript of the hearing is read by Admiral Bradshaw. If I expelled you after that speech, I'd be the worst mother in Academy history. But there's one bit of advice I'd like to give to you."

"Yes, sir?"

"Man, there's only one thing dumber than a dumb Irishman, and that's a smart Alabaman."

We were restricted to quarters for a month on half-pay and put on permanent probation for the remainder of our senior year, which meant that one demerit would expel us. But our confinement sent our grades soaring and my own soared somewhat higher than O'Hara's since he played solitaire. When our confinement was lifted, we were in the best shape of our career to celebrate and the M.P.s were gone from in front of Madame Chacaud's.

We arrived on Friday night at Madame Chacaud's and left Sunday morning so broke we had to hitchhike back to the Academy in zero weather. We were walking through an area of cheap stores and pawnshops when the aroma of boiling coffee drifted through the March air. I sniffed again. It was coffee boiled with chicory, and nostalgia pierced me more deeply than the cold. Someone was making Alabama coffee.

We were passing an abandoned store building and I
noticed a sign, crudely lettered, posted in the window:

SAILOR BEN'S HOLINESS MISSION

Come In and Pray . . . . . Free Coffee and Doughnuts

Inside, a service was in progress. I slowed O'Hara. "Red,
could I treat you to some good old hellfire religion, South-
ern-style, plus a cup of coffee?"

"I could use a little of both."

We entered and took a bench at the rear, not wishing to
tempt the wine-soaked derelicts crowded near the pulpit
with the odor of fine whisky on our breaths.

From the pulpit, Sailor Ben was preaching on the evils of
drink, in the accents of my home. "Boys, I was soaking in
booze till Jesus wrung me dry. I stunk so loud of moonshine
it was a pure wonder the revenuers didn't raid me for a
still. I tell you, if I'da died and gone to hell, I wouldn't have
burned, I would have boiled."

His voice dropped from a tone of braggadocio to one of
reverent thankfulness. "But then I met the best woman God
ever gave a sinner, boys. She was a dilly. She set me on
course to Jesus, afore she died, leaving me with that little
bundle of joy you know as Sister Thelma, and I been sailing
a straight course, ever since. . . . Play, Sister Thelma."

Brother Ben switched on a light which was beamed on a
girl at an upright piano who had been lost in the shadows.
She was dressed in a simple gray skirt with a white blouse
and the light threw an aura around her ash-blond hair.
Then I knew why the winos were crowding near the pulpit
as she began to play "Shall We Gather at the River."

The hymn is ordinarily a funeral song, but I felt it was
appropriate for Brother Ben's sermon and I rose to sing, in
a quavering tremolo that raised the hackles on my own
nape.

After a prayer, Sister Thelma took up collection. She
was not more than eighteen, and she floated down the aisle
with a sidewise sway to her hips that was both ethereal and
feminine. She moved in serenity, her blue eyes glowing
with spirituality, and when she came back to us and smiled
at me, I felt an angel's wing brush my cheek.

But I was embarrassed, both for myself and for Red, for
we had nothing for the offering. When I glanced down at
the plate that I handed over to Red, I was embarrassed for

the girl. There was nothing in it but pennies, a few nickels and a rare dime.

Red seemed to hold the plate a long time, so long, in fact, I feared he might be following some obscure Irish-Catholic ritual and counting the take. When he nudged me with the plate, I handed it back to the girl without looking. I was astonished to hear her say, "Why, I thank you, Brother O'Hara."

Brother Ben led us in a final prayer and invited us all back to the pantry for coffee and doughnuts. "Were you holding out money on me, you bastard?" I whispered to Red.

"Not at all, my boy. I wrote the girl an I.O.U. for twenty dollars, payable next Sunday."

Coffee and doughnuts in the church kitchen was like a homecoming for me. Once Brother Ben found I was from Alabama, he cornered me in conversation while Red cornered Sister Thelma. Brother Ben, I found, had been a loom-fixer in a Jackson, Mississippi, cottonmill and had worked for a season on a shrimp boat out of Pass Christian. He had gotten the Call while at sea, and hence the name "Sailor Ben."

Once in a lull in Brother Ben's conversation, I heard O'Hara say to Sister Thelma, "Lassie, I'll pluck a feather from an angel's wing to grace your bonny hair," and I knew he was zeroing in on Thelma. Glancing their way, I noticed Thelma was slinging her pelvis toward Red as he talked, and again nostalgia assailed me. I had forgotten how the girls hunched down South and I had not seen such hunching since my last Baptist Young People's meeting at Jacksons Gap.

When I finally squeezed in a few words with Thelma, I apologized for Red's I.O.U. "That's the way they pledge contributions in Ireland," I told her, "and I'm pledging twenty dollars myself."

"I'll declare," she said (but she did not hunch for me), "that's the most generous thing, Brother John. Why don't y'all come back Saturday for a chicken supper."

I promptly accepted. Forty dollars is a lot of money for a chicken supper, but I was determined Red should honor the I.O.U., and if Brother Ben's mission did not get the money by Saturday night, there'd be nothing left from Madame Chacaud's to put into the plate Sunday morning.

Once on our way again, I said, "Red, you're honoring that I.O.U."

"Certainly, Jack. Thelma's a lovelier lass than any at Madame Chacaud's."

"Whoa there, boy," I said. "If you've got any ideas about Thelma, drop them. To circumnavigate that little behind, you've got to get a shotgun away from her pa, assistance from a preacher and learn to speak in unknown tongues to show you got religion."

Thereafter, Brother Ben's Mission became our favorite charity, and Brother Ben's sermons spurred me to reread the New Testament. It surprised me how appropriately the Scriptures could be interpreted in the light of the New Relativity. Once when discussing the parables from the Sermon on the Mount with Red, showing him how they could apply to the Space Age, Red agreed.

"Yes, Jack. The meek shall inherit the earth because it takes guts to blast off from this planet."

Red quit cheating at solitaire during those days and after a month's attendance at the mission, he dropped cards entirely and took to reading love poetry. I approved. Any man who read poetry couldn't criticize a man for reading the Bible.

O'Hara pulled no stops to get to Thelma Pruitt's heart, if that was truly his direction. He wore his green polka-dotted drawers on their first date, but his space charm did not work on Earth. In May, he "got the spirit."

It's hard to fake the unknown tongue. When Red rose to his feet and began to shout in the midst of a sermon, he fooled me completely. His language had the accents and rhythms and nonrepetitive phrases of a genuine Pentecostal experience, and I was so convinced that he had been touched by the Holy Ghost that I was even adding "Amen" behind the logical pauses in his shouting.

Blasphemy and sacrilege!

With unfocused eyes and waving arms, he stood before that congregation, and all were clapping their hands and shouting encouragement to this new member of the church. Brother Ben was thanking Jesus, and Sister Thelma, her face glowing with pride, was moving to the piano to begin softly playing "Come to Jesus." Then Red, in his final fervor, shouted out a phrase I recognized: "Erin go bragh."

Red O'Hara's unknown tongue was unknown to Mandan but familiar to Dublin. He was shouting in Gaelic.

So he entered into the brotherhood of the Holiness Church, with a false passport. Thelma wept for his salvation but she would not yield. He got her, finally, but not the way he intended.

Late June at Mandan is a season of sentiment. From the needled spires of the Academy, the prairies lay green to horizons purpled by heat haze. Alfalfa blossoms sweeten the air. The axial tilt of the earth seems to toss the Dakotas toward the sun in apology for the winter. Rivers are flowing once more, birds are returning and the senior class is going.

But life orbits. Circles of farewell merge into circles of greetings and circles are wedding bands. Graduating midshipmen, freed of matrimonial bans, marry and start other circles of honeymoons and sowings to forget, for a spell, the approach of another farewell, their first cruise into outer space.

O'Hara and I got orders to lift-off in early January, to scout a sector near Lynx. Buoyed by my growing faith, I felt no trepidation about our coming probe, but O'Hara resorted to conventional methods of allaying apprehensions. Red married Thelma Pruitt and left on a six-month honeymoon of sun and fun in Jackson, Mississippi.

When Red broke the news of his honeymoon site, I broke for the clothes closet and prayed that his bride be given the strength and the nuptial talents to divert Red's mind from both our coming probe and a real and present Jackson. Once I had spent five hours in Jackson, Mississippi.

For me it was a pleasant summer spent in fishing up and down the Tallapoosa, meditation, prayer and quail-hunting in the fall. Fishing was good, I got the Call and the birds were numerous.

By meditating, I learned that the Lord's Will was for me to carry His Word to other galaxies, but there was a law against missionaries in space. Before the union of nations, the law had been put through by former colonial nations. After the union, the law was retained by the Interplanetary Colonial Administration, with full agreement of once underprivileged countries, to permit Earth colonization of planets inhabited by nonbelievers.

I had the Call to preach to beings of alien species, and the Call was in violation of Navy Regulations.

Red O'Hara was having his troubles, too, over in Mississippi. Four days before I was scheduled to leave for Mandan, a rented auto pulled up at the farm and Red got out.

After the introductions and after Papa had taken him out to the barn for a drink (Papa still sinned), I showed Red over the farm.

"Thelma and I were staying at her Aunt Ethel Bertha's, the one that raised her after her ma died," Red explained. "Thelma didn't want me to fly back. She got a little nervous on the flight down and swore off flying, for both of us. She thinks I'm driving back, with fourteen feet of snow on the ground. So I thought I'd drive over here and fly back with you, without letting Thelma know. Thelma says if God intended man to fly, He would have given him wings."

"How was the honeymoon?" I asked.

"Tell you the truth, Jack, that was about the best honeymoon I ever had."

"Were you married before?"

"No. Never had to before."

Red had never been one to burden others with his problems and Jackson had added to his maturity, but inadvertencies occurred.

When he returned the car to the rental agency, I trailed him in Papa's car to drive him back. Not once did he suggest that we stop at a bar, nor did he inquire about the pleasure parlors available at Jacksons Gap. I commended him on his righteousness.

"Thelma's Aunt Ethel Bertha was pretty strict about those things. She was dead set against drinking and smoking. She caught me in the woodlot one evening smoking a cigar and she blessed me out. You know, Jack, I'm tolerant with you reformers. But it doesn't set well with me to get blessed out for smoking by a woman with a dip of snuff."

"Didn't Thelma defend your right to smoke?"

"Well, Thelma was the reason I was smoking in the woodlot. My little angel didn't want me to defile our bedroom with tobacco smoke."

Red was taciturn for the few days he spent with us, but Mother loved him. He begged off quail-hunting and spent his mornings with Mama watching "The Pitfalls of Love," "Life Can Be Golden" and "The Sadness and the Glory." Aunt Ethel Bertha and Thelma disapproved of television, it seemed, because it showed girls dancing with bare legs. Red had not seen a soap opera for over five months.

When Papa drove us to Montgomery to board the plane for Mandan, Red, gazing out of the car window, commented idly, "Jack, I can see why there are so many mulattoes around these parts."

On the plane to Mandan, I faced our coming lift-off with the calmness of one whose fate was in other hands, but Red was raring to go. After marriage and Jackson, the void offered no perils for O'Hara.

We lifted off from the Mandan pad near midnight, January 3. He tied his green leprechaun above the instrument panel and said a few words aloud to Mary while I spoke silently to Jesus. Since I was flight commander because of my higher academic rating, I ordered Red to take the con.

The night was moonless. The air seemed crystallized by the cold. Beneath a vault of stars the prairies stretched white around us to the rims of the world. Above us, Cassiopeia beckoned as the window onto Lynx slowly opened and we completed the chant of spacemen.

"Power on?"

"Power on."

"Struts clear?"

"Struts clear."

"Ports closed?"

"Ports closed."

"Ignite pods!"

"Pods ignited."

"Countdown commencing!"

Red's face in the glow from the panel reflected only joy as he repeated aloud the readings on the panel: "Four, three, two, one . . . zero. Here goes nothing!"

Glare from our pods on the snow dimmed the stars as the ship creaked from the stress of the launch and Gs forced us back into our rests. We were rising, and inside me a sense of purpose was rising.

"Pods away!"

Our ship lurched and surged as the assist pods dropped and the lasers cut in, and the *sough-sough* of their pulsing chimed oratorios through my being.

"Cepheus three points off the port bow, Captain," Red sang out. "On course for Lynx."

As I watched Uranus drift astern, I knew that my own course was not plotted on the ship's flight-recorder, but it lay as clear in my mind as that triangulated on the star chart before me.

As the gold of the stars shifted to violet and the blackness before us grayed, as our weight stabilized to the constant acceleration of one gravity, Red turned and asked, "Well, Jack, my lad, how about going below for a cup of java?"

"Sounds good," I said.

So vast are the meadows of the void that the bleat of one lamb can be lost. It was not given me to know that my voice would be amplified and reinforced by the most unlikeliest of channels. In my exaltation and pride, I could not foresee—and no one could have guessed—that the boy who unlocked himself from the seat beside me would become, in the fullness of time, the god of a far galaxy.

CHAPTER
THREE

Time telescopes nearing the speed of light and ceases at the Minkowski Barrier, but the hiatus must be filled. For me, entering the one-space continuum meant mediation, the Scriptures, prayer and reading Navy Regulations. Red chose the four horsemen of romantic poetry, Keats and Shelley, Yeats and Fraze, reruns of soap operas procured from the culture bank and Navy Regulations.

Red spoke little of his marriage and in his infrequent references to Thelma she was "my little angel." His term of endearment became suspect in my mind, however. Once I attempted to engage him in a discussion of the Christian concept of Heaven, but he dismissed the subject. "Lord spare me, Jack, from Heaven with its angels and deliver my soul to Fiddler's Green."

Fiddler's Green is the paradise of space sailors, a meadow whereon the brooks flow with whisky and maidens gambol in birthday dress.

Because I understood O'Hara, I made no attempt to convert him. Full well I knew that O'Hara was beyond the capabilities of any fledgling evangelist.

We had taken the Scout's Oath and were pledged to

spend a measure of the one-space in the study of Navy Regulations, particularly the codes governing the classification of alien humanids. Man was the standard of measurement in the universe, and if the aliens qualified as *homo sapiens*, their planet was exempt from occupation by the Interplanetary Colonial Authority. Alien status was determined by the high command on the basis of scouting reports.

Qualifications were strict, touching on many aspects of the alien, his person, his organizations and even his taboos. Humanid societies must use water closets (social), and there must be separate water closets for male and female (taboos). To be classified as *homo sapiens*, a humanid had to possess an opposing thumb, and a belief in a Supreme Being, such Supreme Being not to exceed a triune godhead, and statute law and order must exist among humanids. Reading over the qualifications, it struck me that the only item overlooked was that the postulant was not required to wear saddle oxfords.

Biological practice was a particularly vulnerable area for alien claimants to human status. An ability to cross-breed with Earthmen was an understandable requirement, but even that was invalidated if the gestation period was less than seven months or more than eleven. Coition must occur face-to-face. Group participation disqualified. Public nudity disqualified. Oral contact with primary erogenic zones disqualified. Reading over that list caused me to rock with laughter: Red O'Hara could not have qualified as a human being under the alien codes.

I took the biological section of the codes across the passage for Red to read. He read them gravely, closed the manual and handed it back to me. "No matter, Jack," he said. "I'll continue to think of you as a human being."

Let him without sin throw stones.

As midshipmen, we had been exposed to the study of Navy regs, but the pressure of classes prevented any in-depth analysis and midshipmen habitually skipped footnotes. In the section concerning alien governments, there was a footnote that aroused my curiosity. It read: "Addendum. See Public Law 36824–I.C.A."

With microfilms of Earth laws and legal systems in the ship's culture bank, Red and I went below and flashed P.L. 36824–I.C.A. onto the viewer.

To qualify as members of the World's Brotherhood, inhabitants of an alien planet must possess a defense system with
capabilities for interspace warfare sufficient to relieve Imperial Earth of the responsibility for the aforesaid planet's
defense.

As I clicked off the viewer, Red commented, "The message from Earth is clear—if you can't defend yourself, we're
coming after you. Jack, these codes aren't designed to qualify a planet for brotherhood. They're designed to disqualify."

I disliked the subversive tone of Red's remark. "Government policy is not our responsibility," I said. "It's not for
us to question the law but to obey."

"You're absolutely right, Jack," Red said, "for reasons of
personal sanity. If you're going to worry about the sins of
the flesh as instrument of such policy, you're as crazy as a
man cleaning the ashtrays in a car careening through a
crowded schoolyard."

" 'Render unto Caesar that which is Caesar's,' " I quoted,
but in truth I could not be too condemnatory. Already I
was planning in my heart to do a little fudging on Caesar
myself.

Throughout my inner turmoil within the hiatus, the flawless technology of Earth continued to function. Our laser
thrust slowly died. Mass loss weight. For a little while,
O'Hara and I floated free, playing basketball in the ship's
gym and using each other as balls. Then our retro-jets
phased in and we returned to the deck as deceleration replaced acceleration. Finally we came again into light and
time, but the configuration of the stars was strange. A new
galaxy hung in the sky and the Milky Way was a point of
light astern.

"The luck of the Irish" is no chimera. When we surveyed
the galaxy on the screen, Red looked over the star cluster
with the eye of a housewife selecting strawberries and said,
"Now, there's a likely-looking star."

I brought it in and scaled it up, checking its planetary
system. It was double the magnitude of the sun, so I
bracketed in an area one-third again as large as Earth's orbit,
and lo, there on the outer rim of the screen floated a planet.
We brought planet and star onto opposite rims and set the
computer. In an hour we had an estimate: the planet had

a thirteen-month year, a twenty-eight-hour day and water vapor. It had an axial tilt only ten degrees greater than Earth and polar icecaps.

"Red, you're a genius."

"Credit my polka-dot drawers," he said and took over the helm.

From one thousand miles out, we saw a planet of greenery, blue water and clouds. As Red swung into our first orbit, our sensors picked up heat lines veining three land masses and reaching almost to the poles. We circled closer, dropping to the springtime, or Northern, hemisphere of the globe, and the signs were good. That grid had to be an artifact constructed by beings with a high degree of organization and engineering skills.

I went aft to the con, leaving Red at the helm, and switched on the viewer. Below me, I saw mountains and rivers and grassy plains, and once, over an ocean, I picked up the father of all hurricanes moiling the width of my frame. But there were no signs of cities, railroads, or roads, and no indication of why a gridwork of heat should lay over the continents. As we passed into terminator on our fifth orbit, sinking lower, my eyes caught the glint of an object on the west coast of the largest continent. Immediately, I locked the viewer in, enlarging. Below me in the early morning sun, I saw an artifact.

As it registered, I hit the "position fix" button and yelled into the intercom, "Red, I saw an observatory, plain as day. . . . An astronomical observatory."

"Mark it, Jack. We're going down."

Red made a four-fifths orbit and retroed, mushing into the atmosphere as easily as falling onto a featherbed. He shifted to air jets, and the jets coughed, wheezed and bit in. Our lasers were burning oxygen.

"Yippeeee, yeeeow!"

"Erin go bragh."

How beautiful the turbulence of air! How sweet the sounds outside of hulls! Once more for us, "up" was up and "down" was down without reference to the ship, and the pull of real gravity to the spaceman is as welcome as the arms of his beloved. More, as we planed lower into the thickening air, I saw herds of gazelle-like animals grazing on the plains, and once a string of copper needles stuck into a prairie, possibly communications relay towers of some

sort. Suddenly I dropped to my knees on the control-room
deck and offered up thanks for Red O'Hara's green polka-
dot drawers.

"Jack," Red's voice interrupted, "none of these mountains
top at more than six thousand, so I'm going down and level
off at angels eight. ETA at the co-ordinates is twenty minutes, and I've got one helluva tailwind."

"Roger."

Out of the port, I could see the terrain below, looking for
all the world like the Great Smokies and cut by winding
streams. I could distinguish between the dark of evergreens
on the northern slopes and the lighter green of deciduous
trees on the southern slopes. These mountains were older
than Earth's, but the flora seemed very similar. All that was
missing were signs of habitation.

"I see your observatory, Jack. South of it there's a large
cleared area. . . . Commencing approach circle."

Red banked the delta wings and I got a glimpse of the
observatory among the trees. A balcony circled its dome.
Near the building, I spotted another of the copper needles
peeking above the treetops. Now we were over the mountains again, turning back and leveling off, gliding down. I
felt the nose tip up, heard the supercharger cut in and Red
was standing the ship on its tail.

"Gyros!"

I cut in the vertical stabilizers, calling, "Gyros in." The
ship quivered from the torque. My seat tumbled in its gim-
bals, and the final approach panel was in front of me.

"Compressors."

"Compressors in."

The retro-jets bit into the air and the ship was falling,
stern down, as gently as a leaf.

"Struts!"

"Struts extending."

There was a clunk, a long creak and a final clunk as the
struts extended and the pods locked. Without reference to
panel, I could estimate our distance from the surface by the
changing pitch of our jet whine, but I was reading the board
with interest. Give or take a few pounds air pressure, a few
percentile points favoring oxygen and a fractional difference
in G forces, the life-support system of the planet was very
similar to Earth's, and the temperature reading told me that
a balmy morning in late spring awaited us outside. As I

heard the jet sibilance change to a roar and the roar grow muffled, I braced myself.

Except for a slight initial cant to the ship and a lurch as the landing struts righted it, the terror of the spaceman, touchdown on an alien planet, came off as smoothly as an elevator dropping to the lobby floor. Not once had I burdened my Creator with prayers during the descent, so confident was I of the skills of O'Hara.

"All readings A-Okay, Red. Lay below to lower the ramp and roll out the carpet. I'll rig the pavilion boom."

"Aye, aye, sir."

"And mind your manners, O'Hara. I've got a feeling Mother Earth will be getting a batch of new customers, today. . . . And, Red?"

"Yes, sir."

"If the customers are quadrupeds, keep in mind Navy Regulation 3,683,432."

"Which one is that, sir?"

"Bestiality—punishable by a confinement of not less than six months and not more than ten years."

"Glad you have it memorized, sir."

As I opened the hatch on the pavilion locker and swung out the boom, I smiled to myself. Red considered my words as banter, which I intended, but I had not roomed with Red O'Hara for four years without picking up a little of the con man's art.

In a con game, the most spontaneous gesture should have long-range ends in view. With the hatch closed and the locker empty, the pavilion storage compartment was also a brig with an outside lock on the door and the bulkheads padded. In the event of stalker's fever overtaking a crew member, the canvas tent could be jettisoned in flight and the lunatic confined. Shoreside, the compartment would serve beautifully as a brig.

When I opened the hatch to rig the boom, the compartment was flooded with the perfume of growing things, and as I stood in the hatchway I heard birds warbling from the woods. Below me a meadow, brightened with flowers, sloped to a natural amphitheater surrounding a flat field in the valley about 500 yards from the ship. Beyond the oval field, the valley rose again to a bare knob and beyond that hillock more trees. Through the trees, I could see with my binoculars what we had taken to be an observatory, a

white circular building topped by a dome that was surrounded by a balcony.

Above us, a few clouds floated in the blue and off to the
west, the ocean gleamed against the sweep of a wood-
covered and far-jutting peninsula.

"Look alive, sailor," Red called from the ground, thirty
feet below.

I looked down. He had lowered the ramp and leveled
the square of red carpet which would form the floor of our
exhibition tent.

"There's no door to the observatory," I called as I swung
out the exhibit case.

"Maybe it's on the far side," he yelled up. "They could
see us land, so they should be coming over in a few minutes.
Shake a leg."

I lowered the container and then hauled out the tent, a
pyramidal suspended from a telescoping boom a little
thicker than an auto aerial, to let it balloon downward, and
closed the hatch to preserve the symmetry of the ship. By
the time I walked down the ramp, Red was anchoring the
sides of the tent with dowlings.

Within fifteen minutes, the Earth exhibit was ready. We
lolled in camp chairs beside the marquee of the pavilion,
uniformed in dress silver with the blue lightning bolts on
our epaulets, our silver ship behind us with its blue Navy
stars on its wings, with the gold, blue and yellow stripes of
the pavilion soaring to a point of stars above us.

Our display cases flanked the entrance with their assort-
ment of beads, bracelets, earrings, toys and models, gifts
for the natives. Inside, seats were arranged for the three-
dimensional movies of Earth's wonders, natural and technological. Placed unobtrusively behind us inside the tent,
its viewing lens protruding through a flap in the canvas, our
language computer was set up and waiting. From the apex
of the tent, a concealed loudspeaker sent the jerk and jive
melodies of the Grave Images rolling down over the
meadow.

I was recording data orally into the captain's log as Red
scanned the treeline across the valley to pick up a sight of our
first customers when he motioned me to turn off the recorder.

"Why don't we tune down that racket?" he asked. "I
can't hear myself see."

"Regulations," I answered.

"Up regulations," he snorted.

I returned to the log, recording observations I could make from where I sat. Then I clicked off the log and shoved it into my tunic case, joining Red in his scanning of the distant treeline. There was nothing alive out there. We waited—fifteen minutes, half-an-hour, forty-five minutes—and there was nothing.

"Why don't I go over?" Red suggested. "At least I could get an idea what the building is."

"Regulations," I said. "You could walk into an ambush."

He looked at me. "I never thought Jack Adams was a book officer."

I am not an officer who goes strictly by the book, but I did not want Red to know it.

"You're learning, boy," I snapped. "Scan the sector from twelve o'clock to four o'clock."

He lapsed into a disgusted silence as I continued to sweep a zone ahead of me with the glasses, twenty degrees to right, twenty degrees to left—procedures established by Navy Regulations.

We saw them simultaneously, bipeds at ten o'clock, that broke from behind the knob across the valley, rushing down the slope wearing primitive leg armor and brandishing clubs. As I clicked off the Grave Images, Red said laconically, "Thanks. It looks like your ambush couldn't wait, or they don't like the music."

In the silence, we could hear their war whoops drift across the valley and Red said, "Better start some martial music—for us."

He reached back to our Earth-gifts display case and drew our laser rifles from a concealed drawer. I laid the weapon he handed me across my lap as I counted the warriors, twelve in all, armored but running at a speed no loinclothed Apache of Earth could have matched as they charged down the slope.

Suddenly they stopped at the flat area in the amphitheater, apparently for a war conference, and spread out into a line of battle. They planted markers on each flank of their skirmish line, and, suddenly, they began to kick a ball around.

"Forget our war, Jack," Red said. "It's a soccer team."

Not exactly soccer, I decided, as I put my weapon away. They were playing a combination of soccer, lacrosse and tenpins, kicking the ball with tremendous force toward a wicket of three pins guarded by a goalie who guarded with a stick. The object, apparently, was to score a strike on the pins behind the goalie, and one player succeeded as I turned the volume up on the Grave Images, hoisting it a few decibels to let it carry to the playing field.

But the players did not look up.

"Maybe they're nearsighted," I was saying when Red shouted, "Saints be praised, Jack. Look at *that!*"

Fifty yards below us and to the right, a girl had emerged from the line of woods.

"Jesus Christ!" I breathed—and I had not taken the Lord's name in vain—as I swung my glasses onto her figure.

For an approximation of the girl's stride, take the flow of a tiger's pacing, the lilt of a springbok's leap, and mix with the grace of a ballerina. Her whole movement was visible. She was less than five feet tall, but fully three of those feet were dedicated—no, consecrated—to legs. Bare feet, ankles, calves, knees and bare thighs swelled in diapasons to the glory of her buttocks, which swooped back and in to her narrow waist. Her dress, loosely gathered by a belt of ribbon, barely reached below her hips.

"This is no country for thigh men," O'Hara sighed.

She walked toward the amphitheater at an angle that would carry her face beyond our view and I reluctantly lifted my attention upward along her torso. Twin mammae protruded from her chest in the configuration of *homo sapiens* and a near-human head was balanced on her neck. Her face was bare of fur, as were her arms and legs, and she had eyebrows arching above two dark eyes, larger and farther apart than a human's. Her skin was white and her hair was black.

" 'All that's best of dark and bright,' " Red said, " 'meet in her aspect and her eyes.' "

"And her arse," I added, for the swing of her walk jostled the hemline of her skirt to reveal new prospects. Female she was, and not solely on the evidence of her breasts. She wore no panties.

"*Homo sapiens,*" Red gasped. "Proof positive!"

"Not by regulations," I snapped, still studying the girl's face. Not once had those eyes lifted toward us, and the guitars of the Grave Images beat against her unheeded. "She must be deaf," I said.

"Who in hell wants to *talk* to her?" Red asked. "Look!"

An irregular host of the long-legged beings trailed behind her from the woods, all moving with the same grace, with females outnumbering males. All wore the same short tunic. They walked singly, and the females were without jewelry or make-up. None so much as cast a glance toward our ship or our gaudy pavilion. No one talked, no one smiled.

"They have no curiosity," I said.

"Maybe they're more interested in soccer than in space ships and the Grave Images," Red answered.

"But there's no animation on their faces. They don't talk. They're drifting along like a herd of gazelles. Perhaps they're beasts, dumb brutes."

"Animals don't go to soccer games," Red said. "Anyway it looks like we're getting a couple of customers."

We were indeed. Two of the beings had detached themselves from the group and were walking up the slope toward us. They were children, a boy and a girl, and Red reached back into the toy case, pulled out a basketball and inflated it with a cylinder. He was spinning it in his hands when they glided close and stopped, keeping about twelve feet away and ten feet apart, looking at us with wide, expressionless eyes.

They were the equivalent of eight-year-olds on Earth, with rosy cheeks that might have come from the north of England. Their tawny hair curled back from their forehead and we could see ears beneath the hair. Their eyes were the same brown color as their hair.

"If eyes are the windows of the soul," Red said, "these beings must have great souls."

He smiled at the children, and his words and gesture revealed that he was making the common error of a spaceman—personifying aliens. To an alien, a smile may be an expression of hostility—even on Earth a laughing hyena is not noted for its sense of humor—and a hand extended in friendliness to a nonhuman may result in a broken arm. And Red's assumption that these beings had souls was against Navy Regulations.

"They appear to be evolved from lemur monkeys crossed with kangaroos," I said.

Ignoring me, Red pointed to himself. "Red," he said to the boy. Then, pointing to me, "Jack."

The children merely watched.

"Boy," he said, pointing to the boy. "Girl."

The children watched.

"Here, boy. Catch!" He tossed the basketball toward the boy, who stuck out his hand, palm down, and slanted the ball to the ground, where he caught and balanced it on his extended toes. The little girl sidled away from the boy. He flicked the ball slightly upward with his toes, swung his foot aside and kicked the ball toward the girl, who returned it with a sidewise flick of her leg. Soon the ball was volleying between them as each stood on one leg, the other leg moving like a pendulum, with the ball sounding *thud-thud* between them, moving in a flattening trajectory.

As lightly as go-devils wheeling from dust, they capered before us, keeping the ball between them with a drumming that rose to a whirring as the ball grew blurred to our sight. Yet they continued to look at us, gauging the ball's flight with their peripheral vision as they consumed more energy than long-distance sprinters. Finally the boy faltered. He struck the ball at an angle that drove it too high for the girl to return. She caught it in the crook of her knee, cushioned its recoil and swung it back to him in an easy arc.

He caught it with his instep, balanced it for a second atop his toes and tossed it gently upward and toward Red, saying plainly, "Here, Red. Catch!"

Then they turned and were running toward the soccer field at a speed I could not have matched.

Red held the ball and said, "They have vocal chords. These people are people."

"Not at all," I said. "They practice public nudity."

"Because they don't wish to hamper their hip movements," he argued. "They're not merely ambidextrous, they're ambipedal."

"Exactly," I said, "which makes them upright quadrupeds rather than bipeds."

"Don't take the book too literally," Red said. "We, too, are upright quadrupeds, and a fig leaf could qualify them for the human family."

"Regulations are regulations."

"But we make the scouting reports," he argued, "and we can bend the report a little to fit regulations. . . . Look, the woods are full of them!"

Another cluster of the beings had emerged from the wood at the same spot as the first, moving with the same purposefulness toward the playing field, and none looked up at us.

"Jack, they're all coming from the same direction."

"Probably entire villages migrate as a group," I said.

"I intend to follow that stream of traffic back and see if

I can discover where it's coming from, if you'll mind the store."

Using the ordinary prudence rule of spacemen, Red and I should have stayed together; but ordinary common sense told me these beings were more interested in the soccer game than in an ambush. Besides, I was curious, so I decided not to pull regulations on Red. I had set the tone I wanted, our "store" was about as popular as a kosher delicatessen at Mecca, and I, too, was curious. "Permission granted," I said.

Red removed his boots and stood up to slip out of his trousers. His shirt was longer than the aliens' tunics, but his green polka-dot drawers flashed beneath.

"You're out of uniform," I said.

"My silver breeks might frighten the bairns."

Looking at his gnarled legs covered by the pink fuzz of hair, I let my sense of truth overrule my official manner. "I would take my chances with the trousers," I said. "If they frighten the bairns, your legs will give them nightmares."

But Red was gone, moving toward the point of woods where the walkers had emerged. No sooner was he out of sight than I turned off the Grave Images.

It was pleasant to sit in the sunlight and watch the procession pass. Though the inhabitants were indifferent, the planet was friendly. Balmy air drifted down the hillside pungent with the odor of greenery and a few clouds moved across the sky. On the slope of the hill beyond the valley, a steady but sparse flow of beings were moving toward the amphitheater to sit in rows on the slopes surrounding the field. Except for the absence of sailboats on the distant bay, I could have been in Oregon.

The game began and the procession from the woods dwindled and began to move faster. Watching through my glasses, it was difficult to follow the contest. A player would drive toward a goal and, when his shot was blocked, he would turn and block someone else's shot toward the same goal. No bodychecks were thrown and there was less contact because of the agility of the players than there would have been in basketball on Earth. There was no scoreboard and no referee.

My mind grew vaguely troubled as I watched the scene. Give or take a few degrees of tilt, these beings were humanids. With facile toes and hands, they might well be

trained to work a double-level production line, and the
facility with which they handled their bodies in yonder
game portended well for safety programs. On the basis of
what I could report already, Earth would have a grade-A
colony on this planet. Transistor-radio factories would rise
among these woodlands. Earth's Bureau of Home Appli-
ances would set these beings to producing low-cost kitchen
ranges. Their soccer games would be company-sponsored.
But here, on a planet filled with insurable risks, my first
chore would be to violate the Church-State Clause in the
Alien Code.

And I would need Red O'Hara's compliance.

My attention was distracted from the game by a female
coming out of the woods. Heretofore they had come in
groups, but she walked alone, and she moved so sedately in
comparison with the animalistic swing of the others that
she reminded me of a ballet dancer projecting the image of
a queen. I focused my glasses on her, a handsome female
with hair so black it had a bluish cast. When I lowered my
glasses slightly, I saw that her stride was restricted because
her hips were hampered.

Concupiscence and carnality!

Plainly visible beneath her tunic, skintight against her
broader thighs, she was wearing the green polka-dot
drawers of Red O'Hara.

CHAPTER
FOUR

After my shock at the sight of Red's shorts wore off, my
heart exulted. Here was an opportunity to gain Red's
compliance. Not two hours on this planet and he had
been undrawered. He was married and adultery was a sin.
He was a space scout, and commingling with an unclassified
alien female was statutory bestiality—a misdemeanor violation of Navy Regulations. Literally and figuratively, the

Lord had permitted me to catch Red O'Hara with his trousers down.

I would swap him a misdemeanor for a misdemeanor, my silence for his. Under the Scout's Oath, we could not tell a lie, but we both could refrain from telling all of the truth.

When Red burst from the woods twenty minutes later at full gallop, his shirttail flapping in the breeze, officiousness was set on my face. O'Hara ignored my expression—if he noticed it—for he was talking before he came to a stop.

"Jack, you may think me daft, but do you know what those spires are?"

"Phallic symbols," I snapped. He was wearing a tiny maple leaf pinned to his shirt.

"Hell no! They're markers for subway stations forty feet underground. They've got trains. An express came by at ninety miles an hour."

His words almost shook my composure, but I had long-range goals and so I kept to formality. "What happened to your shorts?"

"I met a female in the woods, a fairy child," he grinned. "She took a fancy to my drawers, so I swapped them to her for this maple leaf."

"Come off it, Red. You'd never trade your luck even-steven for a plastic button."

"Why not?" He noticed my coolness and began to weasel. "I have sixty pairs. . . . Fifty-nine, now."

"Red, you're incorrigible, and you with a bride on Earth."

"Jack, that little angel's not even born yet, Earth time."

"Don't mess up the theory with your facts," I said. "When we re-enter her reference frame, Thelma's going to be the maddest woman in Christendom."

"Not necessarily," Red said. He pointed toward our ship. "I could ram that baby through the barrier fast enough to get back to Earth before the marriage and call the whole thing off—if you had guts enough to stand the Gs."

Red was trying to divert me, and he succeeded. "That's only a theoretical possibility," I said. "If it can be done, why hasn't it been done?"

"Don't mess up facts with theory," Red mimicked. "It hasn't been done because the Navy won't allow it. How could they court-martial a scout for violating regulations on a trip that he hasn't made yet?"

Red was beguiling me from my purpose, another example of his con art. "Speaking of court-martials," I said, removing the recording log from my tunic pouch and simulating a click of the "on" switch with my fingernail, "I am charging you, Ensign O'Hara, with commingling with an unclassified alien female. How answer you these charges, Ensign O'Hara?"

When I shoved the recorder toward him, I could have struck him in the stomach. He staggered back a pace, his face turned ashen beneath his freckles, and snapped to attention, his bare heels sounding with a thud instead of a click.

"Probe Commander Adams, Ensign O'Hara answers the charges in his native tongue." From that point, Red launched into a stream of Gaelic which was unintelligible to me but which, from his expression, was loaded with ancient Irish curses.

When he finished his defense, he saluted and I simulated a click of the "off" button. "Very well," I said. "Your Erse will be translated by the court."

"And the charges will be dismissed," he said. "But what's come over you, Jack? As a goat at Madame Chacaud's you were a prince. As a lamb your wool is getting in my teeth."

"For the record," I said, "these beings are subhuman."

"But we are the record," he protested. "If we declare these beings subhuman, the Harriers will be landing and yonder lads and lassies will be weaving carpets with their toes."

"What difference does it make to you?"

"I'm Irish. We learned sympathy the hard way. What matters if these beings have long legs, don't smile, or don't hold face-to-face . . . ?"

His declamation skidded into silence, for in his anger he had almost admitted to the misdemeanor, in English. The phrase he did not complete was "face-to-face coition."

His remarks, delivered in the conviction of his wrath, made me abandon my plan to blackmail acquiescence from him. Now, my scheme subordinated, my curiosity held sway. If it wasn't face-to-face, then what was it?

"Off the record, Red," I said, my voice dropping to a soft and confidential pitch, "how was the lass?"

"I'm telling you nothing, my lad, for my answer is on the

record, in Gaelic. It will prove my innocence. But I will make this prophecy in plain English: That cloak of piety you wear will rip like tissue paper once you have felt the toes of these lassies."

Now it was my turn for anger. Red had sneered at my deepest convictions as a "cloak of piety," had, in effect, placed a bet that my carnal longings were stronger than my faith.

"Catch, you bead-counting Mick!" I tossed the log to him. "And try to read back the pig-Latin you spoke for the record."

He juggled it in his hand for a moment. He knew that the tape could be replayed though it could not be erased, and he realized he would hear nothing. He tossed it back to me, wonderment written on his face. "Just what are you up to, Jack? If you've got a game going, deal old Red a hand."

"I'll deal you in," I said, "when you tell me why the lassies can't qualify face-to-face, for I'll never learn from experience."

A whirring came from the sky and we looked up. An air hover was descending toward us from the sky in the direction of the building. There were three beings seated on the craft around an object on a tripod.

"Jack, my boy," Red said, "not everyone on this planet is a soccer fan. Here comes our welcoming committee."

They were dropping to the ground, less than ten yards distant, and Red walked forward to meet them, his hands clasped high above his head in the regulation manner to show we were unarmed and came in peace. But the movement of his arms hoisted his shirt above the plimsol mark, and he wore nothing beneath. Red O'Hara, one half of a diplomatic mission from Earth, awaited to greet the emissaries of a foreign planet with his front and behind hanging out.

Of course, we expected no ambassador on a planet where we had arrived unexpected and uninvited, but I had hoped to be greeted by a mayor, police sergeant, or at least a rookie patrolman. We got an elderly female pilot of the hover craft who never moved from the controls, a girl who shouldered the box on a tripod and stepped down and a graying male who waved our salute away with a backhanded sweep.

Although he wore nothing but a tunic with no insignia of

rank, the male was in charge. He pointed to the concealed
scanning lens of our language computer and said something to the girl, who set the lens of her camera-like box
before the viewing scanner of our translator.

"Saints be!" Red voiced my own amazement. "She's setting up a counter-translator."

Gallantly Red stepped inside the tent to bring the translator out while I stood speechless.

Technically, the Mark XIV language translator is the
most sophisticated computer on Earth, yet these beings,
observing from a distance, had spotted its scanning lens,
deduced its purpose, and brought over a translator of their
own to exchange vocabularies.

We had landed on a planet with a technology as advanced as Earth's.

Covertly studying the older man, who never once looked
at Red or me, I got an impression of mixed wisdom and
idiocy—he resembled a moronic owl. But the girl was a
prize. Her green eyes contrasted with her light brown hair,
and her hands, as she adjusted the dials on her machine,
were as deft and as graceful as those of a Balinese hand-
dancer. As she adjusted the knobs with her hands, her toes
were leveling the machine on its tripod. Once she lifted her
leg to focus with her toes the viewing lens of her machine
and Red was fascinated by her agility. Fortunately, the machine blocked my line of vision; still it was her eyes that
drew my attention. Though without expression, they seemed
to exude the serenity of a woman kneeling before an altar
after benediction.

She set the machine to recording, signifying to O'Hara
that she wished him to transmit data into her translator.
When the light flashed green atop her machine, after five
minutes, she had O'Hara receive her machine's vocabulary.
After five more minutes, broken only by the whirring of the
machine and shouts from the soccer field, the lights again
flashed green.

The girl leaned over her machine and said something in
a sing-song, pushed a button and the machine's speaker
emitted in English, "One-two-three-four . . . testing."

We were ready to converse, and the gray-haired man
bent to his machine, looked into my eyes for the first time
and spoke. Seconds later his machine emitted, in the man's
own tone of voice, "I am Hedrik the Language Teacher.

The girl is Harla. The planet is Harlech. You have landed near University 36."

"I am Jack Adams," I said. "This is Red O'Hara. We are from the planet Earth in the Milky Way." I spoke into the translator, which repeated my words in Harlechian with the exception of the proper names.

"Why do you come to Harlech?"

"To learn, to teach"—I followed the formula—"to communicate and to establish the bonds of brotherhood or unity."

That "or" was an escape clause in a verbal contract drawn for the I.C.A. by Earth General Insurance. Scouts were coached not to use the phrase "brotherhood and unity."

"Learn you may," said Hedrik, "though the course in any single science takes four Earth years. Teach you may, though your courses may not be offered for credits. We are now communicating. We seek no bonds of brotherhood and/or unity with other planets."

This man was a space lawyer and he was rejecting my contract point by point.

"Do you speak for your government?"

"There is no government. Harlech is an association of self-administered universities. I speak as an advisor to Bubo the Dean of 36."

"Is there no industry?" I asked into the machine.

"Industry is automated. Our primary occupation is scholarship."

It was as if the heavens had opened and I saw before me a great opportunity to lead these beings to the Light. "We would like to teach," I said.

"What can you teach? Our technologies are the same."

"I can teach Earth customs, philosophy, government . . . perhaps a few courses in Earth religion," I said, throwing the last phrase in as an apparent afterthought, "to broaden the backgrounds of your students."

"And what can the red one teach?"

"Let him speak for himself," I said, quite unaware of Red's qualifications as a teacher.

Red stepped to the translator. "I could teach Earth folklore, poetry, drama, perhaps a few courses in Earth biology."

"Your word 'poetry' does not compute," Hedrik said.

"Let me define by example," Red said, and I noticed he was fingering the machine as he spoke into it. "I will compose a poem to Harla. Listen:

On this hilltop where I stand
  Green meadows slope to the sea.
Bright are the waters that gird this strand,
  Glittering far and free,
But brighter than oceans and greener than land
  Are the eyes of Harla to me.

He accented the rhythms he fed into the computer and
the sounds that came from the machine rose and fell with a
melody too lovely for my telling. And the translator crooned
with a tremolo and huskiness seldom achieved by the machine—O'Hara had slackened the diaphragm on its speaker.

If the girl's eyes could have formed an expression I know
that they would have glowed with pleasure, for she lifted
her foot and slapped its instep against the calf of the leg
she stood on to applaud the poet, Harlechian style. Her
gesture shamelessly revealed her nakedness.

Hedrik bowed to his translator and fed into it the longest
speech of the day. "We will add your courses to the university curriculum as electives, but first we offer you lodging
and linguistic tapes to let you learn our language. Select
such subjects as you wish to teach and submit them to the
registrar to be entered into the university catalogue. The
summer term begins fourteen days from this date. I go to prepare your quarters. You may assemble your teaching aids.
You will be summoned at six, if no storm intervenes. You
may roll up your tent. Harlechians are not attracted by lures."

He was turning to step back on the platform when the
girl said a few words to him and he turned back to the
translator.

"The girl, Harla, wishes for Red, with the maple-leaf
award, to tutor her in Earth biology."

Red reached for the translator, beating me to the button
by a hair. "In honor of the girl with green eyes, the greatest
wish of my heart is to tutor her in Earth biology."

Before the machine could emit the translation, I was
pressing the "input" button and feeding it a question:
"What does the maple-leaf award signify?"

They listened and Hedrik spoke again into his translator,
turned and stepped on the platform. As Harla hoisted the
machine aboard, its answer came loud and clear, branding
Red O'Hara an adulterer and the girl with the aura of
spirituality a harlot.

"Excellence in fornication."

As the hover craft dwindled in the sky, I turned to Red. "Despite their technology, doesn't it strike you as strange that they cannot predict the weather six hours in advance?"

He was taken aback by my subject and my mildness, but he answered promptly, "Not with a jet stream of 500 knots 10,000 feet above the surface."

"I recall you said something about a tailwind. . . . Stow the trinkets, Red. . . . There's something I wish to check."

I turned to the translator, pushed the "input" button and asked, "Translate Harlechian equivalent of word 'God.'"

Throaty and intimate from its relaxed diaphragm, the machine purred, "No Harlechian equivalent of word 'God.' Closest concept, the word 'Dean.'"

I fed the machine the word "Heaven."

"Exact Harlechian equivalent of word 'Heaven' is word 'Harlech.'"

"Hey, Red," I yelled. "Guess what? These gooks think their planet is Heaven."

"I'll buy that!" Red yelled back, with unseemly gusto.

For different reasons, I, too, felt elation. With no concept of God, Harlech was ripe and ready for the willing gleaner's hand. These harlots with the faces of angels would be given souls.

Our microtapes were packed and ready, our pavilion rolled and stored, the ship's sensors set to administer an electric shock to any who entered without my authorization, and all soccer fans had gone from the landscape when a youth broke from the woods, dressed in a black tunic and moving with the speed of a marathon runner. He carried a roll of parchment in his hand and sped up to us, stopped and handed the roll to me. It was written in English.

To the men of Earth, Bubo the Dean sends greetings.

The bearer of this scroll, Jon the Student, will conduct you to your quarters in the teachers' section of University 36. Bring only material you will need for classes. All other wants will be provided. Linguistic tapes have been prepared to assist you in learning our language.

Within eight days, submit your list of classes to the registrar. Total academic freedom exists at the university. No restrictions are imposed as to subject. Since your classes will be noncredit electives, it is recommended that you teach only subjects which will attract students.

Bubo the Dean

"Bejesus! A magna carta," Red said. "Teach what you wish, it says."

"If we can find the students," I pointed out. "With the curiosity quotient of these beings so low, we may find ourselves teaching to blank walls."

"Advertising will be the answer," Red said.

Our guide pointed toward the woods and we lifted our valises and followed him. I had expected a hover craft to come for us, but obviously Harlechians did not stand on ceremony. We were taking the subway.

And no porters had been provided, a fact which spared me embarrassment since I would not have permitted anyone to carry my library. In it were microfilms of all the known sciences, institutions and history of Earth deemed suitable for alien consumption. The only science not touched on was the military science, probably the one subject Red and I were both expert in and the one we were most qualified to teach.

Though military science was eradicated from our files, it was uppermost in my mind. We were trained to estimate the military potential of a planet, analyze its defense capabilities and assess its points of tactical vulnerability. If this planet were found to be subhuman, as I suspected, its potential for colonial exploitation would be invaluable.

Then, when the great, gray ships of Earth returned, wisping out of the fogs of space in battle formation, those squadrons would be deployed in part by the information made available to the admiral commanding by the Adams-O'Hara Probe. We both should get lieutenancies for this discovery.

Despite the emoluments offered, I felt that the burden of the observations would rest on me, for obviously Ensign O'Hara regarded Harlech as an extension of Madame Chacaud's. My junior officer would have his troubles until he sublimated his carnal appetites to the greater glory of the Empire of Earth.

As we neared the trylon I could see gleaming through the trees, O'Hara spoke in words that reflected the truth in my evaluation of him. "I'm offering a course in emotions, Jack. That fairy child who was so accommodating, right about there"—he pointed to a spot off the path as if he planned to erect a historical marker on the site—"functioned like a jeweled watch, with as much enthusiasm."

We had broken into an open glade with the tower soaring above us, three piers set in concrete and converging to an apex. There were no crossbeams between them and they seemed to be made of an alloy of copper. In the area beneath was only bare ground. Whatever the device, it was too elaborate merely to mark the entrance to a subway, but it was not a subspace laser-ray projector.

We descended a spiral ramp to the subway platform. Counting my paces and calculating our angle of descent, I figured 35 feet, not the forty that Red had estimated, as the distance of the platform below the surface. A number of earth-piercing bombs zeroed in on the towers could wreck the transportation system of the planet in short order. Below on the platform, I casually glanced at the tunnel walls, for the tunnel was as well-lighted as the platform. Light reflections from the glazed surface of the tunnel indicated it had been bored by lasers.

Harlech had the science to defend itself from an attack from space. Whether it could mobilize that science rapidly enough after a sneak attack had knocked out its transportation system was another question.

Tactically, one obvious point of attack would be the towers, I mused, as a whirring from the tunnel mouth rose to a rumble and a three-car train pulled up at the platform. At a nod from our guide, we entered the third car and walked down the aisle and took seats. Not an occupant of the car looked at us, although no one was reading or talking to his neighbor. For all the animation in the crowd, we could have boarded a hearse enroute to a crematorium.

"Yes, Jack," Red muttered from the seat beside me, "these beings could use a few episodes from 'Life Can Be Golden' to teach them emotions."

Among underground installations I have seen, including that relic of intraplanet warfare, the Norad hole, nothing could touch the complex that housed University 36. Before we reached the central station, the train passed through a marshaling yard at least twenty tracks wide. At the station, there were no escalators up. All passages led out into a mammoth warren, brightly lighted, ventilated and kept at an even temperature. Down the centers of all but the shortest *culs-de-sac*, two-way passenger conveyor belts moved at an eight-mile-per-hour clip. Weighted with our bags, the belts demanded an exercise of agility when we hopped aboard.

We rode half a mile to an intersection where Jon changed belts to carry us another three-quarters of a mile. "Not lemurs," Red commented. "Moles."

Jon stepped off the belt and led us to a door marked with three Harlechian characters, pointed at the inscription and said, "Red."

We went into a large office with a high settee and two desks. A girl sat at one of the desks, and when we entered she spoke into an intercom. Then she lifted her eyes to Red and the voice from the intercom came to us in English. "I am Veda the secretary of Red the Teacher. You may speak to me, Red, through this intercom or another on your desk."

Already these beings had wired the interoffice communicators to a central cybernetic translator. Red's living quarters were bugged.

Jon led us through the door to a spacious office with desk and other furniture, through it to a library lined with Harlechian books and into a bedroom with closets and an adjoining toilet with a high commode and stall showers. There was even a small kitchen in the rear with sink, refrigerator, table and high-legged stools. All the rooms were painted and carpeted, except the tiled kitchen, but no pictures were hung on the walls.

After our tour, Jon returned to the desk and pulled out a map of our underground complex. Speaking into the intercom, he showed us where we were in relation to the overall complex and nearby facilities, commissary, infirmary, stores. "On Harlech," he added, "it is not considered proper to look at one whom you are not addressing. Personal references or questions should not be used with another until an agreement is made by the use of 'thou,' the familiar form of address, between them. Personal conversations should not be carried on within the hearing of a third person. You will find a list of lesser taboos in your desk."

Red glanced at his wristwatch and suggested to me that we meet in an hour in the commissary. Our guide apparently noticed his act, for he said, "There is a twenty-eight-hour day on Harlech," pointing at a small clock on the desk. "If you wish to carry a timepiece, you may obtain one here." He pointed to a spot on the map.

"What do I use for money, Jon?" Red asked.

The word "money" was emitted from the translator in its English form, so I know it did not translate, but the Harlechian interpreted the word from its context. "All things on Harlech are to be had for the asking."

My quarters, fifty yards farther down the tunnel, were the duplicate of Red's. My secretary's name was Risa, but in the brief office conference with Jon, the boy added a sentence for me he had omitted in his talk with Red. "If you wish sex, call Risa."

"Why didn't you tell this to Red?" I asked.

"He wore the sign of the maple leaf, so he would know. Can I be of further service?"

Bending to the intercom, I spoke rather harshly. "Yes, fire that girl and get me a male secretary."

On Harlech, things were done with dispatch. When I emerged an hour later, showered and shaved, a pimply-faced lad said, "I am Hal the secretary of Jack the Teacher."

Our commissary was an automat, the foods similar to those of Earth, though mostly vegetables, with a meat that tasted much like beef. Around us, about forty diners sat at the tables, and all observed the primary taboo. Over Harlechian coffee, Red and I discussed the ban against the direct gaze. "It must spring from a need for privacy in such confined living areas. And casual chit-chat is ruled out by the private-conversation taboo."

"Oh, yes," Red said, "and wonderful it is to make love without the hurdle of vacuous female chatter. There can be no pillow talk where there are no pillows."

"Don't tell me you've bedded your Veda already?"

"Hoisted is the better expression," Red said enigmatically. "But all in the name of biological science. If these beings can cross-breed, they are two legs up on acceptance to human status."

"Your experimentation is pointless," I retorted, "since they are godless beings who have no military."

"I have my own ideas about that."

His was a cryptic remark but I questioned him no further, for I had a few ideas of my own which would not stand questioning. So we shifted to theorizing why these beings chose to live underground. We agreed that some past intercontinental nuclear war or threat of war had driven them below.

That theory began to look somewhat tenuous after we went under narcosis and devoted fourteen hours of the twenty-eight-hour day to learning the Harlechian tongue.

It took me four days to learn the language, which had no connectives, no conjunctions and no subjunctives—conditions contrary to fact were not accepted by Harlechians. The entire vocabulary, technical and otherwise, consisted of less than 40,000 words, despite the fact that the flora of the planet was similar to Earth's. There were far fewer animals, however, on this planet.

Words were formed from simpler combinations. For instance, "flow" was the word for life and movement. Air was "sky flow," water "ground flow," tides "sea flow," electricity "power flow." Once the root words were learned, it was simple to construct variations on the roots and be understood. Going to a movie, for instance, could be expressed as "Leg flow to light flow."

I broke somnolence only for meals, and by the second day I was picking up snatches of conversations around me. At that time, the students were taking their final exams for the winter quarter and their talk was limited to academic subjects. The rhythm of the speech was similar to Earth's Scandinavian.

By the third day, I had mastered the language well enough to visit the installations on the campus, and I was surprised when I visited the school's infirmary. It had a large and lively maternity ward for coeds, but there were no fathers pacing the anterooms. A nurse informed me that no record was kept of the fathers since the matter was of academic interest only, even to the mothers.

In one small way, this planet its inhabitants called Heaven did resemble the Christian Heaven—there was no giving or taking in marriage. Harlech was a planet of bastards.

On the campus, I could follow the life-cycle of an individual, for the cryogenic mortuary had a viewing window facing a gallery for student observers. Corpses were carried to the mortuary and dissected for the organ banks in public view without ceremony. If a corpse was too old for salvage, it was carted back to the crematorium. I was appalled by the cold efficiency displayed with pagan disregard for ritual.

Very few teachers were visible in the tunnels. Most of the adults I spotted among the students were service personnel.

It took Red five days to master the language, and our meager difference, if any, in linguistic ability could not account for his tardiness. I suspected Red of breaking somnolence for long periods, and my suspicions were verified on the evening of the sixth day. I sat in my library, reviewing Earth training films, when my phone rang.

The merry voice of the Celtic star rover came over the line, speaking in Harlechian, "Jack, my lad, let's lift a brew in celebration of my graduation. Meet me in the neighbor-hood tavern at 22:00."

"What tavern?"

From my vocabulary studies, I knew that strong drink existed on the planet, but I had no idea where to obtain such spirits.

Red gave me tunnel co-ordinates not far from Faculty Row.

"Why not now?" I asked.

"I'm interviewing a new secretary at 21:00."

"What's wrong with the old one?"

"Nothing, Jack. That little old thing's still perking like a horizontal coffeepot. But she needs an assistant."

"What qualifications are you looking for?"

"More torque," he said.

"Red, are you drunk?"

"I've fungoed a few. Go on over to the bar and catch up with me if it's not against your religion."

"Well," I said, "the Good Book says we can drink a little wine for our stomach's sake."

So it was that I agreed to go ahead of him and meet him there. Navy Regulations permitted drunkenness to be en-tered as a defense when space sailors stood accused of minor breaches of security, loose talk, or conduct unbecoming an officer. This night I intended to sound out Red with some carefully selected loose conversation. If drunkenness was the price one must pay to advance a high purpose, then the nobler angels of my nature would have to wobble in their flight.

Sustained by my righteousness, I advanced to the bar. Not only was I willing but suddenly I was eager to down a few boilermakers with the companion of my wilder days.

CHAPTER
FIVE

R ed must have found the bar with a dowsing rod or some
Irish instinct for whisky. There was no neon sign to mark
it and no military policemen stationed before it, only let-
tering on the door which translated: "Power groundflow
here" or "Firewater served."

It was a cocktail lounge with soft lights, lounge chairs,
tables, a bar with stools and the click of Harlechian voices
beneath flutings from a juke organ. I ordered a whisky and
beer at the bar, feeling actual nostalgia for the old days of
brawls, drinking and sins of the flesh, and my poignancy
was enhanced when a girl rose and came to the bar with an
order for her table. As she waited near me, she spoke out of
the corner of her mouth, softly. "How's it for a bit of hip
slip, Big Boy?"

"Hip slip" is slang for "hip flow," the formal term.

Coldly and formally, I answered, "Ni lik flick," as she
turned back to her table.

Stifling my nostalgia, I downed a whisky and sipped my
beer chaser as I meditated on the good life and the rewards
of virtue—freedom from bruises, hangovers and Monday-
morning remorse. Before I had finished my second boilermaker, the door opened and O'Hara, three sheets in the
wind, staggered in.

Nude and lewd!

For once, the Harlech taboo against staring was threatened with a mass violation. Red wore the plaids of a High-
lander, a green tam-o'-shanter and a folded tartan angled
over his shoulder. A leather pouch was strapped to his belt
and his legs, gnarled oak trunks covered with pink moss,
jutted from beneath kilts so short they would have made a
Scotsman blush. He wore no shorts. Arranged like military
decorations down the forefront of his tartan were five
maple-leaf awards.

"What in the name?— Where in the?— How did you get those mini-kilts?"

"At a tailor's grotto," he roared in Harlechian, "corner of South Sixth Tunnel and West Eighth Burrow. What these little frog-eyed kangaroos can't do with their fingers, they do with their toes. . . . Mac, set up my regular."

Since the bartender's name was Mac and he had commenced pouring a double whisky with a beer chaser, I knew O'Hara had not merely found the place but that he was already an habitué.

"Lower your voice," I said. "Some of these lads might take offense."

"Let them," he bellowed, scowling over the seated drinkers, "and I'll bounce a few of these swan-necked heads off the ceiling. . . . But never fear, Jack. Biologically this planet has gone to seed." His voice sank to a stage whisper that carried through the closed door and across the tunnel. "You know why these moles live in holes? They're afraid of the weather topside. . . . Well, here's to Earth, lad, the planet that raises hell and men."

"To Earth," I repeated, clicking glasses.

"We're in a pure democracy, Jack, and you know why? These owl-eyed grasshoppers haven't got the energy to organize a government. They can't breed leaders. Ah, lad, and there I see a golden opportunity. On a planet of multiple amputees the one-armed man is king."

"O.K., Red. We'll flip for the throne. Tails I'm king and heads you're prime minister."

"That's an O'Hara flip," he said promptly, proving he wasn't as drunk as he pretended.

"Another round, boy," I called to the bartender.

I could act drunk myself, and I smelled a confidence game other than my own.

"Jack, we could set up our own little colony, here. We don't need the I.C.A."

"Watch it!" I snapped. "These walls have ears."

The Interplanetary Colonial Authority was a quasi-military intelligence agency, and Harlechian agents could be planted in this room. In English I added, "If you're proposing a conspiracy to deprive Earth of a colony, there won't be enough of you left to donate to an organ bank. Now, tell me," I shifted back to Harlechian, "what's the reason for the kilts."

"Advertising, lad. Look at this." He reached into his

pouch and pulled out a packet of printed cards. "We're teaching electives, so I'm drumming up the student trade."

Glancing at the engraved card pasted atop the packet, I read:

Jack the Teacher
Specializing in Out of This World Subjects
The only blue-eyed teacher on Harlech

I was touched by his thoughtfulness in finding a printer and ordering the cards printed for me, but I had to point out an obvious mistake. "Red, I'm not the only blue-eyed teacher on Harlech. There's you."

"Oh, no," he said. "Your card must be read in conjunction with my own. Here."

He handed me his card, which read:

Red the Teacher
Specializing in Out of Any World Subjects
The only blue-eyed, red-headed teacher on Harlech

He was upstaging me, but I expressed no resentment because I was more curious about another item of his dress. Pocketing my cards, I remarked, "Thanks, but how'd you earn the maple-leaf cluster?"

"You know how I earned the top one," he said, "and the rest were awarded for excellence in language studies. I ran through four tutors before I mastered the brogue. This bottom one came from Harla. Remember the girl who adjusted the translator's scanner with her toes?"

"Indeed," I said. "The inspiration for your love lyric."

A pensive look came to his eyes. "When that little girl kinked her knee at me, it was love at my first sight. . . . She taught me irregular verbs."

"There aren't any irregular verbs in Harlechian," I objected.

"So!" He shook his head sadly and signaled for another round. "That pecker-plucking lik flicker was just putting me on. . . . Jack, you're a theologian. Love is a giving, right?"

"In part, yes," I said.

"My charity's wearing me out. I'm beginning to feel like a one-man Community Chest."

"Try celibacy," I suggested.

"Not on your life," he said. "Generosity's my one virtue,

and I intend to keep my virtue. By the way, you floored that lad, Jon, when you asked for a male secretary. Are you trying to ruin the good name of Earth?"

Since I had not mentioned getting a male secretary to Red, I was more surprised that he knew than I was at his interpretation. Obviously rumor-mongering existed among the students of Harlech.

"No," I answered. "I fired the girl to retain what little was left after you got through with the good name of Earth. Carnality is evil."

"I'm with you there, lad," he said, "100 percent. It's wearing me down. Maybe I should get a male secretary."

"Tired of bedding the lassies?" I oozed sympathy.

" 'Hoisting' is the word, Jack. Seventy pounds can be heavy when held horizontally. But the problem's not only physical. The laws of economics are setting in."

"How do economics figure on a planet without money?"

"When goods are in excess supply, their value goes down. I'm losing my interest, Jack. There's no challenge, except for a weightlifter, and I don't really enjoy myself unless I'm breaking some law, moral, social, or legal."

"Such as Navy Regs?" I suggested.

"Especially Navy Regs," Red said. "And I'm drunk, so you can't bring charges."

"I'm drunk, so I'm listening," I said.

"I wish you'd teach a course in chastity, Jack. You're an expert. Maybe you could come out and denounce carnality, teach them that promiscuousness is sinful."

"Another round here, boy," I called, mostly to hide my consternation. From where I read the helm, it looked like Red was on the course I had plotted.

Turning back to O'Hara, I shook my head. "Sermonizing against sex to Harlechians would be like arguing against hopscotch with children. Even their word for it sounds like an all-day sucker. " 'Lik flick' just doesn't sound dirty enough."

"Aye," Red shook his head sadly. " 'Dirty'! Now, there's a good word. Sex is no fun lest it's furtive. If we had Brother Ben here he could put the fear into these bairns. A shot of old-time religion would put guilt feelings in their crotches. *That* would give chastity a value, lend dimensions to romance, make love a challenge."

"And violate the Church-State Code," I reminded him.

"Forget the Codes," he said. "We make the report. At

best it will be two years before a survey team checks the
planet to verify the report."

"Even so," I said, "these beings have no concept of sin,
primal or otherwise, so how can they be delivered from a
bondage they're not aware of?"

"Jack, my lad," Red said, and I sensed he was coming in
for a landing, "I spring from a long line of acolytes, though
none ever made the priesthood. My genes believe in succor-
ing souls, but I only hallow the soil, I cannot harvest."

"I don't read your message," I said.

"What I'm saying, Jack, is this: I'll teach 'em to sin if
you'll save 'em."

Wild ideas were an O'Hara specialty, so the very im-
plausibility of his scheme gave it sincerity. Still, I shook my
head, not wanting to seem too eager. "Sin hasn't been
'taught' since the Hebrew children studied Baal."

"I've given thought to the lectures," Red disputed. "With
visual aids from Earth, I think I could swing a course in
Elementary Human Emotions. The females are educable. I
taught Harla to smile, and she's learning to whimper and
moan. . . . The way I figure it, I could hit them low and you
could hit them with the hellfire-and-damnation angle."

"Let's go to the table and figure out a curriculum," I
suggested, taking my drinks from the bar. As I led him
from the bar to our first faculty conference, I felt like a Judas
ram leading a sheep to slaughter. O'Hara, the master trick-
ster, had outwitted himself. He had conned me into doing
what I had intended to con him into letting me do. Now,
instead of a silent witness, Red was an accessory before the
fact.

Within two hours, Red and I had worked out a schedule
of classes. I was to teach three quarterly courses in succession: Human Customs, Ethics and Values, followed by
Earth Religions 1 and Earth Religions 2. Red was to parallel and support my classes with Elementary Human Emotions, followed by two survey courses: Love, Courtship and
Marriage, and Earth Rituals, Folklore and Superstitions. We
agreed to eliminate all but a passing reference to Buddhism,
Islam, Hinduism and to touch on Judaism, in Religions 1,
only as a background for Christianity. My wild-card course
for each quarter was Aesthetics and Awe. Red's would be
Earth Drama. We both took a once-a-week class in gym
featuring Earth Games and Sportsmanship.

In the area of Christianity, primarily Religions 2, we

struck a snag. Red held out for the Seven Mysteries of the Catholic Church but I balked at Mary's bodily ascent to Heaven and her crowning as Queen of Angels. Red persisted in his support of the woman until I asked him pointedly, "Look, Red, do you really want to see an angel given authority over men?"

He cogitated only for a moment. "You're right, Jack. Uncrown her."

We completed the schedule and Hal sent it to the registrar's office. The registrar's student assistant assured our student assistant that she would okay it immediately and see that it got into the catalogue. With the exception of the language teacher, we had not met an instructor since our arrival on campus.

Because our courses were electives with no credits given, there was a possibility that we would have no students at all. We could not rely on our value as curios because intellectual curiosity among Harlechians seemed minimal, even in the presence of Red's revealing kilts and my modest, full-length trousers. Red was a walking billboard in his kilts, but his advertising was not reaching the right market. Otherwise it was successful to a point where, when we met of evening in the taproom, his morning's effervescence was gone and he looked pekid.

"Aren't you feeling well?" I asked.

"A little of my edge is gone, come evening."

By now he was tottering under a load of maple leafs pinned to his tartan. "Why don't you strike a gold leaf for every ten green leaves," I suggested, "and lighten your burden."

He took my suggestion, but he was still tottering, the next day, under three gold leaves and five greens. "It's killing me, Jack, but I can't break these lassies' hearts with an outright rejection."

Our morale was not helped any by a bulletin that appeared on the refectory board on a morning two days before classes commenced:

Pursuant to the suggestion of the Registrar, the Department of Primitive Anthropology has added elective courses to its curriculum which will be presented by the alien instructors, Jack the Teacher and Red the Teacher. Students desiring to take these courses are cautioned against commenting on the malformed legs and eye structure of the aliens.

Bubo the Dean

When Red saw the notice, he exploded with a stream of expletives which would have offended even a nonpious man and stalked from the commissary.

"Where are you going?" I called.

"To corner that frog-eyed will-o'-the-wisp, Bubo."

For myself, I was amused by the notice. In the days of prespace mythology, the universe had been peopled with bug-eyed monsters. The myths were wrong. Space held only two squint-eyed, bandy-legged monsters: Red O'Hara and me.

Red couldn't find Bubo. He telephoned to report that evening, but he had gotten satisfaction from Bubo's student secretary, a male. He had written the notice in the first place, at the suggestion of Hal, thinking he was doing us a favor by advertising our classes. In the morning, a new notice had been placed on the bulletin board:

> Pursuant to the suggestion of Red the Teacher, courses offered by the aliens have been transferred to a new Department of Liberal Arts. Students desiring to take these courses are cautioned against commenting on the malformed legs and eye structure of the aliens.
>
> *Bubo the Dean*

Arriving late for breakfast, Red commented on the change with pleasure. "No Earthman is taking orders from a bug-eyed department head. I've got my pride."

On the last day before the opening of the semester, we climaxed our campaign with large posters spotted throughout the dining halls. In circus type, printed in beautiful red against a background of pale yellow, they extolled the wonderful courses offered by Jack and Red the Teachers. The tagline was pure O'Hara:

> Thrill to leprechauns!
> Experience the miracle of Salvation!

Red, I felt, was promising more than I could deliver with the last item, but it was morning and Red's seltzer still fizzed. "Have faith, lad. You can do it with an assist from O'Hara."

From Hal, I learned that class lists were not given to the instructors until after the beginning of lectures and that forty students was the maximum any one instructor was permitted for a single class. We were working blind as far as our advertising campaign was concerned, so Red printed up an advertising placard for my wall: "Hit forty!"

If we could have used television, I'm sure Red would have tried it. There was a television set in the dining hall, and there was a broadcasting studio on campus with a continental hookup, but it was never used except for official announcements. According to Hal, they had tried television on Harlech but had given it up.

On the day school opened, Bubo the Dean appeared on local television to welcome new students arriving on campus. He was a bald-headed little man whose broadcast lasted less than a minute. He told the new arrivals to ask their teachers for information if such information was not covered in the catalogue.

When the catalogue reached our office, we found our classes listed alphabetically among 420 other subjects being offered.

Opening day was a disappointment. Eight students attended my first class on Values, six were in my first class on Aesthetics. My afternoon class in Values attracted twelve, but the afternoon class in Aesthetics sank to six. Even so, it was not the scarcity of students that caused me greatest concern.

Classrooms were arranged in four tiers rising from the lectern to the back wall. There were no desks, only high stools, and the stools were so arranged that each could be seen from the lectern. In my ordinary relations with the students, their nudity had caused me no problem with my greater height, but looking up, the view was embarrassing. Moreover, the taboo against looking into the faces of one not spoken to directly conflicted against the Earth taboo against looking at the nakedness of a female, and the classes were largely female.

Yet, I had to call the roll, and call it I did, trying to identify voices by the shape of the midriffs. For my introductory lecture, the same for all courses, I had not brought visual aids, so I could not darken the classrooms to show slides. I drew a celestial chart on the blackboard, using twenty minutes for a demonstration originally scheduled to last ten, to show the relation of Earth to Harlech.

Finally, I had to turn and face the class, extolling the beauty of my home planet, the joys of life lived on its surface and the purpose of space scouts. I lifted my eyes to the ceiling, saying, "Our stars and moon by night, our cloudscapes by day, are visions of surpassing loveliness. We, too, once dwelled in caves, but the beauty above us drew us out of the darkness to face the perils of life on the surface."

One I had lifted my eyes to the ceiling, surveying imaginary skies, they stayed there. I could not drop them again, and I hoped that my students would consider my posture merely another of Earth's strange customs.

That was the longest day, but my opening remarks on modesty as an Earth custom was delivered with the fervor of an evangelist. Concealment as an art in Aesthetics was not described but declaimed and, when I finally unglued my eyes from the ceiling at the close of each class, the indecency was still there. Above it, I could glimpse the faces of my students, staring with blank eyes forward, not taking notes, merely listening, as unashamed in their nakedness as so many Adams and Eves.

It was a sad meeting I had with Red at our tavern. In comparing notes, I found with some gratification that his classes averaged one and a half students less than mine. His advertising campaign had been a failure, but mine had failed less.

"Perhaps you suffered from overexposure," I suggested. "Maybe it would help if you wore shorts under your kilts."

"Aye, Jack," he said. "Your trews must be the answer, they wonder what is hidden there." Suddenly his face lighted. "Jack, we're going to get more students!"

"How?"

"I'll wear my lucky drawers."

"You've already played your ace," I said. "You have no hole card."

"No, the drawers will do it!" he insisted. "There was my error. Besides, my voice is so weak I can hardly lecture, so the drawers might help fend them off. I've got to be more selective without offending the generosity of the lassies. And that gold star gave me an idea. . . ."

"Were you distracted by their nudity?" I asked, rubbing my sore neck.

"Hell no! I called the roll by it since all their faces look alike."

I told him how I had evaded matters by staring at the ceiling.

"Pretend you're a gynecologist," he suggested, "and look upon them as objects and not as subjects."

"Tonight I'll meditate," I said. "Some answer will come to me."

"Good," he said. "With the aid of the Lord and my polka-dot drawers, we'll salvage this semester."

That evening, alone in my study, I meditated on the problem of nudity, my own discomfort in its presence and the attitude I should adopt toward the Harlechian indifference to nakedness. As an astronaut, I had been trained not to overreact to bizarre practices, and in theory I should have been as indifferent to these beings as I would have been to baboons. They were not humans but humanids, and their practices barred them forever from the World's Brotherhood. But the very fact that I meditated denied me exit through the doors marked "Arrogance" or "Pride in Species."

O'Hara's suggestion that I should adopt an objective attitude was valid but would take time. Too long had I considered these matters subjectively. In a word, I was "involved." My stimulus-response mechanism had been overtrained to respond until Brother Ben Pruitt had taught me the wisdom of self-denial. Now, I wondered if I had substituted prudery for my former prurience.

Finally, I hit upon a solution.

My first attempt to avoid confrontation had been the coward's way and theologically unsound. To face temptation and to resist it would strengthen my spiritual muscles. I would accept the situation as a challenge and a blessing, for it would have me overcome the biggest rat of sin which still gnawed at my vitals—lust of the flesh.

It is one thing to confront a theoretical devil in the quietness of a study: it is another to engage the devil in hand-to-hand conflict. The next day, my classes were increased by three and a half females, on the third four and a half, on the fourth by eight. Hal, my secretary, explained it: "Academic freedom also extends to students. Your classes were monitored the first day by various scouts, who sent their reports back to their departments. You should hit forty."

Within three weeks, both O'Hara and I had hit forty. Once all stools in the room were filled it was no longer necessary to call the roll, but I did so for aesthetic reasons.

Nowhere among the cultures of Earth are the pubes considered objects of beauty—*toujours le fig leaf*—and tradition conspired with my innate modesty to cloud my observations the first week, but now I dispute the cultures of Earth. Though I never attained objectivity, I did achieve a balance between prurience and prudery which allowed me to simulate indifference and to observe and to evaluate my observations with growing refinement.

"Down with the fig leaf" will never become the cry of Jack Adams, and my lectures on modesty continued with zeal. I relied heavily on slides of ladies' fashions taken from the era when legs were referred to as "limbs" and an ankle revealed was a blush aborning, but I must give the devil his due.

As Red had suggested, and as the classroom architect obviously intended that I should do, I continued to call the roll in the Harlechian manner, never violating the taboo against gazing into faces. In fact, the faces of my students remained blurred and nameless while that which Shakespeare so quaintly called "the forfended places" began to assume personalities—grave Orlis and laughing Alita and Cara with the golden hair.

Cara floated within my ken in grace and beauty, plus a quality at first indefinable. Cara, I think, more than any other, inspired me to introduce the English word "beauty" into Harlechian to replace the clumsy compound word they used. She was my golden girl, the teacher's pet, and I never looked on her face from fear of disillusionment. Her mound of Venus swelled as a perfect ovate spheroid tasseled with cornsilk curls. A faint ellipsis to the outer labia gave the whole that strangeness of proportion without which there is no true beauty, and the curve gave it an air of joy blended with a feeling of peace which seemed to exude happiness and serenity. But still its aura defied definition until, one morning, inspiration provided me with the word which encompassed the whole—Cara's had character.

As I struggled to retain celibacy, O'Hara struggled to attain partial abstinence without offending his "lassies." To set up controls that permitted him selectivity, he installed the Order of Saint George, donated by a medal hung by a wide red ribbon from the neck of the recipient. The medal itself, a Cross of Saint George, was cast from bronze, its surface anodized a deep green with an interior cross of white. It was a beautiful object that served a secondary function in a world Harlechians had never known: it was O'Hara's backhanded swipe at England.

By publicly posted terms of the Order, no maiden could

become a Dame of the Order of Saint George with a frontal assault on O'Hara. To earn her cross, the applicant had to tempt Red with her wiles. Luring him into courtship was merely the first hurdle. She had to resist his advances for at least one-half of a Harlechian hour of seventy minutes.

Through this simple device, which he credited to my gold-star suggestion, and from his donning underwear, Red gained a rebirth of energy, which he transmitted to his teaching.

Drama was his favorite course, but feminine guile and wiles were taught in his course on Elementary Human Emotions, with the use of visual aids. One half of each hour was spent viewing Earth soap operas with subtitles in Harlechian.

Once I called for him during a session on Earth Dramatics and I got an inkling of his teaching methods. Standing outside the door, I listened as he spoke.

"When, *poof*, the fire-breathing dragon vanished, and there stood the leprechaun in his little green suit, laughing, *heh heh heh, hee hee hee, hah hah hah.* Now, all together students, *heh heh heh, hee hee hee, hah hah hah.*"

There, for the first time on Harlech, I heard laughter from the throats of Harlechians, and pleasant it was, like the tinkle of tiny bells, rising to peals of genuine laughter.

Still, when Red joined me, I was troubled. To the literal minds of the Harlechians, leprechauns and dragons were real—Red the Teacher had spoken. And O'Hara's Celtic imagination was peopling their minds with demons which I would have to exorcise before leading them to the Cross, when Religion 2 would be taught.

As we walked away from the classroom, I let his enthusiasm die in praise of his students. They could memorize their lines at one reading and their art of mimicry was unsurpassed. "They're all method actors, Jack, for they believe in their roles as the gospel truth."

"Speaking of the Gospel, Red, you may do them harm by feeding their minds with superstitions."

"No, Jack," he demurred. "I'm preparing their minds to believe when the day comes for you to tell them of God speaking from a burning bush, of manna from heaven and of our Blessed Savior walking on water."

O'Hara always took the long view.

Slowly my lectures on modesty began to have effect, at first among the coeds. As the summer semester drew to a

close, more and more students appeared in my classes wearing underwear, and one morning when I surveyed my
classes, I found, with the poignancy of farewell, that the
ellipsis of Cara had been covered. Only then did I cease to
call the roll, and my students sank into anonymity.

Underwear became a campus fad. Males as well as females were swept up in the craze. Understandably, the
dominant fashion for undies was green polka dots.

Then another fashion note was sounded on the campus.
One morning a petite miss with lustrous dark hair and eyes
made an entrance into the class. Around her neck was a
wide red ribbon drawn to a V between her breasts by the
green and white of the Cross of Saint George. Red had
awarded his first decoration.

Within a week I spotted another on a female passing me
in the corridors. She, too, was brunette, a lissome wench
who walked with undulations extreme even for Harlech.

It was several days before I could compliment Red on his
choice of recipients because the press of work had forced
us to cut our tavern meetings down to the Sixth day,
roughly Friday of the eight-day week. Then I commented
on the fact that both dames were dark-haired.

"I've had my fill of golden-haired angels," he said, "and
I'm recruiting a cast for a television drama and none of my
girls wish to play Juliet because she is killed. Since she's
Italian, she has to be dark-haired."

"You're presenting Shakespeare!"

"Ninety minutes, prime time, on a nationwide hook-up,
Sixth day, next fortnight."

"How did you arrange it?" I asked. "I thought Bubo had
a monopoly."

"Nobody has a monopoly. The students run this school.
A few of my communications majors in the drama class are
handling production."

"Which play are you presenting?"

"I open with the murder of Macbeth by Mrs. Macbeth. . . ."

"Hold it, Red," I said. "I read Shakespeare in high school.
Lady Macbeth didn't kill Macbeth. Banquo killed Macbeth."

"That's a technicality," Red said. "I have Lady Macbeth play Hamlet's mother to give more punch to the incest
scene when Hamlet accuses his mother of murdering his
father in order to bed down with Macbeth's brother, Iago."

"How does Juliet get into the act?"

"She's fleeing Shylock, who's after his pound of flesh, and she winds up in the castle, where Hamlet falls in love with her."

"What happened to Ophelia?"

"That part doesn't play too well," Red explained, "so Hamlet packs her off to a nunnery in the second act. She was too wishy-washy."

"You're casting a blonde as Ophelia?"

"What else?" Red snorted his contempt.

CHAPTER SIX

Incredibly, Red pulled it off, a pure Shakespearean soap opera, with some of the best lines the Bard ever wrote worked into the melange.

O'Hara asked me to review the play for his cast since there were no newspapers on Harlech and no drama critics who could estimate the quality of the performance by Earth standards. I turned down an invitation to the studio and agreed to meet them after the telecast at the tavern because I wanted to watch from the mess hall to judge the crowd's reaction.

"Hamlet Macbeth" was staged against a microfilmed backdrop of Earth scenery that changed with the scenes, opening on a lonely Scottish moor where witches cackled and prophesied doom for the House of Macbeth. The camerawork was excellent, and when the camera zoomed in for a close-up, the emotions revealed on the face of the actors were Earth emotions. Juliet, played by an actress named Kiki—whom I recognized as the medal-holder from my Aesthetics class—was beautifully bodiced in lace and purple velvet with a flaring gown that reached almost halfway to her knees. Her hair was pinned high around a medieval henning.

In the last scenes, Hamlet was brought to a towering rage

by Iago's hints that Iago had not only indulged in the delights of his sister-in-law, Lady Macbeth, but also those of his daughter-in-law by marriage, Hamlet's own beloved wife, Juliet. In his jealousy, Hamlet kissed his sleeping bride farewell, then stabbed her with a bodkin he removed from her hair.

But Iago was hidden behind the arras with the castle's men-at-arms to witness the murder. When they charged into the room, Hamlet knew his wicked stepfather-uncle had tricked him into murdering his innocent Juliet. Hamlet then delivered his poignant farewell address, beginning, "To sleep, to dream . . ." and ended it all with the bare bodkin.

There was an audible intake of breath from the audience when Hamlet plunged the skewer into his breast and stumbled backward, slowly, to fall over the body of Juliet. There was a slow fade-out as the camera focused on the scene and swung up to hang directly over the purple bed where the two corpses lay, criss-crossed like the Cross of Saint George behind the superimposed credits which flashed on the screen. After the screen went empty and the lights came on, the students stood and slapped the soles of their feet against their calves, applauding and continuing to applaud the dead television set.

Definitely the laity had scored over the clergy, and far beyond the confines of P.U. 36, I had to admit as I stepped aboard the belt for the tavern. I stifled pangs of jealousy as I composed a critique of the production for the cast.

Iago had been overacted by the boy, Draki, who had done too much mustache-twirling and peripheral leering while working his machinations, but I could not blame the student. Behind it all, I spotted the fine Irish hand of the play's writer-producer-director, Red O'Hara, and he was vulnerable. The melodrama's theme of incest had been in bad taste and inappropriate on a planet where a son seldom knew his father.

Red had arrived at the tavern before me with the principals in the cast and production crew. Kiki still wore her velvet gown, draped now with her order of Saint George, and Draki, without the make-up of Iago, was a fresh-faced lad with blond hair. My biggest surprise came when Red introduced me to his cameraman, Tamar, the girl with the undulating hips who also wore her Saint George's Cross. Remembering the quality of her photography and Red's difficulties in casting Juliet, it occurred to me that O'Hara was using sex to gain his ends.

My praise of the students was fulsome. "Any one of you could make it big on Broadway. And you, Draki: your Iago would have earned you hisses on any stage on Earth. You oozed villainy."

Around our table the conversation was a subdued click and whir, even after four or five toasts to various members of the cast, but I had learned to gauge the tempo and pitch of Harlechian voices. The students were engaged in an animated, at times even vociferous, conversation, and Red was the focus of their enthusiasm.

But I received my mead of attention as an Earth drama critic and more from the peripheral glances of Tamar. They listened avidly as I told them of the audience reactions, the intake of breath, the sustained applause. "It was good for you, Draki, that you were on television, otherwise you would have been pelted with tomatoes and eggs."

Under the spell of good spirit and strong spirits and impelled by the eyes of Tamar, my old Mandan syndrome revived and I rose to propose a toast. "To the artist of the production staff, the young lady whose genius with a camera and other talents would make her the first choice of any producer in Hollywood were she transported to Earth. I drink to Tamar of the Gliding Hips."

"Hear! Hear!" Red chanted.

Tamar, across the table, lifted her eyes to me, dark and glowing either with spiritual effulgence or from the reflections of her Cross of Saint George, and said, "I would forego all honors to be led to the cross of Jack the Teacher."

Her remark, which I took for the first glow of dawn in this pagan night, shrived me of all Mandan dross, and I answered, "Dear lamb, it shall be so, when the Dean of Deans so wills it."

"Careful, laddie," Red whispered in English, probably assuming that I was moving in on one of his Dames, which I confess was my intention. Then he raised his voice: "Children, our next project at the beginning of the winter semester will be a musical, televised from on stage in the gym before a live audience to let you feel the audience reaction. I'll show you films of the Rockettes to give you an idea how a chorus line operates. Tamar, you're made for the role of lead dancer. And we're going big for this one. It'll be colossal."

Now the click and whir stepped up to a faster pace around the table as the students, one smash hit behind them, began to plan anew. Suddenly all conversation stopped.

I had not seen the boy in the black tunic come through the door, for I was entering a plea for Red to use film clips from the Corps de Ballet of Earth when the silence stopped me. Looking up, I saw the Dean's messenger standing at our table, pulling a slip of paper from his dispatch case. He handed the paper across the table to Draki, bowed, turned and left the tavern.

Draki glanced at the paper, slowly folded it into a quarto and slipped it into his tunic pocket. In the dead silence, I leaned over and asked, "Bad news, Draki?"

"I have been expelled by Bubo the Dean for misconduct," he said simply. "I tricked Hamlet into killing Juliet."

"But that was a play! You're not Iago."

"The elders do not understand, Jack."

"Give me that slip, lad," Red bellowed. "I'm taking it back to Bubo and making him eat it."

"He would not like the taste of paper, Red," Draki said.

"When I get through knocking his teeth out, he'll have to make it into a broth and sip it through a straw." Red got up and started around the table when Kiki rose and pounced on his back in one flowing and fast movement. Her eighty-odd pounds would never have brought Red down, and such was not her purpose. Her legs locked around Red's legs just above the knees. Compared with hers, Red's legs were oak trunks, yet he was manacled and going nowhere. Like a koala bear cub on the back of its mother, Juliet turned to Tamar and said quietly, "Tell him, Tamar."

"We do not dispute the decisions of the Dean," Tamar said. "We are here to learn, the teachers here to teach. They do not interfere with us. We do not interfere with them."

Draki rose. "It does not matter, Red. You must not let Bubo harm you. I was studying communications and there is nothing to communicate. I will take the works of Shakespeare that you gave me back to the hinterlands and write plays so there will be something to communicate. Farewell, esteemed teacher." His voice faltered slightly when he added, "Farewell, beloved friend."

He turned and left. Juliet released her chastened prisoner, who, shocked and saddened, sat down. "How could Bubo punish me? He has no weapons," Red asked.

The boy who played Hamlet answered him: "He would punish you as Iago punished Hamlet, for Bubo is wise."

"On Earth we call it 'clever,' " Red said.

A gloom had settled around the table, giving me my second inkling that Harlechians had feelings. For minutes no one spoke, until finally Red clapped his hands. "Drama students dismissed."

As they rose and filed out, Red said, "So, Bubo's the Dean because he's the best con artist. That's interesting."

"The same can be said of college deans on Earth," I reminded him. "Their artistry there is used to increase endowments."

"But imagine expelling the lad for playing a villain. . . . The concept of justice needs to be taught on this planet, Jack. There should be courts set up to appeal such offhand decisions."

"Harlechians are literal-minded," I said. "Perhaps Bubo figured that a boy with Iago's wiles might take his job. . . . But forget Bubo and tell me: Why did you choose the theme of incest for your play?"

"Hamlet and Juliet were teaching the students the joys of going steady," he answered with a detached air. "Iago and Mrs. Macbeth were teaching them the evils of lust. . . . But somebody's got to teach Bubo a sense of justice!"

"You're not challenging Bubo," I told him.

"You're right, Jack. I'm not." He rolled his glass around its edge. "Justice is your department. You shall teach Bubo justice."

"Fat chance," I snorted. "I can't even find him. . . . Red, now that you've shown the students the wages of sin, why not inspire them with a more elevating drama?"

"The musical extravaganza is just such a drama." I could see his spirits reviving. "The dancing chorus, the Maids of Bethlehem, will be dancing to celebrate the birth of our Blessed Savior."

"You're planning a musical Nativity Play?"

"Aye, lad," he answered, leaning forward, "for I have this fantastic idea. To put more punch into the chase scene, I'm making the inn at Bethlehem into a brothel. When Herod arrives looking for the Christ Child, he meets the madame of the inn—she's a whore but she has a good heart—and he hits on an idea for making her talk. Since she's a madame, he figures she'll know all the local scuttlebutt, and he's going

to make her squeal, literally. You see, Herod's been tipped
off that J.C. is in the village. . . ."

"Tipped off by whom?" I gasped.

"By the Star of Bethlehem. . . . It's a dead give-away.
. . . What's the matter, Jack? Are you ill?"

After the incident in the tavern, it was obvious that Red
had established a relationship with his students on a visceral
level, but I shunned such contact. If I were to become
shepherd of this flock I would keep them sheep and preserve my integrity as Jack the Teacher. Never would I
become "beloved friend," as Draki the dropout had referred
to Red.

Nonetheless, I acquired popularity of sorts because of my
gym classes, where I introduced basketball modified to fit
Harlechians—players were allowed to pass with their feet
and the basket was raised four feet because of the leaping
ability of the players. Five teams were organized from my
class and pitted against each other. By creating team spirit
and the will to win, I hoped to instill militancy in my
players. Some of these boys would become my light-bearers
into the darkness of Harlech.

A cup was designed for the champion team, to be
awarded in the exam-week playoffs, which, borrowing from
Red, I decided to televise continents-wide, but in truth all
of my players were champions. One forward, by the name
of Frick, would have made the Boston Celtics on his first
tryout.

One week before final exams for the summer semester, a
messenger interrupted my final class, on Values, with a note
from Red:

> Urgent. Request earliest possible conference *re* Dramatics
> and Theology. Am in my office.
>
>   *Red the Teacher*

I read the note rather ruefully and caught the conveyor
belt for Faculty Row, thinking it poor taste for Red to inter-
rupt a class on so trivial a matter. O'Hara's success with
Shakespeare had confirmed his belief that he was a born
producer, and he was taking his Christmas pageant seriously, I knew. But I could not see where that play would
even remotely touch on religion.

After passing through his outer office with its moil of
students, I reached his inner office to find him sitting atop

his desk, dictating a "Guide for Establishing University Drama Departments" to a girl student. Red dismissed her and she glided out, brunette and long-legged even by Harlech standards.

"How goes the Christmas extravaganza?" I asked. "And have you cast the Virgin?"

"No, I'm still in the writing stage. But the script's shaping up. I've got a terrific opening. Sort of a *Tom Jones* banquet scene where Dean Herod sends his centurions out to corner the Christ Child."

"Herod didn't use centurions," I objected. "Centurions were Romans and he was a Jewish King."

"I know, I know," Red said impatiently. "I'm making him Roman to protect the Jewish image because Jesus was a Jew before John converted him. . . . Incidentally, I'm thinking of calling John 'Jack the Baptist' to give you a little prepublicity. . . ."

"Oh no you don't! But speaking of images, what are you doing with the Dean's image by calling Herod a dean?"

"These bairns can't relate to kings, since they've never heard of a king."

"No matter. You call him 'King Herod,' and that's an order."

"Aye, aye, sir. But get this, Jack. The very last scene, in the manger, will be the climax of the play. Herod's centurions are closing in. Enter the girls of the brothel—the Maids of Bethlehem—and lure the soldiers upstairs. When that squad of centurions traipse up the stairs at the end of that chorus line, the audience knows damned well they are going to be up there a long, long time. Get it? Curtain! Now the curtain slowly rises on the manger scene. Enter three kings of the Orient, bearing gifts and singing. They kneel. In the background you hear the angels singing. The lights sink lower, lower. It's a living creche. Only the backlighting for the Holy Mother and the Star of Bethlehem remains bright. Mary, safe now, spared by the evil lusts of the soldiers, gazes down on her child, bathed in light, and the hopes and fears of all the world is focused on her face. Slowly the light fades—into total darkness? No. Above the audience the Star of Bethlehem still gleams, for the light of the world will not go out. Then the houselights rise on the last notes of a carol, but the star burns into the rising houselights. Get the symbolism? The play can never end. The light is eternal."

Red's voice, charged with enthusiasm and awe, died into silence, and I sat stunned. He had taken liberties with the offstage story, but the play remained true to the Nativity story as we knew it, with a dramatic impact that would impress the manger scene forever on the minds of the audience.

With all his faults, Red had the touch of a poet.

"Well, what do you think?"

"Red, it's beautiful." My voice broke as I repeated, "Just beautiful."

"I knew it would shake you. But there's something missing in the production. Religions 1 doesn't cover Christianity. The audience won't know the Christ Child from any other babe in swaddling clothes."

"That's true," I nodded absently, my mind still glowing with the vision of the manger scene.

"Jack, with four-month seasons on this planet, Christmas will come at the end of the fall semester. The pageant has to be presented on the twelfth month. You can remedy the situation by installing a crash program for Christianity."

"You mean teach Religions 1 and Religions 2 in the same semester?"

"Exactly."

"Red, I can't. I don't have the time. As it is, I plan to devote three periods a day to Religions 1."

"I'll join you, Jack. I'll drop the course in Comedy. I'll tell them about Moses and the Hebrew children and let you concentrate on Christ. Jesus is more your cup of tea anyway."

Except for a single flaw, his proposal was sound. If he taught a class in religion, he would become guilty of a misdemeanor and his silence would be guaranteed when the reports were sent in on Harlech. That was an attractive prospect, but not the determining factor. I, too, wanted the manger scene to arouse all possible connotations in the minds of the Harlechians. But still I was troubled.

"Red, you aren't qualified to teach Religions 1. Your students would end up knowing nothing but a few of the spicier passages from the Song of Solomon."

"Lad, I'll spend two days under narcosis studying the Old Testament. You can mark out the passages you want me to emphasize in class."

"Let me meditate," I said.

"Of course, of course."

He pulled a bottle of whisky from his desk and poured us both a drink into shot glasses. Now I knew he was planning another crime, and that if I didn't go along I couldn't report the conversation. I took a sip and waited.

"Jack, as soon as Herod and my centurions leave that stage, they'll get a pink slip from the Dean's office, and I want to give them some protection from Bubo, the bastard —some recourse from his decision, preferably to an impartial judge and jury. What do you say to you giving a course on law?"

"I'd say you're crazy," I exploded. "Teaching law to unclassified aliens is a felony."

"Well, I didn't think you'd go along. It would have been a great help to me, teaching the law as given to Moses. Else these bairns won't have the faintest concept of law. You're a good Christian, Jack, when it comes to misdemeanor. Too bad you lack the guts to be a felonious Christian."

I flared. "It's easy for you to sit there and propose that I commit a felony."

"I just made myself your co-conspirator," Red pointed out.

"I still think it's stupid. If we set up student law courts with student judges, we'd be playing with mudpies. Any decisions the students made would be overruled. There's no recourse from the decisions of Bubo."

"You're wrong," he said. For a moment he looked at me. "We could pull the students out on a strike."

"There are five thousand students in this university."

"Aye," he said. "Already one-twelfth belong to us. By the end of next semester, we'll have one-third. As the twig is bent, so grows the tree."

I went over his figures in my head, and he was correct. "I'll meditate," I said.

Before I meditated, I made a grass-roots survey by talking to Hal the Assistant. "In a general way, Hal, have you heard any reports from the students complaining of the teaching methods of Red the Teacher or me?"

He said nothing but reached into his desk and pulled out a card file. "Halfway through the semester, Jack, I quit taking applications from students who wished to enter your fall classes, regardless of what you taught. . . . There are over four hundred such cards in my files. Your students are tutoring others in what you teach."

"Isn't this rather unusual?" I asked.

"You and Red are the only teachers who teach in person. All others televise their lectures."

"No one mentioned this to us."

"You didn't ask," he said. "Besides, the students did not want you to know. Then you would televise, too."

"But you don't have that fear?" I said.

"No, Jack. You would not be trying to 'hit forty' if you could not count your students."

Here was gratifying information, indeed, but it did not impel me to recklessness. As a guest of the university, I had no desire to launch myself on a collision course with the school's administration, but justice is a virtue and there were wrongs to be righted. Besides, there was the need, as Red pointed out, to structure the students' minds to an understanding of law in its legal sense to grasp the concept in its higher meaning. But the teaching of Earth law to colonials was a felony under the Codes because equal laws cannot be applied to separate and unequal races. That principle had been demonstrated in United States history in the flames of several cities. I would not let myself slip into a life of crime no matter how innocent my motive.

An incident created by the basketball playoffs changed my mind. In playing the aggressive game that I taught him, my star, Frick, committed six personals in the televised championship game. He was expelled by Bubo for fouling out.

When the pink slip came for Frick in the dressing room, I was complimenting the boy on his play and he read the anger in my face at the sight of the paper.

"It is nothing, Jack," he assured me. "I will go into the hinterlands and organize basketball teams. It is more to my liking than pottery-making. Farewell, my esteemed teacher, farewell my respected coach."

"Farewell, Frick," I said with genuine sadness. "Keep in touch with me. Perhaps my teams can play your teams in the future."

"I will write, Jack the Coach—and will you tell Red that I must resign my commission as captain of centurions?"

"That I will do, Frick."

Suddenly he saluted me, using the circular arm movement with open palm forward of the Irish military. Involuntarily, I returned his salute as his bare heels clicked together with an audible sound. He did an about-face and marched from the gym. His behavior puzzled me until I recalled Red's remark that all Harlechians were method actors who believed in the roles they played.

The knowledge did much to relieve me of guilt feelings. If Frick was a captain of centurions in Red's Christmas play, he was already marked for expulsion.

Over drinks that evening, in the tavern, I accepted Red's compliments on the televised basketball game and passed along Frick's message. "You told me," I mentioned casually, "that you had not begun casting for the Christmas play."

"I haven't," Red answered. "Frick was a captain of centurions in my gym class. I got tired of doing push-ups as an exercise and taught my lads close-order drills."

"Perhaps we should forget the idea of a student strike," I said, "and send your little army over to capture and court-martial Bubo. Running a university by whim deserves no punishment short of a firing squad. This planet could use a little law and order in administrative circles."

"Are you telling me, Jack, that you'll teach law?"

"I'll take the high road if you'll take the low road."

"Then, my lad, I have something to show you." He reached into his pouch and brought out a slender volume printed from Earth microtapes: *The Old Testament with Annotations*.

Dramatically I removed from my coat pocket a volume of my own, twice as thick as Red's volume, and laid it beside Red's. It was *Blackstone's Revised Commentaries and Earth Statutes*. We lifted our glasses and hooked arms to drink in the astronaut's pledge of loyalty. We had sworn by the books.

Before we unhooked, the hidden television screen above the bar clicked on and the subject of our pact became visible: Bubo welcoming the new students for the fall semester. He gave the same set speech as before, advising students with problems to consult the catalogue first before applying to their department heads. This speech, too, lasted less than a minute. Suddenly, I was jolted by an idea that struck me with the force of a revelation.

Bubo the Dean was nothing more than a television tape programmed to play at the opening of each semester.

Hal had told me that all other lectures were televised. It could well be that there was not even a faculty active on this campus, that Red and I were two Don Quixotes organizing to joust with an administration that existed only on television tapes.

Even the pink slips from Bubo the Dean supported my theory. If I assumed that the pink slips were not whimsical, then Draki's had been given to a boy whose observed behavior would have appeared as that of a scheming, unprincipled manipulator. Frick's had been given to a student whose behavior on the playing court had been that of a tiger with aggressive instincts dangerous to society. But what mind could be so literal as to take their behavior out of the context of the play and the game?

The answer was simple. Only one analytical device would evaluate solely on the basis of observed behavior without grasping the connotations, and that device was not a mind, human or subhuman. I rolled the Harlechian words over my tongue silently, and suddenly I knew—Bubo the Dean was a computer hooked into the television circuit.

Since the logic of Harlech was the same as that of Earth, and the scanners on our first overflight had shown the continents connected at the north pole by the continental grids, it followed that the computer was interlocked with other university deans. He who controlled Bubo controlled the planet.

Back on our starship was a microtape on cybernetics.

Red was telling me he had brought Draki back as a scriptwriter and Draki was translating *Hamlet* into Harlechian. I feigned an interest in the project. "Why not have him translate the Bible?"

"That's your department," Red said. "Besides, Harlechians wouldn't buy it without a deal of editing."

One day's deep narcosis would allow me to learn the language of computers. Fifteen minutes alone with Bubo the Dean would permit me to do more to establish justice and mercy on this planet than a thousand student strikes.

Harlechians would "buy" the Bible as written, for through me, Bubo the Dean would issue a simple edict—read, believe, worship.

Red O'Hara, contemplating his navel, Drama, could not and would not know that he was having a drink with a new Paul modified by Luther. All universities on this planet could be programmed to a single course of study. Out would go basket-weaving, poultry-breeding and pottery-making. In would come Humanid Engineering, abetted by the latest conditioning techniques, to mesh these beings with the Absolute. Outward from University 36 to the

whole of Harlech would go the Word—amplified and reinforced by solid-state circuitry.

True, the I.C.A. might reprimand me, but in the light of
eternity even the I.C.A. would thank me. In their present
state, these bug-eyed ground bees lacked the aggressiveness, the sense of struggle, the perfectionism demanded of
a productive working force. Infusion of the Protestant Ethic
would transform Harlech into a first-rate colonial possession
of Earth.

"You seem preoccupied, Jack."

"Semester-end fag, I reckon. Would you excuse me, Red?
I have a few errands to run, and for the next two or three
days I'm going under to do a little reading." I tapped
Blackstone, pocketed the book, said my good-bye and left.
Outside, I caught a belt downtown and transferred to the
belt for the station. There I caught a train south to the
soccer-field station and walked once more through the woods
of late summer, heading for the ship and its culture bank.

Sooner or later, my sidekick would come to the same con-
clusion I had, and it was imperative that I alone know the
art and science of cybernetics. Else Red, with his new interest in religion, would turn all Harlech into a planet of bead
counters with a bleeding heart in every bedroom.

Sooner or later, Red would realize that the name "Bubo"
was an acronym made from the Harlechian words "barstung
undel borflik," which translated "grid-patterned powerflow"
and meant in English, "systems-analyst computer."

On Earth we called him "Saco."

CHAPTER
SEVEN

R ed had created a viable relationship with his students on
a visceral level before the summer term ended. It was a
week into the fall term before I established intellectual
contact with a single student. But my day dawned with a
burst that dimmed the memory of my night.

As I have mentioned, the concept of beauty was not clearly defined on Harlech because, I reasoned, of an absence of contrast and color to life underground. In my first course on Aesthetics, I had relied heavily on slide projections of Earth paintings from the great masters. From the rather incredible results obtained on the final exams—the class average 3.8 on a scale of 4.0—I knew that the paintings had created interest, and I repeated them at the beginning of the fall semester. Aesthetics fell on my last period on three days of the week. In my mid-week period, I had run through a showing of the great paintings in Earth's history, saving for last, Kramer's "Sunset." It was my favorite and I liked to linger over it.

"We have all seen and felt the glory of sunsets," I rhapsodized, "for nowhere is nature more lavish with such spontaneous outpourings of color. For me, this painting epitomizes that glory more than any actual sunset. When I remember sunsets, I remember Kramer's. His vision altered my vision. It is not so much what he sees as how he sees it, and how much his vision affects our manner of seeing. This is true of all great artists. Earth's concept of romantic love between man and woman was enriched by Homer's vision of Helen, and my vision of sunset has been altered by the brush of a long-dead artist."

In my admiration, I had completely forgotten that I was speaking to a nonhuman audience. When the buzzer sounded and the lights came on and the class began to file out, I felt somewhat chagrined as I turned to put away my notes. For long I had striven to establish myself as an austere man of the spirit, but I had let myself get emotional over Kramer. I felt I had lowered my image in the eyes of my students.

"Jack," a student asked, "may I speak to you about sunsets?"

Rather pleased by a request that must have been prompted in part by curiosity, I turned to face a female, green-eyed and golden-haired. "Of course, my dear," I replied.

"You speak of that which cannot be weighed or measured. I have listened without hearing. Today, I heard when you spoke of Kramer's 'Sunset,' but I did not hear with my ears. Your words held a different truth. Go with me to the observation tower and show me how to look at a sunset."

I glanced at my watch. Sunset was near on the surface.

"Gladly, my dear," I said, feeling for the first time the pride teachers feel when they awaken a vision in the mind of a pupil.

We hurried. Days were getting shorter and it was almost a mile to the circular ramp which led to the observatory. Striding beside the girl, I could not help but comment to myself on her beauty of form and carriage. She flowed in grace and all about her seemed a sweep and a glide, save for two high and widely separated breasts, like the forequarters of kittens coiled to spring in play, which jiggled against the fabric of her gown. So palpitant and palpable they were, I jerked my peripheral gaze from the sight and silently muttered a prayer.

At length we emerged into the tower, glass-walled and furnished with lounges, and walked out onto the balcony, into an air tangy with the scents of autumn. The sun was still above the horizon. Frost had fallen since my last visit to the surface and the woodlands stretching below were aflame with colors.

"Look at the trees!" I breathed the words in rapture.

"Their leaves are dying," she explained, "because the cold is coming and the sap is falling."

"Don't think of causes," I told her. "Enjoy effects. Look how the sunlight slants through the leaves, taking yellow from the maples and scarlet from the oaks. Let those colors sink through your vision to stain your soul. Savor October's nutty ale, now, dear girl, for soon it will go and we will be gone. Beauty is a wisp of smoke blown on a wind. Mate its transience with a sense of your own mortality and share with me its passing. Out of eternity this moment has come to us, so let you and me, who are young and dying, treasure these red and golden flarings which shall so soon subside again into eternity."

What my words lacked in poetry they made up in sincerity, for there was something about this girl which inspired me to such expression, a quietness, a hint of perfume whirled on the eddying air, or the way the sunlight burnished her curls. She walked to the rail, laying her hands on it, and looked toward the beginning sunset. Perhaps to share the flame of my vision by my touch, I laid my hand on hers and stood beside her. We watched in silence as the sun of Harlech sank lower, became a huge scarlet ball and melted on the gun-metal horizon of the distant sea.

My student seemed enraptured and the air was growing

chill. Quietly I slipped from my coat and draped it around
her shoulders as the red died into the deepening purple of
the night. We said not a word as the first stars flickered
and a night wind rustled her hair. Then she turned and
looked at me, twilight reflecting in her eyes, and said, "I
have taken your coat, Jack, and you must be chilled."

"I hardly feel the cold," I said truthfully.

"We must go below, so you can have some warm soup.
But I do hate to say good-bye to the sun. Your beauty has
such sadness, Jack."

"When you say farewell to the sun," I said, "you are
welcoming the stars."

"Yes, that is true. Which star is your home, Jack?"

"Yonder," I said, pointing. "In that faint haze of light."

"That is the galaxy we call M-16," she said.

"We call it the Milky Way," I said, "for inside it the
stardust trails the sky like a milky veil."

"The Milky Way," she repeated. "I like your name better. . . . Jack, who was Helen?"

"She was a woman of Earth, dead long ago, whose
beauty launched a thousand ships and burnt the topmost
towers of Ilium."

"Then she must have been very beautiful," the girl said.
For a fleeting moment I thought I read sadness in her eyes
as she added, "Too beautiful to die."

"But surely no more beautiful than you," I said.

Strangely, I was not beguiling the girl. The remnant light
from the west bathed her with a luminosity that filtered
whatever mote of dross there might have been from her
face and form, and her grace was that of a disembodied
spirit. To flatter such a girl was to compliment the notes of
a skylark.

"It pleases me to be called beautiful, as Helen was."

Again a breeze eddied around us and I caught the fra-
grance of her hair. "You are more beautiful than this night
sky with the stars out to play," I said.

"Your words make me wish for that which I cannot name,"
she said.

"You are undergoing a spiritual awakening, my dear."

Suddenly she looked up, "Would you like to take me,
Jack, here beneath the stars?"

There was a strangely tactful quality in her voice, as if
her remark sprang from some ancient acquiescence, diplo-
macy rather than desire.

I almost laughed at her naïveté. "Why do you ask me that, dear child?"

"Your eyes were asking for me."

"My eyes speak only for my flesh. My spirit tells me no."

"What is spirit, Jack?"

"You will understand better, my dear, after you have taken my course in Religions 2."

"Are you saying that you want me but won't take me?"

"I am saying that unless I also join with you in spirit, then I cannot join with you in flesh."

"Then will you join me below in a cup of tea?"

"I would be pleased and honored," I said, escorting her into the rotunda, "but I don't remember your name."

Entering reluctantly and turning to look back once more at the stars, she said softly, "Cara."

With that one word, Kramer ceased to influence my sunsets and I knew that thereafter all my memories of sunsets and night skies would belong to Cara.

It was my girl of the golden vagina.

We took supper together in the student union, and I tried to re-create for her the old loves and legends of Earth, Aucassin and Nicolette, Tristan and Iseult, Helen and Paris. I spoke of Troy and Camelot and fabled Cockaigne, spinning around her a web of mythic wonder that brought to her eyes a softness I had never seen on Harlech. Yet, though my ancient legends charged her with enchantment, I was bound more straitly by the spell the girl drew around me with an even older magic.

She came from the northern mountains, she told me, where the salmon ran, and she was majoring in piscatorial hydroponics.

"When I was a little girl," she said, "I used to stand for hours and watch the fish leap in the water as they rushed upstream to die in the joys of lik flik. My mother could not understand and she called me 'the watcher.' To Mother, the fish were but food. To me, they were flashes of gold in a spume of silver. Today you stood by my side and watched with me, and now I know why I watched. For you are a watcher, too, who knows why he watches."

What she told me fascinated me less than her manner of telling, and she listened with a quiet attentiveness that flattered me. Her loveliness of face and form, her charm of manner and her poise were all the equal of her primal

attraction and they combined to divorce me from an awareness of her nether beauty. Only the heightened clatter of
dishes from the clean-up crew made us aware of the lateness
of the hour.

I saw Cara to her train and on the way she said, "Jack,
I don't wish to presume on your teaching, but if you could
take the class into the woods and show them beauty as you
showed me, they would understand better."

"A field trip would be fun," I agreed, "but would the
students come?"

"You invite them and some will come."

"Will you help me, Cara?"

"It will be an honor and a pleasure," she said.

We stood together on the platform until her train arrived, and just before she boarded it, she said, "Jack, I
would like to learn your language."

"You shall have my language tapes tomorrow," I promised.

O'Hara greeted my news of a breakthrough with reserved enthusiasm. "I wish you luck on the field trip, but I
would feel more confident if you had been approached by
a lad."

"Why so?"

"The lassies have taken to this idea of whetting the male
appetite."

"How does that affect Cara?" I asked.

"Wiles, my boy. Womanly wiles. These females have had
them all along; they've just been dormant. Since you're such
a challenge to the lassies, you may not return from the
woods as virtuous as when you entered."

"Red, you've acted from nefarious motives for so long
you downright believe everybody else does."

"Not so, Jack. One of my girls was asking me if you
were capable."

"What color hair did this girl have?"

"Dark brown."

So it was not Cara.

"And what did you tell her?"

"I could not lie to the lass and tell her you were not
normal. On the other hand, I could not tell her you were
repenting from your sins of fleshly lust. Yet one must give
these students a reason, and I am hard put to give reasons

for celibacy. So I was adroit. I told her the cross you gave was of such quality that it made all others worthless."

"Red," I said, in genuine appreciation, "you may be a Catholic but you've got a Protestant heart."

"Don't be too grateful," he warned. "These folk have literal minds. I might have loosed on you hordes of Harlech's wiliest females, all out to gain some golden bauble studded with diamonds. As yet, they have no concept of the Cross of Christ."

"In the fullness of time, its meaning shall stand revealed."

"Aye, in the fullness of time. But I'm thinking of your field trip next week. Be sure there are lads in the class. Your lassie may be luring you into the woods for a Bacchanalian feast, and John Adams may become the *pièce de résistance*. By the way, Jack, what is the girl's field of study?"

"Fish-farming."

"Aye?" Red was becoming adept at acting. His face registered instant concern. "Avoid her, lad. She is an expert at spawning."

Red's warning I dismissed as another example of his low-level thinking. Nonetheless, I checked the group of twelve students who gathered on the station platform that seventh-day morning and noted with gratification that four of the twelve who volunteered for the field trip, excluding Cara, were males. We took an eastbound train into the foothills of the coastal range, and certainly we were the most unusual safari in the history of higher education. A spaceman, member of perhaps the least qualified profession on Earth to expound on the subject, was leading a field trip into the woods to teach aesthetics by example and exhortation.

We got off at the fourth station, marked with its soaring trylon, and I gathered my group together in a small meadow where I called the males to attention to give military flavor to our excursion and instructed them. "We'll advance to the ridge through that defile. Males take the point, front and rear. Cara and I will take the vanguard. Keep a sharp lookout for fire-breathing dragons that might attack the girls."

One of my soldiers went *"Heh-heh-heh,"* in the imitation of laughter which O'Hara taught, and I asked, "What's so funny, soldier?"

"We can't protect against the fire-breathing dragons," he said.

Red had conned the boy into believing his dragon stories, I decided, and only said, "Well, give me warning when you see one."

We trooped into the woods, following the course of a small brook that wound through a deep glade, and it was as if the woods had decked themselves for our coming. A carpet of multicolored leaves crunched beneath my boots and rustled beneath the bare feet of my wards. Beside us, the brook tumbled over mossy rocks and glided between its banks. Cara, walking beside me, asked the English equivalent of the various trees we passed. With her power to absorb, she was already using English phrases on me.

We wound our way through woods, which resembled the woods of Maine after the first frost but were far more primitive. Wind-fallen trees made barriers for me to clamber over which the Harlechians cleared by leaping. So close was the flora of this planet allied to that of Earth that the names of the trees came readily to my tongue, and there were squirrels and chipmunks which were hardly disturbed by our passage. We came finally to the source of our brook, a large pool where we amused ourselves by skipping stones across the surface. For me, skipping the stones to the far side was easy with my Earthman's strength of arms, but only one Harlechian boy succeeded and was applauded.

Above the pool was an opening in the forest caused by a marshy swale. Across the swale in the sunlight stood a majestic tree, with the yellow leaves of hickory, and I halted my troop to let them concentrate on the scene. "See how the sun's rays slanting into the vale are broken by the golden patterns of the leaves, pay attention to the dust motes dancing in the sunlight."

So saying, I took a windfallen limb from the ground nearby and hurled it across the glade to fall beneath the tree and stir the dust motes.

"Now, you can see the rays through the leaves. It gives a visual quality to silence, a silence as golden as Cara's hair," I added on impulse. "On Earth, we paint such scenes to capture the quality forever."

Then, as I set myself to observe the silence, a dark-haired girl spoke up. "Cara is more beautiful than Helen, Jack the Teacher, but Red the Teacher tells me I am more beautiful than Deirdre."

Her riposte astonished me. There was a thin edge of jealousy in her voice directed at Cara, but her words told

me that even the most private of conversations were discussed among these girls. Looking at the speaker, I saw she
was, indeed, beautiful, with raven hair and eyes so dark
they were luminous.

"You are more beautiful than Deirdre," I agreed, "who
was the most beautiful dark-haired woman on Earth, but
Helen was the greatest beauty with golden hair. . . . Notice
the oak tree beyond the hickory, how red its leaves are. An
Earth artist would cloud the form of the oak to bring out
the yellow of the leaves in the foreground."

We mounted to the summit of the ridge, climbing atop
a mass of boulders grayed by lichen and greened with moss,
and looked down on the valley. A small lake shimmered
below and mirrored the colors of the ridge beyond. Far
beyond the ridge rose a line of purple mountains, their
summits sharply outlined in the crystalline air.

"Students, we have walked through beauty," I said.
"Now we look upon it with the eyes of an eagle. Say after
me, 'Oooh . . . ah!' "

Obediently they *oohed* and *ahed* aloud.

Casting a quick glance at their faces, I hoped to catch
some faint stirring of awe, but their eyes could have reflected rapture or boredom for all that I could see.

Still, the beauty was there for my taking, and I walked
alone along a spine of rock to a point that flattened into an
overhang. Casting one final glance behind me at the students, I noticed that they were still mouthing their *oohs* and
ahs without making a sound. I turned back to the scenery
somewhat saddened by the display. They were learning
form without substance.

Suddenly, my attention was drawn again to my group by
a sudden flurry of sound, like the beginning whir of a
covey of quail taking to flight, and I turned to see the students bounding back into the woodland at incredible speed.
Only Cara remained, still mouthing those silent *oohs* and
ahs as she stalked me, moving cautiously out on the spine
of rock.

O'Hara was right. She had lured me here with the aid of
her cabal. At her signal, they had vanished, leaving me
trapped on the point of rock. Watching her move toward
me, gliding one foot ahead of the other as a cat might creep
along a limb toward a bird, I was hypnotized by her movements.

Stirrings long suppressed exploded within me and I raised

my arms in surrender. My time had come to feel the touch of the toes of a girl of Harlech.

"No, Jack! Not that! Not here!" she almost screamed. "We must flee, for the fire-breather comes."

"Child, there are no dragons, not here, not anywhere."

Suddenly she spoke in English. "Not dragons, Jack. A 'lectric storm comes."

"How can you say that?" I asked. "Look, the sky is clear from horizon to horizon."

I swung my upraised arms toward the horizon as she answered, "My ears tell me . . . from the pressure."

Following the sweep of my arm, I saw the horizon. Now the clear line of the ramparts was obscured by a blue haze which, even as I watched, grew darker and rippled with lights.

"Jack, the power flow kills. Run with me!"

Around us, a wind was stirring. The trees began to sough, and I remembered Red's remark: "Forecasting might get tricky when a storm front rides in on a jet stream at 500 knots."

Then I moved off the rock, over the crest and down the glen, hurtling wind-fallen trunks I had clambered over on my way up. Cara ran beside me, leaping bushes I crashed through. Now the trees were moaning. Soon the roar drowned the thud of my footfalls and I knew the springbok girl beside me was retarding her speed to match my rhino charge.

"Run ahead, Cara," I shouted. "Save yourself. I can find the trylon."

"No, Jack," she shouted. "When the dark comes, you will not see. I can see in the dark."

No runner on Earth could have covered that mile in five minutes. Skirting the pond and crashing downward, I had to think as I ran, gauging barriers and the heights of hurdles, and a gray mist was staining the sky. My lungs were aching at the halfway mark, my pace was slowing and the light was dying into an unnatural and deepening gray. Behind us, I heard the beginning rustle of rain.

It grew dark seconds before the rain rolled over us with the speed of an express train and Cara reached back to grasp my hand. Now I knew why she had stayed behind, for running through this blackness would have been impossible for me alone. When the rain struck, it boiled around us in solid currents of water. Behind its roar I heard a deadlier sound, the crack and sizzle of lightning that began to illuminate the darkness to reveal we had reached the meadow. Beyond the meadow loomed the trylon.

I slogged the last fifty yards in five seconds, but the last two seconds were the longest I have lived. Lightning bolts came from all angles. I could have sworn one zipped horizontally along the ground to strike the trylon. We dove into the station entrance, gagging from the reek of ozone, and continued to run until we stood wet, with me panting, on the station platform.

"Cara," I said as I caught my breath, "are the demands of hospitality such on this planet that Harlechians are required to risk their lives for alien visitors?"

"Oh, no, Jack. I was the only Harlechian there."

"Yet you knew the horror of those storms and you waited for me. . . . How do the trees survive?"

"By ferrous oxide in their sap. When they die they burn. But the lightning is good for us," she said. "We lead it through the trylons and it drives the trains."

For the first time I understood the meanings of the towers. Somehow, these amazing beings had learned to convert static electricity for their use, but at the moment I had little interest in applied science.

When my students turned and fled, they had been driven by the oldest fear on Harlech—an instinctive terror of lightning, their real and present "fire-breather." Yet this wisp of a girl had defied a terror bred into her by eons to lead me to safety. There was no human equivalent for such bravery or the unselfishness which prompted it. "Cara, if you had not led me through the darkness, I would never have reached the trylon. I owe my life to your courage."

"I almost stayed with you on the rocks."

"Why?" I took her gently by the shoulders and looked down at her.

"Because your eyes were asking me to take you."

Then Cara smiled at me.

It was no winsome twitch of the lips, but a smile, the most radiant I have seen on the face of a woman, and above the smile her eyes were laughing.

I took her in my arms and kissed her as a lover kisses his beloved after a long absence, and as a boy kisses his first sweetheart for the first time. In that kiss I put, perhaps unconsciously, all I had learned of ardor from the cornfields of Alabama to the cathouses of Mandan, but mine was not a carnal embrace. In my arms I crushed the violets of spring-time even as I held and admired the roses of summer, but a power gave dimensions to that caress above and beyond what O'Hara called "the duty of devotion."

This girl whom my arms bound to me, whose fingers fluted my hair, had a body surveyed and charted in my mind, from the tapering ankles to the swell of her thighs and the golden glory between, to the kittens couchant on her breast and the furze of her sun-burst hair. But only by her acts had I come to know her truly—the sharing of a sun-set's sadness, her selflessness which spared my life and now a smile which vaporized the terror of a storm. From her outer beauty to her inmost core, I loved this girl called Cara, a name I murmured over and over into her hair.

My love would give her a soul, and by the Word I would bring to her, that soul would be saved.

"Cara, I will show you the way to the Cross," I said.

But a train had rumbled up and we boarded it, and for once I caught sidelong glances that the passengers threw at us and I commented on it to Cara. "It is because we are wet from the rain," she said. "They cannot understand why I should be caught in a storm. They can see by your legs why you should be caught."

Her eyes were expressionless as she looked at me, and I chided her: "Your eyes have quit talking to me."

"I know," she whispered, "for it is indecent the way your eyes are talking to me. Please quit saying such things in public."

"I'm sorry, Cara."

"Now, you are sad because you think I rebuked you. . . . Look away. . . . On Harlech, when you choose one, you reject others. On Harlech, we do not reject one another."

"But your eyes *can* talk," I said. "They were speaking to me on the platform."

"Did they? And what did they say?"

"Well, they weren't exactly rejecting me."

She covered her face with her hands, for she was no longer merely smiling, she was giggling. When she again raised her eyes to me, they were proper Harlechian, as expressionless as a gambler with a royal flush.

When she spoke, she spoke in English so perfect it could have been rehearsed for this occasion. "My eyes were telling you, dear Jack, that I love you above all others."

Surreptitiously, I took her hand in mine and answered in English, "And I love you, Cara, above all women, on Earth or in Heaven."

As I plighted my troth so prosaically, on a subway train now gliding into University 36 Station, the power of my pledge raised the hackles on my spirit. As I pledged the words, I could hear the iron gates of space swing shut, for I knew I was cutting myself away from Earth, forever. In honor and with decency, I intended to mate with this girl and defect to Harlech.

O'Hara would have to be told.

If he returned to Earth without me, our ship's flight recorder would reveal the route to Harlech, and the next ship from Earth would be far different from our little argonaut.

Harlech's next visitor from Imperial Earth would be a huge vessel, colored black, and it would be loaded to the gunwales with crew-cut young men. They would wear black uniforms with death's heads on the lapels and they would come with laser rifles. Defection by space scouts was not taken lightly. Naval astronauts, with their military knowledge, could arm and equip a grade one planet to make themselves satraps ashore and freebooters in space.

When the cry "Havoc" was raised for defectors, the huntsmen of the Harrier Corps shot first and asked questions later.

And they would come, if O'Hara left without me.

CHAPTER EIGHT

"Jack, are you daft?"

Red was not acting. He was confused and angry.

"I'm in love, Red."

"Same difference," he snorted.

I had come straight from the station where I had said good-bye to Cara and shouldered my way through a moil of sloe-eyed brunettes, reeking of perfume, who waited in

Red's outer office to be interviewed for the Christmas musical.

No childish evasion of the Code this time, with the pouring of drinks. I had rolled the dice at Rubicon and now it was up to Red to fade me or pass. In a matter of life or death, I had faith that Red would fight beside me. If not, I had a back-up policy—we both had enough on each other to hang each other.

"Come along with me," I pleaded. "I'm in a position to make you temporal king of this planet. All I want out of the deal is the church. . . . We'd make a tremendous pair, Red King O'Hara, and Archbishop Adams, first primate of the Primitive Methodist Church on Harlech."

"Jack, this society's gone as far as it can go. I'm willing to spread the word, straighten out Bubo and provide a little laughter and recreation for these bairns, but you and I are men, for better or for worse. For us, there can be no comfort station on the way to our cross. If you like the underground life, spend your furloughs mining coal in West Virginia, not among these lotus-eaters."

"These people have not been saved."

"So you're calling them people. . . . Jack, when our allotted twelve to sixteen months are up, we're going home, if I have to return you to Earth in a straitjacket. Your skills as a spaceman are worth more to Earth than this entire planet."

"What have we got on Earth?" I asked.

He grinned for the first time. "I've got my blond angel in Jackson, and you have Madame Chacaud's in Mandan."

"There's no woman on Earth who approaches Cara in glory," I said. "I want her, in honor, as soon as I have ordained a minister. My work is here, Red, leading these lost souls out of darkness, and the Lord has provided me a helpmeet in my crusade."

"You are daft. If you want the girl, take her! Just whistle and she'll come to you, my lad." He was angry and growing angrier. "You'll find they're all alike, on Earth or Heaven. The only variations are the ones I've taught in my classes—"

Suddenly he stopped. I could see his mind skid into an idea, and I waited, breathless from such arrant cynicism.

"Jack, I've got it. Let me pour us a real drink to celebrate." I waited as he reached into his desk and poured us both a stiff jolt.

He leaned forward, and his Irish eyes were laughing. "So you're in love, lad. The Good Book says it's better to marry than burn, though you can marry and still burn. What do you say to a legal marriage, with all the trimmings—altar, candles, robes, miter, with a chorus chanting a 'Te Deum'?"

"None of your Latin songs for me," I said.

"Name your own hymns. . . . But I can see it now, and it's a beautiful picture. Your bride, dressed in white, marches slowly down the aisle to the altar. Then Jack the Groom, in Navy blues with stars glittering, kneels beside her before the altar. Slowly the chalice, gleaming in the candlelight, is lifted from the altar. . . ."

"Now, boy, just where would you find a church?"

"In the gym, in front of my class on Earth Rituals, Folklore and Superstitions. That ceremony would do more to impress my students with the beauty and solemnity of Earth rituals than ten lectures."

"Who would perform this 'legal' marriage?"

"Me. As probe commander, you can appoint a chaplain for the crew. Navy Regs don't specify the size of the crew."

"You're not of my faith, Red."

"No matter. Let me wear the robes and I'll marry you by any sacrament you choose, including the connubial rites of Trobriand Islanders."

"This charade would solve nothing. I love Cara, and I want to join with her in holy matrimony until death do us part."

"I know the feeling, lad. I've been through it myself. That's why I speak with authority. Twelve months of marriage to the lass will bring you to your senses. By then, you'll be hopping to climb aboard that ship and cast off for Mother Earth."

Red spoke the truth, according to Navy Regs, but his words were sounding brass without the tinkle of a cymbal. It would take me two quarters to qualify and ordain a minister, but I would gird my loins and wait. Never would I permit Red to use my marriage as a showcase sample for his Earth Rituals, Folklore and Superstitions, and I could hardly imagine a less appropriate minister of the Holy Sacrament of Marriage than Red the Adulterer.

"No dice, boy," I told him. "The regulations also specify that a chaplain must be a man of adequate religious convictions. You don't qualify for the appointment."

I got up and walked out of that den of harlotry and re-

turned to my oasis of celibacy. In my quarters, freed from
the reek of profane love, I breathed deeply as my heart
swelled in diapasons to the memory of Cara's kiss, but the
music rang hollow in my empty chambers.

It was well that my classes on Earth's legal system began
when they did. The shift from general permissiveness to a
more restricted sexual behavior among the students was
not installed without some abrasiveness and dislocations.
O'Hara's First Law of Carnal Economics—scarcity enhances
desire—became operative. A few of the boys attempted to
go steady with more than one female. Such perfidy seldom
brought ostracism on the boy, but spates of hair-pulling
broke out between the competing girls. Although I viewed
such incidents with alarm, Red was philosophical to the
point of phlegmaticism. "Gild a female with four million
years of evolution, scratch her, and your fingernails will
still strike a woman."

On Harlech, the males were even more docile in the
presence of females than the men of Earth, but the males
were capable of greater violence. Feet-fights broke out between the boys, and Red, ignoring regulations, expanded his
gym classes in boxing to 180 students and began televising
matches on Fourth-day nights.

Then reports began to filter in of females accosted in
lonely tunnels. Isolated assaults occurred. Graffiti began to
appear on washroom walls. To counteract this trend, I bore
down heavily in my Values class on restraint, self-discipline
and the character-building aspects of celibacy. But the reports continued to grow in volume and I took more drastic
action to curb the mounting violence.

Red had brought Draki back to the campus and installed
him in quarters as a scriptwriter with no comments from
Bubo the Dean. I followed Red's lead and called Frick in
from the hinterlands to act as Chief of Police, hastily installing a criminal court to supplement the law's executive arm.
Not only law but order was coming to Harlech.

Red greeted my new police force with enthusiasm. Some
students did not fit into our activities: girls unable to make
the drama classes and boys unable to make the teams, and
members of both sexes too unattractive to compete within
the framework of the New Courtship. Red saw in my police
department a new dumping ground for those he termed
"misfits."

Already Red had sent such students to me for counseling.

Apparently he reasoned that if they were devoid of other qualities, they must be spiritual. "Take them and mold them in your image, Jack. They may become the nucleus of future nunneries and monasteries."

Of course, I would have no truck with monks and nuns, but I kept an eye alert for future ministers who might propagate my ministery after my departure.

Indeed there was material among them. One of the students, Nesser, became so interested in the Scriptures that I gave him my language tapes to learn in order that he might study the Bible in English. I found myself looking forward to converting and ordaining Nesser in rapid succession to expedite my marriage to Cara.

When Frick arrived, I gave him microtapes of Police Methods, Interrogation and Procedures. Red promptly unloaded twelve centurions from his clumsy squad onto Frick to use as policemen. Frick promptly rejected four of them and requested four replacements, none to be less than a centurion corporal. Red had forgotten that Frick had once been a captain of centurions. Frick made the new men his police sergeants. I turned Frick's rejects into student lawyers and unloaded four females on Frick as policewomen.

Cara was becoming more and more a part of my life. We dined together and each day spent an hour after classes in the cupola of the tower. Her serenity and beauty gave me a quiet harbor to retire to after the frets and worries of my day.

In turn, she channeled to me a flow of information about the students, most of it feminine chit-chat but none the less charming, about who was going steady with whom and who was cut out. From Cara I also got my first report on Frick's success as Police Chief. "The students respect Frick," she said, "because he clouts them if they misbehave."

My association with Cara was having a devastating effect on my periods of meditation.

One night I attempted to meditate when the thoughts of Cara intruded with such force that I found meditation impossible. I gave up and went to bed but found it equally hard to sleep. In sheer desperation, clad only in the Harlechian tunic I used as a nightshirt, I went for a walk through the tunnels, barefooted. I found that my footsteps had unconsciously led me to the spiral ramp which led to the tower, and I mounted to the cupola and out onto the balcony, seeking to order my thoughts around the celestial patterns of the stars and seeking, too, the therapy of cold.

There, on the balcony beneath the stars, I found an answer to the problem foremost in my mind. I would marry Cara and return to Earth when this tour of duty was completed. There I would visit Washington and my mother's third cousin, the branch manager for Alabama. With Cousin Leroy's assistance, I would wangle an appointment from the I.C.A. as a colonial administrator on Harlech. Within a year, I could be back on Harlech, on permanent duty.

All my prestige as a space scout, which would gain me the appointment, would vanish, but what did status matter to me in a world without Cara? I would give more than a kingdom for her kiss. I would give up Earth and at least the seven galaxies that the space scout averaged before he was elevated to admiral.

In the interim, I would bank the fires of my love for Cara lest they flame into lust and destroy me. I had reasoned my way back to drinking—it might well be that I might find the logic to revive my old Mandan Syndrome. Cara's innocence would have to be protected, and my method was clear to me; cease watching sunsets with her, avoid coffee klatsches and suspend all but the most formal of relationships.

At our Sixth-day conclave, Red reacted more strongly to my new plans than he had to my request for a mutual defection.

"Of all the crackpot ideas! I'd rather see you defect, be listed as missing, than turn yourself into a colonial administrator. Quit using religious absolutes as a chastity belt and take the girl. We could qualify this planet for the World's Brotherhood with a little luck."

"The I.C.A. has no jurisdiction over separate-but-equal planets," I pointed out, "and Cousin Leroy could never get me an ambassador's job. He's at odds with the state department. . . . Anyway, we can't qualify Harlech."

"Why not? You're giving it law and working on a Supreme Being. The boys and girls are covered and they've got separate toilets."

"There's no military," I said. "Harlech can't defend itself from intruders."

"It could have a defense in six months. Those trylons could convert to laser batteries and blast any space fleet out of the galaxy."

"But that would be us!"

"Not you and me, unless you were with the I.C.A. Think of what the I.C.A. would do to this planet. In six months, these universities would be factories making low-cost transistor radios. Our students would be weaving carpets with their toes."

"Don't you want a colony?" I asked in astonishment.

"Hell no! I'm an Irishman. This is no planet for a cloacal empire of pissoirs, production, platitudes and parsons."

"You're way out of line, boy," I reminded him, "even for a drunken shanty Irishman. With one exception, these yahoos are walking units of conditioned behavior subject to the whims of a dean who may not exist—" I caught myself. In my anger I had revealed a facet of my secret thinking, and I hurried on to create a diversion. "They're no more to be classified as human beings than are ground bees. You're talking treason."

"Aye, my fellow traitor. But look who speaks of conditioned behavior. You were brainwashed starting with the day you walked into Mandan."

"I never thought this of you, O'Hara," I said.

"You never think, Adams. You're conditioned not to. Now, go meditate on that, meditator."

"I'm going," I said. "But don't you say another word. One more treasonous remark from you and that class of yours will be treated to the Earth rites of a funeral—yours."

I slid from the stool and backed out, my fists up, prepared to charge, but to Red's credit he said nothing, not a word. Minutes later, I meditated, not only over what he had said but what he had not said. Had he held his tongue from fear of me or from the fear that I, in my anger, might commit an act to endanger my soul? With Red, I never knew.

Even though spoken in anger, his words troubled me. I was not conditioned. Astronauts did not preach the Word, and indeed, I, too, considered these beings the equal of humans. Yet, I would seize every technicality, and there were many, which would forfeit any right of Harlechians to co-status with *homo sapiens*.

For my good and personal reasons, Harlech would become a colony of Earth.

Next, without dwelling on the political ramifications, I outlined my plan to Cara, explaining merely that I would leave and return to her at the end of a year. She listened intently as I explained that I could see her no more except during formal occasions, such as class lectures.

Though downcast, she was brave. "Love alters not with brief hours or weeks," she said, "but bears it out, even to the edge of doom."

"Thank heaven," I said in English, for in her tongue the word for heaven was "Harlech," "for your understanding mind. Red wanted to marry us right away."

"Can Red the Teacher marry us?" she asked.

"Legally, yes. Spiritually, no. . . . As my wife, Cara, and flesh of my flesh, do you think you can remain faithful to me in my long absence?"

"I will go into seclusion, Jack my Beloved, at the salmon hatchery. Though love is not love which alters when it alteration finds, I cannot understand this thing of your spirit. Since your love for me is spiritual, as you have said, why cannot we sit and talk of love?"

Her soap-opera English charmed me, apparently there were some fairly good writers practicing in Red's favorite medium of entertainment, but I shifted to Harlechian to explain to her: "My spirit would be willing, but my flesh is weak."

"Oh? I had thought you strong of flesh."

"That's my problem. When I'm around you, I want, in a wordly sense, to merge our flesh, and I might do so if you were willing, but my spirit tells me it is wrong. Still, the hunger of my flesh might overrule my spirit."

"Then your flesh is willing, but your spirit is weak."

"No. At the moment they're about evenly matched. You have seen Red's boxing matches on television?"

"Yes."

To reduce the problem to its simplest terms, I explained: "It's as if my spirit and my flesh were fighting an eleven-round boxing match. Each has won five rounds. The eleventh round is the round of decision. By leaving me until our wedding day, you will be, in effect, climbing into the corner to help the spirit fighter. With your aid, I can knock out flesh."

"But, Jack my Beloved, I am pulling for flesh."

"Would you have me debase your innocence before our vows are spoken?" I asked in horror.

"Yes," she answered.

Her answer, at once both honest and coquettish, made me smile.

But Cara's face was suddenly sad. She rose and said, "But if you wish me to aid your spirit, from my great love for you I will aid my enemy. I have what I think you call fears, Jack, that you may leave me and never return, and I want you as a woman as well as spirit, to know you as much as I can while I can. It is not that I doubt your love for me, but there are perils in space. Your ship may founder on shoals of antimatter."

"Where did you learn of antimatter?"

"In the library. Since my love is a star sailor, I wished to learn more of his calling. In the old days, in the far, far past, starships were launched from Harlech."

So great was my astonishment that I hardly watched her walk through the door. If what she said was true—and these beings did not lie—her planet was so much farther advanced than Earth that to these beings Red O'Hara and I must have appeared as ape men. Yet, because of their gentleness, their culture, their civilization, they had accepted us, even liked us.

Now, by the inexorable logic of ape imperialism, they would be subjugated, and I would be the sole instrument of their subjugation. More than any other Earthman, I was trapped by that logic, for I had to go and come again. From my primordial lair, I had leaped to a cloud and my jungle would no longer suffice. The ape man of Earth, John Adams, had learned to love an angel of Heaven.

It was I who called Red to apologize. "I regret calling you a shanty Irishman, Red."

"You've called me worse."

"Another thing, Red. Knock off all I've said about the Harlechians. Maybe *we* don't deserve co-status."

"I wouldn't go so far as to say that."

"Let me be humble, Red."

"All right, Jack. You could use a little humility."

"None of your lip! I'm trying to turn the other cheek. This is a try at Christian brotherhood."

"No problem. I always loved you more than my brother, who's a wife-beating drunkard."

"Don't push me, Red. I'm still trying to be humble. I've broken off with Cara, temporarily."

"No problem. Go out and stand by the belt and grab another one. They're all good. Some are just better than others."

"But I love only Cara."

"Since you're in such a loving mood, meet me at the bar. There's an occasion for a drink."

"What's the occasion?"

"I'm awarding you the Cross of Saint George."

"You shanty Irishman!" I bellowed. "Stow your medal."

"Now, that's more like Jack Adams."

So we were reconciled and discussed the antiquity of Harlechians, but not once did Red bring up the subject of qualifying these beings for World's Brotherhood. Legally he knew his proposal was wrong, and intuitively he recognized my determination to colonize the planet and accord full and formal honors to my wife, Cara, if she could be qualified as a human by marriage.

Cara herself altered my preliminary plans.

Late one night, clad only in my nightshirt, I was reading in my library to calm my blood with the antisepsis of cybernetics, when I heard a movement in my outer office. I was alarmed but not frightened by the noise. Robbery was unheard of on Harlech since all was free, but, despite Frick's efforts, violence had been on the upswing. Though I had little to fear from creatures so much weaker than I, I leaned over quietly, turned off my reading lamp and crept to the door.

Silently, I turned the knob and flung open the door.

Outlined by the office nightlight behind her, Cara stood before me, her arm upraised to knock. She was gowned in diaphene so sheer that though it covered it did not conceal the wonder of her form. "Cara!" I almost strangled on her name.

Quietly she spoke. "I have come to take you, Jack my Beloved."

Guided by the social instincts of an Earthman, I bowed, flicked on the overhead light and backed into the room.

"Come in. You must be cold."

"Cold?"

"What are you doing on campus so late at night? And how did you get here wearing that gown?"

"I have taken rooms in the tunnel, Jack, to be near you."

"Then, why aren't you in bed asleep?"

"I tried, Jack. My spirit was willing but my flesh was too eager. So, I have come for you."

"Child, we're not married."

"Then marry me tonight and divorce me tomorrow."

"We need a preacher."

"You need the preacher, Jack. I need you."

"I can't debase your innocence without marriage."

"Then don't," she snapped. "I'll debase yours."

"It's a sin," I said hoarsely, for her thighs were quivering and her toes twitched.

"Is it a sin to be ravished?"

"Not for the ravishee," I said. "But the ravisher sins, and sinners burn in hell."

I bent closer, placing both my hands on her shoulder, pleading to her with my eyes. My gesture proved my undoing. Unseen beneath the billow of my tunic, her foot flicked up. "Better that burning than this," she said, and, as Red O'Hara had prophesied, I felt the toes of a woman of Harlech.

In punctured syllables, she said, "You speak your love for me with more than eyes, Jack, and I consign my soul to Hell!"

Her leg was circling my thigh now, and I said, "Cara, I have never denied my lo . . . honey . . . baby-doll . . . sweet thing. . . ."

I could say no more, for I was rendered speechless by breathlessness. Her remaining leg was rising around me, and I bore her weight lightly as she leaned backward as if to rest her head on some airy pillow. There was an adjustment, an in-gliding. As the gates of hell opened for Cara, heaven opened for me, and I knew I was marked forever by the beauty and uniqueness of my golden girl.

Sufficient unto the night are the sins thereof, so let it suffice to say that I could not determine if she qualified under the "face-to-face" clause of the Space Code. Schematically, I was the vertical bar on a T-square and could not determine if the horizontal bar which was Cara was greater or less than ninety degrees.

In truth, I was not too interested in empirical observations, but in a highly bemused manner I recognized the inspiration for Red's Cross of Saint George and the aptness of his expression, "Perking like a horizontal coffeepot."

Finally, Cara started to bend at the waist, her head drooping toward the floor. I scooped her up as her legs went limp and laid her gently in my study chair. She was beginning to weep and I kissed her brow. "Weep, dear girl. Your tears will cleanse your shame and repentance will help atone for your sin."

Cara only sobbed harder, but there was an antidote for her disgrace. I picked up the telephone and called Red. It was a sleepy, irritated voice that answered my ring.

"Red, it's Jack. I've just had Cara!"

"Begorra! Are you waking me this late to tell me naughties?"

"No, boy. I'm bringing Cara over, appointing you chaplain and ordering you to marry us tonight."

"Shove your orders! Anyway, you have to fill out Alnav 2186-C—with twelve copies—and the form is aboard ship."

He had me there. I had forgotten the regulation.

"Jack?" After a pause he was coming awake.

"Yes?"

"There's no hurry. Banns must be posted. . . ."

"Not in your new church," I said. "I'm appointing you a Methodist chaplain."

"All right, you idiot!" He was fully awake now. "Even though it's a forced marriage, we can do it in style. The lass will love a formal wedding. . . . What's her name?"

"Cara."

"Oh, the blonde. Does she qualify under the face-to-face clause?"

"Haven't you qualified them?" I asked, astonished.

"I tried, before you decided to colonize the planet. Afterward, I didn't wish to risk getting my hips crushed in a lost cause. . . . Lest it's face-to-face, I can't perform the marriage. . . . But, be careful! They tighten up when you restrain them, and they're strong as hell. If you can manage again, lad, lay your forearm against her stomach, get a good grip behind her shoulders and bend her toward you. Three degrees of tilt should qualify her."

The sobbing from the chair grew louder. "Red, she's sobbing something fierce. I'm afraid she's getting hysterical. What do you do?"

His voice was calm, clinical. "Do you have her on the desk or on the floor?"

"Neither, she's canted at an angle in my morris chair."

"I don't know, Jack. Usually, I lay them on the floor, lie down beside them and cry along with them. . . . I can hear her now. Jack, you've hit the jackpot! One tear in either eye will earn mine a Saint George. She'd get a fig-leaf cluster. . . . Say, I've got an idea! Bed down with her and qualify her while she's asleep."

I hung up, partly in disgust and partly to comfort Cara.

In a figurative sense, O'Hara was more interested in ends than in means, more in technique than in morality. At the moment, I was concerned with Cara, who needed me.

I sat on the ottoman before her and took her hand. "Dear girl, don't be frightened. If your soul is damned, then take comfort, for I will be with you, always. I'll pray for my own damnation."

Bravely she attempted to smile through her tears. "I'm crying because I'm so happy," she said. "Your hairy hips are hard to hold, but I love you, baby-doll."

Near the end of morning, I qualified Cara as a member of the human species, in one respect, at least. Though I padded my hips with pillows, I did not escape without bruises. But no good end is reached without struggle, and Cara was to an Earthwoman what a Stradivarius is to a ukelele.

After our final last good-night kiss, she snuggled into my arms and shocked me with a remark: "Jack, Red the Producer doesn't like blondes. He wouldn't give me even a tiny part in the Christmas play, and I did so want to play in it. Do you think he will marry you to a blonde?"

"He'll marry us," I said, "and you'll get a part in the Christmas pageant."

"That would be a wonderful wedding present, Jack," she said, snuggling closer.

Her remark disturbed me by its implications. Though I come from Alabama, I don't believe in drawing the color line. We are all God's children, and a blonde is just as good as a brunette. Red was a bigot.

After my long association with O'Hara, I knew as well as any man how to bargain with him. After I swore him in as chaplain in his office the next day, he poured libations while I maneuvered for a position of power.

"Red, I want none of your popish rituals intruding on the dignity of this wedding. The altar and candles are good, so are a few voices, maybe. But I want no choir performing Handel's *Messiah*, full-length, no priestly regalia—a plain purple robe will serve—and only one sign of the cross for demonstration purposes."

Red leaned back and eyed me thoughtfully. "Jack, I love you more than my drinking brother, for you are unique among men—you are uniquely rigid, self-righteous, narrow and bigoted."

"Boy, do *you* disapprove of bigots?" I asked.

"Bigots and Protestants," he answered.

"And blondes!" I shot at him.

"That's prejudice, not bigotry."

"Then why have you excluded blondes from the Christmas pageant and denied Cara a role in the play?"

He looked at me, and I could see in his eyes that the channels of communication were opening. "The trademark of an O'Hara production is realism, attention to details. Whoever heard of a blonde Jewess?"

"Who on Harlech ever heard of a Jew?"

He brushed my remark aside. "I could put Cara in a chorus line with my Maids of Bethlehem," he said thoughtfully, "but she would have to dye her hair."

"You're not mixing that angel into a chorus line of prostitutes," I said. "What about the role of the Virgin?"

"The Good Lord cast that one. Tamar plays the Virgin."

"That girl with the hips?"

"Aye."

"Boy, howdy!" I exploded. "If you can get an audience in *this* school to accept *that* girl as a virgin, Cara could play the Christ Child."

"I took Tamar off the camera—say, Jack, I have it!" He hunched toward me, excited. "I can write a role for your bride that's a natural, one that will top the Virgin."

Alarmed by his enthusiasm, which was obviously genuine, I drew back. "One thing, Red: I don't want Cara gallivanting out on the stage doing a striptease to 'Adeste Fideles.'"

"Jack, you will love her part, and it will not offend your piety in the least. In fact, I'll not let you see it until Christmas. It will be my present to you. Of course, it will take effort, great personal effort."

"Your generosity is appreciated, boy. Now, what do you want?"

What he wanted was nothing minor—a robe, a miter, four altarboys, one of whom was Nesser, a chorus of twenty voices, and a Cross behind the altar that would light up when I sang out, loud and clear, "I do."

Cara was ecstatic. At my request, the incredible artisans of Harlech produced a golden wedding ring with a ten-carat diamond. Frick, in the blue uniform and epaulets of Police Chief, was my best man, and he fumbled for the ring. Cara was a vision in her white minigown with veil, and for the first time I saw public tears on Harlech when her brides-maids were overcome with emotion.

When the Cross lighted behind the altar, the Harlechians applauded. Then we knelt before the altar, were pronounced man and wife and blessed by Bishop O'Hara, who sprinkled us with holy water to symbolize my wife's baptism into the Methodist faith. The ritual was another triumph for O'Hara, and to give him his due, it was a beautiful and impressive ceremony, and was televised. We arose and marched down the aisle, Cara and I, to the strains of "Pomp and Circumstance," beneath the raised billy clubs of Frick's police.

Cara and I had planned no honeymoon since all tunnels look alike and the surface was deep in snow, and it was well that we had not. Waiting outside in the corridor were two black-tunicked messengers from the Dean's office, with pink slips for Red and me.

I accepted mine and read it as the second messenger shouldered his way against the flow of the crowd to serve O'Hara's.

> At the suggestion of my regents, it is requested that Jack the Teacher and Red the Teacher appear before me and the regents concerned at 10.00 A.M., next Seventh day, to show cause why Earth Religions 1 and Earth Religions 2 should be taught at University 36.
>
> *Bubo the Dean*

Cara was disturbed. "You and Red have not been expelled, but a pink slip from the Dean is never good. He may wish to punish you."

CHAPTER NINE

A reception had been planned for after the wedding in Red's office, where Tamar had laid out a buffet table in our honor, Earth-style, and there was a cake and presents. We hurried off to the reception, where most of our invited guests would speak English, polarized along an Osh-kosh-Oxford axis, with the exception of Frick, who had picked up the argot of New York from studying old gangster movies.

Preoccupied as I was by the pink slip, I felt little nostalgia for Earth. In fact, such a remark as "My dear Tamar, you *must* tell me your recipe for this delightful squid dip" rather revolted me since it came from the boy, Nesser.

Red was late in arriving. It had taken time for him to divest himself of his bishop's gear and get back into kilts. When he strode in, greeting the guests, his joviality seemed undiminished by the pink slip, but after a few minutes he called out, "Carry on, folks, but I'd like a few private words with Jack the Teacher."

Since his inner and outer office was taken by the reception, we entered the library, where he pulled the pink slip from his pouch and tossed it on the table. "How do you read this, Jack?"

"Negative-negative," I answered.

"You'll notice, Jack, that these pink slips only arrive after a television show. Bubo must be a fan."

"He knew we were teaching religion," I pointed out.

"Which would mean nothing to him," Red said. "All other lectures are televised and ours aren't. We've never been hooked into his programmed circuit."

"You sound like Bubo is a computer," I said casually.

"To tell the truth, Jack, the thought occurred to me. But now we're having to appear before him. . . . Well, you're the lawyer, Jack. What do we do?"

"We'll defend the course," I said with some heat. "We'll be God's advocate against the Antichrist."

"Now, lad. All these folks understand is logic. . . . We might sell them religion as a tool for conditioning behavior. We must keep strictly to the legal approach."

"On a planet without law?" I snapped.

"But on a planet with logic," Red grinned, "and any good lawyer can confuse a logician. . . . But we don't know what the objections are, so we'll have to improvise on the spot. But I think I see ramifications here that can work to our long-term advantage. . . . Yes," he added, tapping the pink slip slowly, "I think we could win this argument by losing it."

I sensed the gist of his reasoning and followed him. "Blessed are the persecuted," I said.

"Right! Come to think about it, Jack, you'd better let me handle the defense."

I remembered Cara's warning, and I recalled, too, the unspoken slogan of Mandan and the Navy: "Never let the buck stop here." If Red wanted to grab the buck, he could have it. "It's all yours, Red."

With a relieved mind I returned to the reception, where Cara and I cut the cake and opened presents. There were the usual knick-knacks of cutlery, silverware and napery for the bride, but there was one huge, rectangular package for me from my class in Aesthetics, which Cara held to the last.

It was a painting, three feet wide and four feet deep, of a hickory tree standing on the far side of a swale, its leaves yellow in the slanting sunlight of autumn, and each leaf was detailed against the swirled russet of an oak tree behind it. Dust motes danced in the sunbeams broken by the leaves, and on the carpet of leaves beneath the tree lay the limb from a wind-fallen oak I had thrown there. The hickory was done with the photographic clarity of a Kramer, the russet of the oak grove was laid on with the color-mad sworls of a Van Gogh and the skyscape beyond had the dreamy mistiness of the Hudson River School.

In amazement, I turned to Cara. "Who painted this masterpiece?"

"All of us who went with you on the field trip," Cara answered. "I, myself, painted the lower right-hand quadrant of the upper left-hand quadrant."

"Whose idea was it?"

"Mine, dear Jack. I knew that you loved pictures, and I knew that your Earth mind cannot retain an image over long periods, so we painted it for you."

"You went back out there after you were almost killed?"

"No, dear Jack. We painted it from memory."

When the morning of our conference arrived, I found that O'Hara had spoken too soon of my theory that Bubo was a computer. Bubo the Dean was not present. Instead, he was represented by his student secretary, who introduced Red and me to the two Regents, Karlo, a behavioral engineer, and Farb, the equivalent of a primitive anthropologist. "Bubo the Dean sends his regrets," the student said, "but the press of his administrative duties deny him the pleasure of attendance. I will take notes for him to act upon. Teachers and Regents, be seated."

Red and I took seats across a conference table from the two Harlechians. Farb the antiquarian spoke first, in flawless English.

"Teachers, the microtaped versions of your planet's history have been analyzed. In the beginning, we of Harlech had tribal wars and one mate per male. But tribes merged into nationalities upon the three continents and the wars became national. Then two continents allied and subjugated the third, and then there was tension between the two great powers. Space exploration was undertaken and the conflict that was planetary became universal. Freebooters roamed the spaceways.

"A final war came, of such fury that the axis of the planet was tilted. By then, civilization had gone underground and many of the tunnels were flooded. Remnants of the two great powers joined each other with a rapid-transit subway system, for the surface was radioactive.

"We had discovered, as you have discovered, a method for leaping that which you refer to as 'the Minkowski one-space' and which we called 'the time warp.' This discovery left us at the mercy of our own ancestors for any freebooter could go back in time and with his knowledge alter the course of the planet's history to suit his own whim or to favor his old nationality."

"I thought of that!" Red exploded.

"Regency speaking!" the student secretary snapped.

Farb continued as if there had been no interruption: "So we of Harlech shifted emphasis from outer space to inner space and used the remainder of our space fleet to exile the incorrigibles, those with XYY genetic syndromes, to other galaxies. We equipped their ships with self-destruct mechanisms, which operated on a delay principle actuated by their touchdowns. Many were sent into M-16, your own Milky Way."

"I thought of that!" I said.

I, too, was silenced by the secretary and Farb concluded: "We believe that you descend from an exile ship of Harlech. Your leg structure, designed for weightlifting rather than running, would have evolved from life on a benign surface. Much of the edible flora and fauna of Earth could have evolved from our seed animals and plants. You are overspecialized for survival on a planet such as Earth, and even your language resembles ours. The country you call Wales was once called Harlech. . . . Farb has spoken."

Karlo, the behavioral engineer, then spoke: "In the beginning we had gods, but the gods were used to stimulate tribal wars. In the beginning we had mating, but the females became the chattel of stronger males, and the females adopted the rejection pattern as a defense. In the interests of mental hygiene and feminine dignity, we eliminated our gods and did away with sexual exclusiveness. Thus we eliminated 82.3 percent of our nonorganic mental aberrations. The remainder we eliminated by gene control and the inhalation of DNA. In a fully automated society where all citizens are law-abiding, the state withered away. We have now a pure democracy and scholarship is the chief industry of our people. Democracy includes academic freedom to the point where freedom stops and license begins. Thus we ask you to eliminate from your courses, next semester, Religions 1 and Religions 2, as they are considered retrograde and inimical to the best interests of our students. . . . Karlo has spoken."

"Questions or rebuttals?" the student secretary asked, turning to O'Hara and me.

"Since you deny religion, Karlo," I asked, "what happens to your immortal souls?"

"If the life flow is uninterruptable, it exists with or without our approval and is thus no cause for our concern, logically. But any concept which seeks future development of our senses impairs their present development."

His concept was completely canceled by the concept of Original Sin, and I started to rebut him in theological terms when Red kicked me under the table and spoke out, himself.

"Regents, since you have answered our primary question so adequately, then we will discontinue our formal lectures on religion next semester. But since it is illogical to state a premise without arriving at a deduction, I have one request to make. I have now in rehearsal a drama depicting the birth of an Earth god to be presented at the end of this semester. No god should be born without dying. In full agreement with the Regents, I would like permission to logically continue the drama at the end of next semester by revealing the death of that god."

Karlo spoke. "We approve of the death of gods. Continue your serialization by all means, Red the Teacher, for we Elders also enjoy your dramas."

"That was some defense, Red," I commented as we walked down the belt toward Faculty Row.

"I told you we couldn't lose," Red said. "I'm choosing the most popular lad on the campus to play Herod and twelve of my best centurions to play his soldiers. Once they're pink-slipped, we'll have the nucleus of a popular revolt. Then when I throw the Easter drama at them, I'll have Judas, Pontius Pilate and forty centurions to back up our legal appeal against Bubo."

"That takes care of the drama department," I said, "but it wreaks havoc with the religious department."

"Cheer up, lad. The Regents have given us a 'them' to separate from 'us.' And we and the students are the 'us.' We're going underground with our religion."

"How much more underground can we get?"

"As long as we don't televise our religious services, we'll not be detected. And we promised only that we would not give formal lectures. . . . Join me in a drink, Jack, and let's discuss this at greater length."

"Only one, Red," I said. "I promised Cara I'd be home for lunch. She's been practicing Earth cooking, and she wants you and Tamar over for dinner, next Sixth-day night."

"We'll be there," Red promised, as we walked into the tavern, "but tell her to give up any idea of making a match between Tamar and me. The lass is too omnivorous for wedded bliss."

"So I observed," I remarked, as we settled on our stools. "She was giving me the once-over the night Draki was pink-slipped."

Mac didn't wait for our order. He was preparing our boilermakers the minute he saw us walk in. "Here's to the catacombs of a New Rome," Red lifted his glass.

"To a fully automated New Jerusalem," I replied.

Once O'Hara's enthusiasm was aroused, he could communicate better than any spaceman alive, particularly when a conspiracy was involved. By the second drink, I was beginning to feel like a method actor portraying Saint Peter. I could smell the catacombs. By the end of the third drink, I was willing to take on a few lions in the Colosseum. Bubo was Nero. But Red drifted off into new areas of speculation.

"All myths have a basis in fact," he said. "Harlech was our Eden and we XYY syndromers sinned when we tilted the axis of our native planet. Our flood occurred in these rabbit warrens and when Noah's Ark landed on Ararat, it landed with retro-jets."

"Cut it out!" I said. "You're taking from me my Original Sin."

After one more round, I tore myself away, for I was already fifteen minutes late for lunch. When I walked into the kitchen, an anxious Cara kissed me and drew back in disgust. "Jack, you reek of whisky! Have you been out with that Red the Teacher?"

I was contrite, my compliments over her cooking were profuse though thick-tongued, and she was intent on the outcome of my meeting with the Regents. "So they don't approve of my marriage, or your religion. Well, our marriage is none of their affair! If I wish to attempt an interspecies marriage and accept my husband's faith, that's no business of the elders. . . . But one thing is my business, Jack. If you're going to get staggering drunk, I want you to quit wearing Earth clothes. They make you too conspicuous. I don't want perfect strangers walking up to me in the tunnels and asking if I'm the girl who married that Earth sot."

Although Cara said nothing, she was perturbed by my plan to open a secret chapel in my office to continue teaching religion. I was beginning to read the eyes of Harlechians and in the privacy of our quarters, decorated now with the frills of femininity and that magnificent painting, Cara's eye flow was uninhibited.

"You don't approve," I said.

"I approve, but Bubo would not."

"I'd have the students with me, the police force and the law courts. All the strength is on our side. Why should I care what Bubo thinks?"

"There is also strength in weakness," she said, "and Bubo can punish. He is devious, like Iago, though he would do nothing himself. He is an administrator."

"Agreed," I said. "And as an administrator, he does nothing but delegate authority."

"Bubo could delegate the wrong authority," she said.

Her remark tipped me off on Bubo's methods. On Earth the same techniques were used when an executive was assigned to manage a failing branch operation and then was blamed for the branch's failure.

Such resources were beyond Bubo's reach with me—if

there was a Bubo—for I was no part of his organization. Moreover, I planned to return within two years of my departure with enough proxies to take over the whole operation. If Bubo then revealed himself, and if he was well-mannered and obsequious, I might have a managerial job for him in the new operation, perhaps Colonial Ceramics. He could be vice-president in charge of testing Earth lavatory commodes.

Despite the prophecies of Red and the slight friction generated by my drinking, my marriage got off to a good start. Cara had her little secrets. She wouldn't tell me what part she was playing in the Christmas drama and forbade me to watch the rehearsals. "I'll be everything you ever dreamed of in a woman, Jack my beloved, and the role will make you proud of me."

She wouldn't let me in the kitchen when she was preparing the dinner to which Red and Tamar had been invited. She wanted to surprise me with the recipes she had gotten from an Earth cookbook.

She had fire in her make-up, too.

To implement the police power in my hands, I invited Frick, my Chief of Police, to the dinner. Cara approved of Frick, but she turned thumbs down on Nesser, whom I wanted to invite since I planned to use him as an altar boy when I opened my first chapel. "Jack, I want to enjoy the dinner, and I couldn't stomach a bite with that warthead at the table."

"But he's a very warm person, spiritually," I said.

"Good," she snapped. "I'm glad his spirit's warm. His hands are clammy and he likes to touch."

Red asked and received permission to invite Reno, his cadet General of Centurions, who was scheduled to act as our sacrificial lamb. Reno was to play King Herod in the Christmas pageant.

Cara's decorum was at its best on the evening of the Earth dinner. We had cocktails in the outer office, where I received the compliments of my guests on the Harlechian costume Cara had designed and made for me, a tunic of space gray with a matching jockstrap which was drawn loosely around the waist with a sash of navy blue and decorated on the left breast with the word "Cara's" embroidered in gold.

Tamar arrived in a dress that deviated further from Harlechian fashion than my own tunic. Hers was a dress, not a tunic. It flared from her waist in ruffles long enough to conceal all but the sway of her hips, but the material she had spent on the skirt was balanced by that which she had saved on the bodice. It was cut so low that it revealed the very points of her principal area of *embonpoint*.

Tamar whistled a wolf's call at the sight of my legs. "If you ever get tired of him, Cara, throw him my way."

Red, with all his knobby knees, did not seem offended by her remark. "I offered him the Order of Saint George, myself."

Frick arrived dressed formally in his blue tunic with his badge and ceremonial billy club hooked to his belt. General Reno came bedecked in the uniform Red had designed for the cadets, looking for all the world like a kelly-green member of the Black Watch with his gold stars shining on his epaulet. He was a slender youth with a very large head that reminded me of Julius Caesar's bust.

Festivities began on Tamar's note of banter but an undercurrent of gravity soon manifested itself despite the cocktails. Word was out among the students that courses on religion were to be discontinued after the fall quarter. Tamar was sad and Frick was indignant. "Do the Regents think these students are children?"

Reno entered a strange remark. "Personally, I think this planet could use a little Hebrew backbone. Take David. Now, *there* was a man. What this planet needs is not peace but the sword."

"You're right about David," Frick agreed. "He had the right idea. If they get out of line, clout them in the kisser."

It saddened me somewhat to think that the boys would use Old Testament figures as models, but at least they were choosing the right model. It would never do for a police chief or a general to pattern his behavior on Job.

Frick had done such a splendid job of excavating a four-cell cellblock behind his police station that I asked his advice about an altar crypt in the south wall of my office.

As Frick explained it, it was no problem. The area could be excavated and the laser beam adjusted to glaze the walls a deep purple, an ideal background for a white cross. Dirt removal was automated. The knob north of the soccer field had been created by dirt removed from the tunnels.

As I stood and mused over the altar, I heard Reno say to Cara, "To our way of thinking, it would seem deceitful of the Children of Israel to booby-trap a pontoon bridge and drown Pharaoh's army, but it was a good defensive tactic."

Upon hearing this remark, I promptly invited Red to the bathroom for an indulgence in an old Earth custom, shared hand-washing.

"Since when did the Children of Israel lay a pontoon bridge over the Red Sea?"

"The students are logical, Jack. They can't relate to miracles."

"Then how do you relate them to booby-traps and pontoon bridges in a nonmilitary society? Teaching military science is forbidden."

"I'm hedging my bet, Jack. If your marriage works out, you might defect. When the Harriers come after you, these lads could protect my old buddy."

"Do you think I'd fire on my own species?"

"Knowing you, Jack, a military man in a militant church, I think you would. If your home, family and altar were threatened by the Corps, wouldn't you fire?"

"Given those conditions, but only under such conditions," I agreed, "there's nothing I'd enjoy more than to walk a rolling barrage from a laser battery through a landing party of those cocky bastards and blast them from hell to breakfast."

Suddenly I was amazed by my own un-Christian vehemence and enthusiasm. But Cara was rapping on the door, calling, "Chow down, sailors."

We entered to a candlelit table, and at each setting was a steaming dish of hotcakes with sides of bacon and pats of butter. Beside each plate was a glass of white wine imported from the south continent, a pitcher of syrup in the center and a pat of country butter. "Ah, what a lovely sight," Red said.

I was equally enthusiastic over the evening breakfast and after toasting our hostess and guests, we settled down to consume the hotcakes. They were delightful, so good that Red and I had seconds, but it was merely the first course. As we finished up our hotcakes, Cara brought in a steaming platter of southern-fried chicken.

"Soul food," I cried, and Red echoed, "Shades of Brother Ben."

Despite the hotcakes, Red and I dug into the fried chicken with gusto, but during the chicken course an unpleasant incident developed. Dressed as I was in the manner of Harlech, I was barefooted, and as host I sat at the head of the table between Cara and Tamar. During pancakes, my bare foot touched Tamar's. Modestly I drew my foot back, put-ting it under my chair, but later her foot touched mine. At first I thought her movement an inadvertency, until her toes began to stroke my own, lightly and caressingly. When the second course arrived, I buried my consternation in the thigh of a Harlechian chicken, as Tamar's toes continued an upward progress, unseen beneath the table.

Perhaps the wine had touched Cara, or perhaps it was my profuse compliments over the chicken, but Cara put her foot over mine and patted me lovingly. Suddenly, Cara was becoming affectionate with my ankles while Tamar fondled my kneecap. I bent to my plate, stoking in the chicken in my consternation, for Tamar was fondling down-ward as Cara fondled up.

A collision between the two feet was inevitable, and I could not bolt for the lavatory or take any drastic with-drawal action, for such would have constituted a rejection of my wife, and her hurt and anger toward me could never have been pacified by any truthful explanation.

Because I had to live with Cara, I sacrificed Tamar. Halfway between my kneecap and my shinbone, the two feet touched.

Not a word was said. The toes launched as lightly from my leg as two wrens taking flight in different directions.

After a long silence, Cara said sweetly, "Tamar, would you care for more chicken? Perhaps another leg?"

"No, thank you, Cara. I prefer the thigh."

"I have the thigh," Cara said, "but perhaps I might cut out a gizzard for you, or chop up a liver."

"Perhaps Jack the Teacher would like a little more breast?" Tamar said sweetly.

"He has a breast!" Cara said, "but perhaps I could pluck out an eye. But they are dark. Like the eyes of a pig that wallows in the first mud available. . . ."

Cara's hand was creeping toward the wine bottle, so I knew that the situation was getting very tense. But in the most freakish intervention of fate in my life since Red had found the planet with his green drawers, the door burst open and two uniformed policemen entered.

At first I felt that Frick had staged a raid to give a touch of drama to the dinner, but the sergeant of the duo blurted, "Chief, a boy has been murdered in Washroom 23!"

"I'll be right there," Frick said, dabbing his lips with his napkin. "Will you excuse me, Cara? Duty calls."

"Certainly, Frick."

"Commissioner," Frick said to me. "I've never handled a murder case before. Would you . . . ?"

"I'm with you, Frick," I said, rising. "This is serious."

"I'll come along," Red said.

"You stay here, Red!" I ordered, "Stay here and see Tamar home."

"Jack, are you leaving before the main course?" Cara asked.

"Darling, there's been a murder!"

"He'll stay murdered, but I've prepared your favorite dish —pork chops. The pork chops will grow cold."

"Never mind, dear," I said. Then, seized by a sudden inspiration, I added, "I don't care for pig meat."

"The murdered boy's name was Krale," the sergeant told us as we strolled along. "He was studying mortuary cryogenics. This was his first semester at the university."

"Not much time to acquire enemies," I commented. "Were you acquainted with him, Frick?"

"I don't have a dossier on him, yet," Frick said, speaking to me in English, "but I knew him by sight. A pleasant sort. He shacked up with a dame as soon as he got here and has been going steady ever since." He turned to the sergeant, "How was he killed?"

"Strangulation. Someone got him from behind while he was washing his hands. They were still wet."

"First we'll have to look for a motive, Frick," I said. "Since robbery is out, as they say on Earth, we'll look for the woman."

"I've got a line on *her*," Frick said. He turned to the patrolman. "Sprint over to her dorm and pick up Dori. Bring her to the stationhouse but don't tell her why."

As the patrolman leaped forward and ran down the corridor, Frick turned to me. "Dori was Krale's steady."

"Give her the news gently, Frick. She might break up over the boy's death."

"Not Dori. Krale was one of twelve."

"Get all their names."

"I will, Commissioner. But I deduce that Krale's murderer is not among them. Dori's got power hip flow and no lover of hers is going to risk a murder rap."

We arrived at Washroom 23, which was guarded by a uniformed policeman who stood talking to two morgue attendants waiting outside with a motorized litter.

"Hurry it up, please, Frick," one of the attendants said. "Krale was a classmate and we want him on ice as soon as possible."

"You're getting him a lot sooner than anybody expected," Frick said, "including Krale."

For once I was grateful for the Harlechian lack of curiosity. No crowds gathered outside the door, and inside only one officer stood beside the body on the lavatory floor. The body of Krale, a fair-haired young student, lay on its stomach but its eyes were staring directly at the ceiling. Its spine had been severed and the head was twisted a full half-circle on the neck.

The patrolman stepped aside as Frick paused a few paces from the body and stared down at it. Then he moved to another angle and stared. In forty-five seconds, he had four different images photographed in his mind. "All right, cryogenics," he called, "you can haul it to the bank."

"Whoever killed Krale must have been terrifically strong, Frick," I commented. "His head was twisted in a vise."

"Not at all, Jack. Let me demonstrate. Stand down the line, there, and brace yourself as if you were washing your hands."

He pointed three bowls down from the one the victim had used and said, "Now, look in the mirror as the officer walks by."

Outside, the sound of the siren on the litter dwindled down the corridor as the officer sauntered by me, as if headed for the urinals lined against the far wall. Watching him, I saw no preparatory flexing of muscles, but suddenly he soared from the floor, twisting as he rose, to land lightly atop my shoulders. With a single movement he hooked his right leg under my armpit and levered my head with his instep against my jaw.

"Resist his foot, Jack," Frick requested.

With my neck muscles, I Indian-wrestled against the boy's foot, but the boy won easily. Then he uncoiled and dropped to the floor.

"I doubt if he could break your neck," Frick said, "but Harlechians are fragile. . . . Sergeant, dust the mirror."

The sergeant took a small bottle from his tunic pouch and jetted a spray of powder over the mirror above the bowl where the victim had been washing his hands. He turned the bottle around and a jet of compressed air blew away the excess powder, leaving the print of a left foot clearly visible on the glass.

"I deduced," Frick explained, "that the murderer pushed the body away from the bowl after he broke Krale's neck to prevent scuffing his knee or ankle on the faucet. . . . Take a transfer of the print, Sergeant."

With a second flask, the sergeant sprayed a blue gel over the powder. As we waited for the gel to set, Frick turned to me. "What's the penalty for murder, Commissioner?"

"Death by hanging," I answered.

I oversimplified my answer for the student since this was obviously a premeditated murder and I did not wish to confuse Frick with the various degrees of homicide. "Hanging from a public gallows," I added.

As the sergeant cut out the square of gel containing the footprint and peeled it back from the mirror, Frick promised me, "Jack, this murderer is going to swing."

"Frick," I warned him, "it's not your job to judge the case. Your duty's to apprehend the killer. The court will decide his fate. If you find him, there must be no coercion or intimidation of the prisoner. And a lawyer must be present when you question him."

In my own mind, doubts were rising about the legality of this venture. I had introduced moot pleadings in mock courts to impress legal procedures on the minds of student tribunals with the aim, eventually, of permitting them to protect themselves from the whims of an administrator. We had even incarcerated a few offenders for two or three days in misdemeanor trials, but I recoiled from the thought of hanging a boy by a kangaroo court.

I could not act without authority, and the only official who could grant such authority, if he *could* grant it, was the very man whose abuses had created a need for law. I would have to go to Bubo the Dean.

We looked at the transfer the sergeant had peeled from the glass. Whorls and lines on the ball of the foot showed clearly. "I'm not prejudging the case, Jack, but this exhibit will hang him. You can't pay off a judge on this planet."

Superficially, I had to agree, but there remained the task of finding the culprit whose foot matched the print, and there was the problem of authority in the matter of capital punishment. "Draw up your warrant, Frick, and I'll meet you at headquarters in half an hour."

Rather than dampen my student's enthusiasm for the

case, I said nothing about the legal void in which we moved but left immediately for Dean Bubo's office. For me, my task was more interesting than the murder. Krale's death gave me an opportunity to prove that Bubo the Dean was in fact a systems computer.

CHAPTER TEN

D ean Bubo's outer office was larger than that assigned to teachers with a railing separating the reception area from a working area occupied by four student assistants, one the secretary who had recorded the minutes of the Regents' Conference. I spoke to the receptionist: "Will you tell Bubo the Dean that Jack the Teacher would like an audience immediately on a matter of extreme urgency?"

She went and spoke to the male secretary, who came forward. "Jack the Teacher, Bubo the Dean is occupied with administrative matters. Could I help you?"

"No, you could not! This is a matter between the Dean and me."

"Jack, if you could just explain to . . ." he began.

"There's no point explaining what must be explained to the Dean alone. Now, let me see him."

"Jack, the Dean's office is taboo."

"I'm from Earth, and we have no fear of taboos."

"It is not fear, Jack, but respect. It is our duty to keep the chief administrator sacrosanct so that he might better devote his thoughts to matters of policy."

"This is a matter of highest policy and demands his immediate attention."

"Wait here, Jack, and I will try."

The assistant walked back, knocked on the door to the inner office and entered. His absence was protracted, or so it seemed to me, pacing nervously beyond the rail. I was so confident that my theory was correct that I was flabbergasted when Dean Bubo walked from his office and ad-

vanced toward the railing. It was the same man who had
appeared on television. A star decorated his tunic.

"What's this matter of highest policy?" he asked.

"Dean Bubo, in my capacity as your teacher of law, I
wish to tell you that a student has been murdered."

"Don't tell me. Call the organ bank."

"But I come to you because his murderer should be
hanged."

"Why come to me? I'm no hangman!"

"I come to you for authority to seek out, arrest and bring
the criminal to trial."

"You're the law teacher. Try him."

"Are you, then, delegating the authority to me?"

"Of course not. Delegate your own authority. . . . Listen,
Jack. You take care of your problems, I'll take care of mine.
Fair enough?"

"Yes, Dean."

But I was talking to the back of Bubo, who was hurrying
back to his higher-policy decisions. Chagrined, I stalked
moodily back to headquarters and countersigned a Jondoe
warrant for the arrest of Krale's murderer, or murderers, on
my own authority.

Frick entered from the interrogation room. "Jack, I've
got the girl back there and she's willing to cooperate. If
my deductions hold, we'll break this case in a matter of
hours."

"Good, Frick, but have a counselor standing by before you
interrogate."

"I've notified Val and Mon already, Commissioner."

"Val and Mon? Aren't those the two from Red's awkward
squad?"

"Yes, Jack."

"They couldn't defend a blind grandmother from an assault charge," I said. "Get Bardo, Marti and Fisk. At least
they'll give the prosecution a little training."

"Yes, Jack. But a question: How do you build a gibbet?"

Hastily I sketched a gallows frame on a note pad, knowing his totally receptive mind would grasp the principle.
With a bit of twine, I showed him how a noose was tied
and fitted around the neck.

Frick looked over my drawing. "Well, as Moses would
say, 'A neck for a neck.' "

His remark intrigued me. "I didn't know you were interested in religion, Frick."

"Red's a good teacher, and its the duty of a police officer to keep himself informed on methods of punishment."

"Right, Frick, and here's your warrant. . . . It looks as if I've landed on this planet just in time to help you stop a crime wave. Are there many murders on Harlech?"

"Once there were quite a few," Frick said, "but there's been none on record the last five thousand years."

"This may not be the last," I said, thinking of Cara and the wine bottle. "But I've got to go. If any break occurs in this case, I'll be home."

I wanted to stay around the station to hear the result of the interrogation of Dori, but I was worried about Cara. Recalling her mood when I left, it occurred to me that Tamar might not be the next victim of homicide on Harlech. It might well be Jack Adams.

Cara was abed when I returned, but the dining room was a mess from the interrupted dinner. In the center of the table, eight pork chops were stacked one atop one another to form a leaning tower. Looking over the disarray, I felt less disgust than sympathy for the girl whose first attempt at an Earth dinner, so eagerly planned and long awaited, had been interrupted by the attempted seduction of her husband and terminated prematurely by a murder.

As I looked, I heard a lamp click on in the bedroom. Cara was awake and waiting. With sudden inspiration, I picked up a cold pork chop, bit into it and entered smiling.

Cara was not smiling. She sat cross-legged in the center of the bed, her arms folded across her chest. Casually waving my pork chop as a banner, I bent to kiss her lips and received a cheek instead.

"What's the matter, Cara? Can't you sleep?"

"Matter! Let me smell your breath."

I exhaled an innocent breath across her nostrils.

"So, after Red brought that swivel-hipped hussy to your rendezvous you had no time for drinking!"

"Be reasonable, Cara. You know I was out on a case."

"Hah! A case? And after I spend four hours slaving over a hot stove."

"Women work from sun to sun," I said, forgetting there was no sun in her life, "but man's work is never done."

"Quit moralizing," she snapped. "You promised to love, honor and cherish me till death do us part and you leave before dinner's over."

"Death did part us, dearest," I said. "Your dinner was delightful, but a student, Krale, was murdered."

"And why should that keep you two hours? Were you trying to resurrect him?"

"Darling, I'm the Police Commissioner. There are duties I have to perform." Patiently, step by step, I explained the procedures that had occupied my time. The explanation took an hour, and she listened in stony silence. When I finished she said, "You loved it when that Tamar toed you under the table."

"Dearest Cara, I was never so embarrassed. But she was a guest escorted into our house by my best friend, and I could not be rude to her in your presence or in Red's. What happened after I left?"

"Red got her out before I broke her neck. But what did you mean insulting my pork chops in her presence?"

"I was not talking about your pork chops. You had compared Tamar to a pig, so I agreed with you that I didn't like pork. It was an oblique criticism of Tamar. . . . As for your pork chops, I never tasted better. And by the way, where were you when I was pleading to you, with my eyes, for help? . . . Where was your loyalty and devotion when that pig Tamar was slopping at your trough?"

So I attacked, and my scheme worked. With innocent protest, with love avowed, with vehemence, sincerity and adoration for two cold pork chops, I made her large toe twitch. By midnight and third pork chop her thigh quivered. By twelve-fifteen, her jaw began to wag. And at twelve-sixteen the phone rang.

I picked up the bedroom extension. It was Frick.

"Commissioner, the case is solved. The suspect has tendered a full confession with the consent of his attorneys, who were present. It was one of Dori's rejected suitors, as I suspected."

"Splendid, Frick. Is Dori still in the back room?"

"No, Jack. But she left her deposition. When I showed the suspect the print and matched it with his foot, he sang like a canary. It wasn't much of a challenge, really. The murderer is Nesser, your altarboy. He wants to talk to you, Jack, about forgiveness."

"I'll be right over, Frick."

Numbed from shock, I slowly placed the phone back onto its receiver and turned to my wife. She was coiled into a tight little ball in the far corner of the bed, hugging her legs to her with her face buried between her knees. To kiss her goodnight on the lips, I would have had to unravel her. To unravel her, I would have had to use a crow bar.

Cara was being hostile, suspicious and irrational in her jealousy, and still I loved her. But the only portion of her bared to my kiss would have degraded my love had I kissed it. So I merely patted her good-night and turned off the light.

"What's this I hear about you confessing, boy?"

Nesser sat on the bunk in the corner of his cell, staring straight ahead, the closest to a picture of dejection that any Harlechian could come.

"Dori spurned me, Jack," he said. "I couldn't live without her. I followed Krale. I killed him so Dori would go steady with me again."

I didn't have the heart to tell the boy that he was only one cull from a large barrel of apples. "So you permitted lust to rob you of reason."

"Jack, it was love, and your Dean of Deans said, 'Love one another.'"

"He wasn't talking about hip flik," I said. "But he might forgive you if you but go to Him in your prayers."

"I might have gone, Jack, but not now."

His answer dismayed me. "Boy, you'd better reconsider. Prayer might be the only solution to your problem."

"Jack, the Scripture says, 'If thine eye offend thee, pluck it out.' It was not my eye that put me here."

Suddenly I realized that the Scripture had again run afoul of the literal mind of a Harlechian. "The idea is that you should feel such remorse for your sins that any punishment would be welcome. Now, Nesser, Frick tells me you wanted instructions on how to achieve forgiveness for your sin."

"Yes, Jack. Krale cannot forgive me. His poor neck snapped like a broomstick. I wanted to ask you, as a teacher, to go to Dori and order her to visit me so I can plead for her forgiveness because I murdered her steady. I want to get down on my knees and beg her forgiveness as Red the Teacher taught in Elementary Human Emotions."

This boy was not seeking divine forgiveness. Possibly he might even be seeking a liaison with his former girlfriend. Rising, I said gruffly, "I'll see what I can do, Nesser."

Frick was gone, but I left a message with the desk sergeant telling him that his prisoner wished to see Dori. "Tell him to try to talk her into seeing Nesser."

"That shouldn't be hard," the sergeant commented. "She's cooperating with half the force now. There's something about a uniform."

Wearily I trudged home from a day of legal, domestic, police and spiritual problems. For the second time in one night, I entered my bedroom, and the rales of Cara told me she slept. Quietly I undressed, pillowing my head near the balled buttocks of my wife.

Cara was gone from my side when I awakened late on the Seventh-day morning, but a note was pinned to my pillow.

> Jack, my shifty-eyed husband, I have gone to a script conference and from there I will go to a costume fitting and from there to a voice teacher and from there to rehearsals. Your breakfast is on the table, but you will have to take lunch in the refectory. You were out all night, so I let you sleep in.
>
> Was Dori as good as Tamar?
>
> *Cara*

I read the note and tossed it into the wastebasket, where it belonged. Marriage is a two-way street, I thought, and that girl is going to learn who wears the jockstrap in this family. While I had been out on an errand of mercy to the cell of a prisoner who was, to all appearances, condemned, she had assumed that I was out with some female.

Despite her training in logic, Cara Adams was as irrational as an Earthwoman.

It was a pleasant surprise to discover the dining room was again my study, neat and orderly, but the pleasure only lasted as far as the kitchen. In a plate in the center of the table, two hard-boiled eggs were placed carefully on last night's tower of cold pork chops.

Deciding to forego the breakfast for lunch at the commissary, I called Red and asked him over to share the meal. He had rehearsals that afternoon and was in a hurry, but he was interested in my story of the murder investigation and my confrontation with Bubo. "That star on his tunic must mean he's status-conscious. There are few other emoluments for a man in his position," Red commented. "Strange, though, that he should let you authorize a trial. He should see that a legal system could be used against him."

"I'm wavering a little on the trial, myself," I admitted. "If Nesser's hanged, in a way I'll be morally responsible."

"Nonsense," Red said. "There's no morality in an institution. Logically, the only official responsible for Nesser's death is the hangman."

"Frick would probably hang the hangman," I said, "and we'd have one murder trial after another."

"Well, bread and circuses. . . . Say, Jack, we may have a conflict of interests here."

"How so?"

"By law, hangings are public. See if you can drag out the trial until after the Christmas pageant."

"Don't worry, Red. I won't hog your limelight, if you'll do me a favor."

"What?"

"Tell Cara to please come home after rehearsals."

"Oh," Red grinned. "Tamar, eh? Those legs of yours set her in motion. For a while there, I was afraid she was going rigid at the table."

"And you select her to play the Virgin. What happened to Kiki?"

"She's not available. . . . Jack, I find the best defense against an accusation for something you didn't do is to do it." He glanced at his watch. "I've got to move. See what you can do about holding off the hanging."

After he left, I sat brooding over my coffee. I didn't want Nesser to hang. As a freed and repentant sinner, I could use his testimonials in my evangelistic effort. O'Hara had inadvertently shown me a way to free the boy on a technicality if Bardo, Marti and Fisk weren't able to win the legal battle.

Hangmen could only be appointed by state authority, and there was no state authority on Harlech because there was no state.

With my mind eased, I went down to the station to find that Dori had already visited with Nesser and had forgiven him.

Looking over the paperwork in the case of Nesser versus the citizens of Harlech 36, I was amazed at the accuracy and thoroughness with which the students had assimilated and acted upon Earth law. Reno, as general commanding the centurions, was the judge advocate for the court-martial, with three of Red's centurions and the prosecutor comprising the remainder of the board.

Reno was chief reviewing officer, and Reno was earmarked for expulsion. He was to play Herod in the Christmas pageant. Here again I might have a technicality in the making. The court was a student tribunal, and Reno's decision could be void once he was expelled. If Nesser were condemned and Reno disqualified, then I could probably free Nesser under the double-jeopardy clause.

I asked Frick for a rundown on Reno.

"I put him under surveillance only a week ago," Frick said, "so his dossier isn't complete. His mother's skipper of a shrimp trawler. He's a dour sort. Doesn't talk much. Goes steady with one girl. Never much of a scholar. When Red came along with his centurion idea, Reno found a career. I'd say he's a typical military mind."

Even though I didn't like Frick's offhand dismissal of the "typical military mind," I was interested in his record-keeping.

"You had a line on the murder victim," I said. "You knew Nesser, and now you speak of a dossier on Reno. How do you accumulate these files?"

Frick thought for a moment before answering. "Generally speaking, Commissioner, my files are the common knowledge of the students. As Chief of Police, I have to keep myself informed."

His answer was evasive.

"In particular, Frick, why do you get a dossier on persons as diverse as Reno and Nesser?"

"Because they are diverse. Crimes are seldom committed by the average student."

"How can you do it with such a small police force?"

"Oh, I don't use uniformed police for undercover work. I have a much larger staff of secret agents."

"How do you recruit them?"

"It's easy, Commissioner. They're given career opportunities. You see, before you and Red came along, we were all destined for some specialized branch of learning, but we're not all inclined toward scholarship. Can you imagine me at a potter's wheel?"

"What about security?" I asked. "How do you know your organization has not been infiltrated by Bubo's black tunics?"

"It has," Frick answered, "but since they are students they are with us. Bubo's agents are double-agents. We have Bubo under surveillance."

"What have you got on Bubo?"

Frick leaned over and handed me a blank sheet of paper. "This will do for a dossier on Bubo. He's Chief Administrator."

Life is a series of tensions, and the secret is to keep them in balance. With a permanent military under the observation of a growing secret-police apparatus, plus crime and domestic problems, I had a well-organized system of dynamic tensions. At the moment, I felt I must concentrate on achieving domestic tranquillity and freeing Nesser to assist me in my ministry. My second problem was complicated almost immediately.

"Jack, the District Attorney came to me this morning with a peculiar problem: When we hang that hoodlum back there, the hangman will be liable for his murder."

These students were geniuses, I thought.

"So," I agreed, "that does pose a problem."

"I've figured a way around it, Jack. . . . An automated hanging."

"What do you mean?"

"Force Nesser to hang himself."

"How so?"

"Rather easily, Commissioner. We'll use a self-actuated gibbet. On the morning of the execution, we can slip a little DNA from a lemming into Nesser's coffee to heighten his death-wish. We affix the noose at the foot of the gallows here." He began to sketch a gibbet rapidly as he talked. "Nesser climbs the thirteen steps and the thirteenth actuates a timer on the trap door. His noose has one-way retractability arranged through a system of pulleys here. A T-bar, emerging here, forces him forward onto the platform and onto the trap door. After thirteen seconds an explosive charge rips back the bolt and the trap door opens, bang! Then he falls through here, *whoosh!* and the rope catches here, *whomp!*"

Frick's efficiency was marvelous but I might have wished for less enthusiasm in certain areas. However, I had the problem of domestic tranquillity to balance my tensions, and I went home early in order to wait for Cara.

Surprisingly, she returned from her rehearsal bubbling with joy and forgiveness.

"I can hardly wait for you to see my costume, Jack my Beloved—the sheerest of diaphene."

"But, sweetheart," I protested, "wouldn't a diaphene costume be a little too revealing?"

"Nonsense, Jack. Beneath the diaphene is a sheaf of silver that covers my whole body. It even constricts my breasts, so I'm no Tamar if that's what you fear."

I avoided that subject quickly. "Now, what about those voice lessons?"

"Oh, I trill a few notes at the beginning and end of the play. Red says I have a beautiful voice."

After her exuberance had died, and after dinner in the refectory, I waited until we had returned home and retired before I dared question the tenor of the note she had left me that morning. "You must understand, Cara, that murder is not treated lightly on Earth and our sense of duty sometimes overrules our personal desires. I'll never be unfaithful to you, on Heaven or Earth, for you are my only beloved."

"Dear Jack, forgive me for being suspicious and jealous. I know it was wrong to doubt. I know you went to Nesser's cell last night, honey baby, sweet doll."

"Why the change of heart?"

"Because, daddy baby, I checked . . . with Frick . . . this morning . . . and read . . ."

She was not able to finish the sentence, but I understood. Despite the gales of tenderness howling around me, there was a calm eye in my hurricane where I considered what she had meant to say. Frick, my own Chief of Police, had put a tail on his Commissioner. I had never seen such devotion to duty, and I could take advantage of the student's conscientiousness.

As long as my bride was reading my dossier, it would be a simple matter to implement the trust that now bound our marriage. I would put a tail on Cara.

So it came to pass in early winter that Mary and Joseph trekked toward Bethlehem at a faster pace than Nesser approached judgment. Bardo, Marti and Fisk threw delaying tactics at Reno, the judge advocate general, even contesting the legality of the court. Reno ruled that the Constitution of Imperial Earth applied to Harlech, providing *de facto* jurisdiction for his court, and he based his argument on an obscure paragraph from Rousseau's *Social Contract*, ruling that the logic therein was universal.

Sitting as an observer, I was awed by Reno's mind. His command presence was such that Red had appointed him general of centurions, yet his reasoning was so quick and devious that, on Earth, he could have succeeded as anything from a politician to an insurance claims adjuster.

Reno's strategy gained my approval.

Not once had I lost sight of my reason for establishing law courts on Harlech. Observing Reno at the trial, watching him nod or shake his head, listening to his fiats issued in a flat but commanding voice, I knew Red had chosen his sacrificial goat with foresight and skill. Reno was building an infra-structure of student government that would challenge and end forever the administration by whim of Bubo the Dean, and he was building himself into the ideal victim for the *cause célèbre* that would trigger the students into a revolt for law and order.

Reno could have been a partner in the Adams-O'Hara conspiracy judged from the precedents he was establishing with his decrees and decisions. In my analysis of Red's con games, I could see that he was using the boy as a pigeon, but I didn't object because I would share in the victimization of Reno. All the testimony now being taken from the police, from Dori and from the student who had discovered Krale's body would be ruled prejudicial once Reno was expelled. Then, legally, no murder could have occurred since legally the victim had never existed.

Scoffers who doubt the verity of miracles are seldom familiar with jurisprudence.

My optimism was concealed from Nesser. Almost daily I visited him, hoping to arouse his remorse and repentance, and I painted a dismal picture of his fate. He was so frightened of damnation that he asked me to pray for a miracle to deliver him. He would not join me in prayer because he was positive that once he embraced Christianity he would be doomed to the Christian hell. I had faith that the miracle would occur, and I wanted Nesser to give thanks to the proper authority when I sprang him on a technicality.

Most of my free time was spent at the court and in the jailhouse. When I wasn't trying to convert Nesser, I was reading the daily report on Cara.

Around other students, Cara showed less restraint than with me. But even her unbridled speech bore testimony to her love for her husband. Once when approached by an actor who suggested carnal gratification, old-style, she rebuffed him with a bluntness almost naughty: "I'm married to an Earthman, and any girl who embraces an oak tree has no feeling for saplings. Begone, amateur."

In my conversations, I praised my wife highly at the slightest opportunity, for her dossier reported that she read my dossier.

CHAPTER
ELEVEN

B y the end of the third week, it became apparent that Nesser would need a technicality to keep him from hanging.

My three best law students, Bardo, Marti and Fisk, made only feeble attempts to establish reasonable doubt. Generally, they agreed with the logic of the prosecution and were aided and abetted by their client, who nodded in agreement when a point of law was scored against him. His counsel refused to let Nesser testify in his own defense, and I agreed with them.

Frick told me that Nesser eagerly awaited the evening news program, which Red had introduced on local television, because the program largely dealt with his trial, in which he was referred to as "The Harlech Strangler." My impression that he enjoyed the attention was substantiated when, after much haggling, his attorneys finally admitted his footprint as evidence. Then he passed a note back to me.

Jack the Teacher,

If I am hanged, could my execution be shown on television with Red the Teacher directing?

Nesser the Strangler

His note vexed and troubled me. Nesser preferred to die as a heathen than to run the risk of a Christian hereafter.

Trial was recessed during the winter intermission and all Harlech focused on Red's Christmas pageant. Cara obtained front-row seats for Frick and me because, as she put it, she owed Frick a favor.

Despite the planet-wide, full-color, three-dimensional telecast, the pageant played before a packed house, and *dramatis personae* was given to each member of the audience. I was thrilled to see the first name on the list:

Hark, the Herald Angel . . . . Cara Adams.

As the orchestra in the pit—which was literally a pit dug into the floor of the soccer gym for this occasion—played a medley of Earth's Christmas carols, the house lights slowly dimmed except for one bright, tiny light above the proscenium, the Star of Bethlehem. Then, out of a darkness accentuated by the Star, came the voice of my beloved, caroling above the wail of a single trumpet.

> Hark, the Herald Angel, sings
> Glory to the Dean of Deans.
> Come we now to Bethlehem
> To hum hymns in praise of Him.

Draki had translated the old carol well, fitting it to the play and to the locale, and Cara's voice was dimmed only by her radiance when she appeared, in a diffused cloud of light, floating high above the stage on invisible wires. For the period of her singing, the light played only on Cara, adorned in a full-length silver leotard covered with diaphene that extended from her shoulders in a twelve-foot wingspread. As Red had promised, Cara's role topped Mary's by a full twenty feet, for my wife was a golden-haired angel.

Then the light swelled to illuminate a corner of the stage, showing Mary in the manger surrounded by an anxious Joseph and shepherds with crooks. At this point there was only one variation from the original story. A midwife was present to explain the meaning of the scene through dialogue. Mary was undergoing labor pains—another touch of O'Hara realism.

The spotlight shifted to right-center, leaving the manger in darkness, and the main business of the play began—the chase. King Herod, leading a troop of centurions, entered, and tension began to build up between the soldiers, the innkeeper and the Maids of Bethlehem as Herod demanded to know the whereabouts of the child.

Allowing for dramatic license, the remainder of the play was carried out with taste and decorum. After the Maids of Bethlehem had enticed the centurions upstairs, the innkeeper began to operate on Herod. One glance at the innkeeper told me why Tamar had been relegated to the

role of Mary. Red must have imported the innkeeper from
the Southern Continent, and by the time Herod vanished
offstage with the girl, he had forgotten the Child, the Star
and the whole of Bethlehem. That girl was a pure 40 on a
continent where 32 was a good average.

Almost as an anticlimax, the scene shifted back to the
manger, where Mary, now bathed with a halo of backlight,
had given birth to her baby.

But there was a method to Red's dramatics—the qualities
that made him a con artist stood him in good stead as a
producer. In contrast to the raucousness and ribaldry in the
inn, the scene in the manger held a reverence and serenity
that drew *ooohs* and *ahs* from the audience. Only one dis-
cordant note intervened in the final scene in the manger:
The three wise men bearing gifts entered with a soft-shoe
routine, singing "We Three Kings of Orient Are" to the tune
of "Tea for Two."

But that note was quickly banished when—last scene of
all—the lights dimmed and my angel floated above a chorus
of shepherds to sing "Silent Night."

Cara finished the last words of the song in total blackness except for the pinpoint of light high above, the ever-
burning Star of Bethlehem. It did not go out but was lost in
the stronger lights as the houselights shone on a drawn curtain.

There was dead-silence. The spectators looked around as
if they could not believe it was over, as if they couldn't
believe it had happened. Once they were convinced that
the play was finished, they rose, flexed toes grown stiff
with inactivity, and a few stood on their chairs.

Then bedlam broke loose.

Looking around me, I saw for the first time emotion on
the faces of Harlechians. Hooting, clapping, leaping, they
applauded and continued to applaud. Then the curtain
was drawn back to reveal the cast, and the stage manager
had to draw it again to avoid a cave-in in the cavern.

When the noise had subsided the curtain was pulled again
for the second curtain call, and on this appearance each
member of the cast stepped forward, one at a time, to receive an individual ovation. When Cara bowed, the noise
crested at its second-highest peak of the evening. Only
Herod earned more decibels than Cara, and his ovation
was not unmixed with whoofs, the Harlechian equivalent
of a boo.

When Tamar stepped forward to take her bow, she carried the child with her, still wrapped in swaddling clothes, and my eyes were attracted to the baby. There seemed a disproportion to the child, for the clearance between its heels and hips was dubious.

Red permitted five curtain calls for an audience that would have gone to fifteen. When the final curtain came, I hurried backstage to compliment Cara, congratulate Red and to make a closer check of two dimensions, the child's and the innkeeper's.

When I embraced Cara, she was ecstatic, whispering, "Did you notice I got more applause than Tamar?"

"And you deserved it," I whispered. "She was upstaged twice—once by you and once by the innkeeper."

She stiffened in my arms. "Don't get any ideas about the innkeeper," she whispered. "She's Red's charwoman. Without her make-up she's forty years old, and without her cantilever Red designed, they'd fall like a curtain."

"Then, dearest, I'd like to go look at the Christ Child."

"Wasn't she a darling? Come."

The baby was surrounded by a circle of feminine admirers, but now it nestled in the arms of its mother, the long-absent Kiki. Kiki was happy to see me and mildly surprised when I asked to hold the baby, but she granted my wish.

I was delighted with the infant, but I was thrilled when, in answer to my cooing and clucking, it opened its eyes and smiled at me. I had rightly suspected its legs, for the eyes that looked into mine were a watery blue.

There were tears in my own eyes when I handed the baby back to Kiki. Here was proof that interbreeding could occur between human beings and Harlechians, that my love for Cara might be blessed with issue.

Cara was touched by my tears. "Jack my Beloved, if you had the hip movement, you would make a wonderful mother."

As soon as I could draw Red aside, I whispered to him in English, "You're the father of Kiki's baby."

"I rather think so."

"What was her gestation period?"

"Beats me, Jack."

"Didn't you keep a log?"

"I couldn't, Jack. There were so many, and many kept

coming back. If it happened when I was casting for Juliet, the bairn won't qualify under the seven-month clause."

"Red, this is sheer dereliction of duty."

"I know, lad. But the documentation is up to you, so keep careful notes."

I turned from Red in disappointment. Now that I was reasonably certain that Cara and I could have an issue, I was uncertain what the issue would be. If it came less than seven months after conception, I could only be positive of its bastardy, for my marriage to Cara would not be legal even if I were appointed Procurator of All Harlech.

Red broke out a case of wine and I stood sipping with the cast. Since the char lady with the uplift-outshoot bra had gone back to her brooms, most of my attention was directed toward the door. After an hour, the wine and most of the cast had gone, and no black tunic had entered bearing a pink slip for Reno. My hope of releasing Nesser on a technicality also went.

As Cara and I walked back with Red toward Faculty Row, I commented, "It looks as if Reno is off the hook for his part as King Herod."

"Reno was never on the hook," Red said. "When you tipped me off about Bubo's vanity, I had Reno personally assign a praetorian guard, answerable only to Bubo, at the Dean's office. The old man was pleased as punch at Reno's gesture. He doesn't want anyone coming in to catch the Chief Administrator taking a nap."

Red's casual manner lent truth to his words. I had misread Red's intentions to create a *cause célèbre* over the expelling of Reno, and now the fate of Nesser was squarely up to Bardo, Marti and Fisk.

Red's pageant marked the close of the fall quarter and the end of our lectures on religion, but it was the beginning of my underground ministry. I had assumed the sense of injustice aroused among the students by the discontinuance of classes coupled with the impact of the Christmas play would bring postulants flocking to my little chapel in the tunnel. Only twelve students showed up for my first prayer meeting, and they were mostly rejects from drama, law, the police and cadet corps. I could take heart only from their number—twelve.

In the privacy of our inner quarters, I discussed the poor response with Cara. "Dear Jack, you speak so much of doom you frighten us."

"Cara, you say 'us' as if you agreed with the heathens."

"I can't love the Dean of Deans because you are all that I can take care of. If He were a woman, I would not let you be a Christian. Besides, I can't make head or tails of what He says."

"My dear, He speaks in parables."

"Then He should say what He means."

After our conversation, I meditated at length on my problem. Were Harlechian minds too literal to grasp the allegories of the Scriptures? Would logic forever deny them the Truth?

Yet I did not despair. These were my children, and I would lead them, step by step, to a full understanding of the beauty of the parables. But since they were children, I decided to make their first few steps easy: For the winter quarter, I offered a course in *Aesop's Fables*.

Continuance of Nesser's trial into winter provided an interest that alleviated my disappointment over the opening of my new ministry. In fact, interest in Nesser's trial was becoming general through word carried by itinerant students and through letters home, and a summary of the proceedings was commenced on planet-wide television. 36 was getting a reputation as a campus where things were happening, and I reaped a windfall bonus for my ministry from the interest.

Frick was interviewed on the newscast and his references to me created a public curiosity I gratified by granting an interview. In it I strove to explain why murder was not merely a crime but a sin, and I discussed my attempts to salvage the spirit of Nesser in the event his body was lost.

After my interview, I was deluged with mail, which was almost evenly divided between those who were interested in the length of my arms, legs and other appurtenances and those seeking a clearer definition of the concept of a soul. I solved my correspondence problem with two form letters: one giving my dimensions where proper, and one defining the soul.

Reasoning that my questioners were good mathematicians but poor theologians, I described the soul as a no-space continuum between two unified fields.

As a law teacher, I was disappointed in Nesser's defense attorneys. They were adept at delaying justice but inept at thwarting it, and they made clumsy errors in nomenclature, referring to the "alleged murder" and the "alleged victim" when, in fact, both the crime and its victim had been legally established. The final straw came when, nearing the end of the trial, they asked for a month's recess in order to produce new witnesses.

Reno granted the request, perhaps from curiosity. Everyone remotely connected with the crime had been cross-questioned by both the prosecution and the defense. It was obvious that Bardo, Marti and Fisk intended to dig up character witnesses. To perform that task for their client would have taken a millennium: it was becoming increasingly obvious to me that Nesser had no character.

Nesser was going to hang, unless some impassioned plea could be made at the summation of his trial to sway the jury toward mercy rather than justice.

There was only one man, on Heaven or Earth, who could arouse Harlechian emotions, and that was the congenital confidence man, Red O'Hara.

I made an official call on Red.

Since he was seated at his desk cheating at solitaire, I knew he was ruminating over some problem of his own. He looked up with a preoccupied grin when I entered and said, "Hello, Jack. How's the trial coming? They going to hang your lad?"

"Looks like it, Red."

"Aye, that it does. How's the marriage? Cara still weeping?"

"Like a baby. . . . But, Red, I'm not here looking for marriage counsel. I'm worried about Nesser."

"Beat him!" Red exclaimed, laying down his final cards, a two of spades appended to a three of clubs and a deuce of diamonds to a trey of hearts. He slid the cards together into a neat pile, snapped them and shuffled them with the riffle of a riverboat gambler. "Yeah, I know how you feel, Jack. I'm worried about a problem with my Easter play. I might have to call on you for help."

His remark surprised me. Drama was his department, pure and simple—a sacrosanct area in which he invited no suggestions and accepted no advice. So I told him, "That's what I'm here for, to get your help. Drama's not my dish."

"This is different, Jack. I'm planning a Passion Play directed toward a noble purpose."

"That's precisely what I want from you," I retorted, "passion directed toward a noble purpose."

He ignored my remark and looked at me quizzically. "Turn your head to the right, Jack. I want to study your profile."

I did as he requested.

"By God," he exclaimed. "Perfect! That stern unyielding brow, that jutting jaw. Jack, did anybody ever tell you that you project martyrdom and self-righteousness?"

"What's this all about?"

"Realism is one of the qualities that make an O'Hara production great, so I've decided to hold the Crucifixion scene outdoors. . . ."

"Wait a minute, Red! You get your cast and audience on the surface, transfix their attention with one of your magnificent pageants and a spring storm strikes. It would be slaughter."

"The Holy Virgin would sure spare us a half-hour, considering our purpose. . . . Anyway, nothing could make a Harlechian forget the popping in his ears when a storm's coming, and the audience would only be yards from an escape burrow. . . . I want this one to be a colossus with a whole phalanx of centurions, the Jerusalem rabble, the Apostles—the whole magilla. You've seen that knob north of the soccer field?"

"Of course."

"You were looking at Golgotha. The spectators' area will be just below the knob, so they'll have to look up at the Crucifixion—to give them proper awe. After the hand-washing scene in the soccer gym, audience and cast will transfer to the surface."

"That's no problem."

"Not that. Beards. The play's being televised for the off-campus audience. I can get by with stage beards on the Apostles, but Jesus Christ is another story. The camera will be focused on Him. Particularly in the Last Supper scene when He projects the whole tragedy of Judas' betrayal in one sad smile. Nothing is faker than a phony beard and I want no hint of phoniness to touch my J.C."

"Red, you don't *know* that Jesus wore a beard," I interjected.

"All the pictures show a beard."

"Those aren't photographs. They are artists' conceptions. Chinese artists don't paint Him with a beard."

"What about that old expression 'Swear by the beard of the prophet'?"

"That expression refers to Mohammed."

Red looked at me dubiously. "I remember no verse in the Bible saying 'Jesus shaved.'"

"Chances are He wore a beard," I conceded, "possibly a red beard, since He was a Nazarene, and they didn't have razors. . . . But I didn't come here to discuss the tonsorial habits of Jesus. There's a boy in jail who's going to hang."

"Aye? That's too bad. . . . A red beard you say?"

"Possibly auburn. Red, I need help in the legal department from a man who can trick judges, sway jurors and confuse prosecutors. . . ."

Red was again concentrating on his cards and laid a nine of hearts beneath a ten of diamonds.

". . . From a man capable of cheating himself in a game of solitaire," I added.

"An oversight, but let it stand. . . . My mind is distracted by the saddest event in all the universe: the Crucifixion of Our Blessed Savior. . . . As I see it, Jack, the climax comes when the cross is raised, on a Golgotha littered with plastic bones. After the slow ascent of Calvary, I expect to hear *oohs* and *ahs* from the bleachers when that twelve-foot cross is slowly tilted to the sky."

"It would take a squad of centurions to drag a twelve-foot cross to the top of that knob," I pointed out. "Harlechians aren't built for lifting."

"Aye," he nodded. "And there's my problem. . . . It must be done somehow to make the audience grasp the symbolism of the cross."

"Easter's a long way off," I said. "Nesser will be sentenced within the next ten days. I'm faced with an immediate problem—how to keep Nesser from death by hanging."

"Have him drawn and quartered," Red suggested, reshuffling his cards. "It would be a mite more dramatic and would be a convenience for the boys in the organ bank."

"Cruel and unusual punishment is forbidden by Navy Regulations," I reminded him.

"Oh, *that* book! But mine is also an immediate problem. These productions don't just happen. They are planned. I must begin casting right away. . . . Do you think Cara would play Mary Magdalene?"

"She'd love it," I said. "But whoever heard of a blond Jewess?"

"I could write in dialogue explaining that her father was a Viking sea-rover. . . . Now, here's a tremendous scene."

Red's face glowed as he looked up from the cards. "A tavern somewhere in the tenderloin of Jerusalem, a drinking orgy in the Tom Jones manner, Mary's bragging that she can drink any Jew there under the table. It's her Scandinavian genes, see. It's wild! Then enter Jesus. A quiet falls over the room. Mary Magdalene looks over the new man. She's hooked, converted on the spot. . . . But here's the snapper. How can she express her feeling, this dumb little broad? By dancing. Now, get this, Jack. All she can do is shimmy. She prances up to Jesus and starts this belly-dance. . . ."

"A very sensual dance, eh, Red?"

He laid an eight of clubs below a nine of diamonds, so I knew the edge to my voice had cut him. "These girls can shimmy. You've noticed how their hips quiver before they hop. But Cara's would be dramaturgy . . . a holy hootchy-cootchy."

"I would not permit my wife to perform on the surface," I told him bluntly, "because I value her life. I would not permit her to shimmy on the stage below before some heathen impersonating Christ because I treasure her immortal soul."

He focused on me an unclouded gaze. "It would be a proper part for Cara because her husband is going to be my Jesus."

"What?"

"You're a natural for the role, Jack. You have the long face, the air of righteousness, you can grow the beard and, with your strength, you could lug the cross easily to Calvary."

"It would be sacrilege for me to impersonate Jesus."

"Not at all. In the old Passion Plays it was always the most devout who was chosen for the role."

"Play your own Jesus," I said. "I know I'm unworthy."

"Agreed," Red grinned. "But I am even less worthy."

"Agreed!"

There was a six of diamonds turned up on his shuffle and the only seven on his line was in spades. "Beaten," Red said.

"Why don't you play the six of diamonds on your seven of spades?" I asked.

"Is it Jack Adams suggesting that I cheat?"

"It would be cheating for Red O'Hara not to cheat."

"No more," he said, shaking his head. "Not in your presence. Your air of deep peace and spiritual serenity daunts me. . . . How's the Crusade for Christ coming?"

"Poorly. No converts. Cara tells me that Harlechians fear our Christian hell."

"Then tempt them with heaven."

"Red, listen and think." I was becoming impatient. "Nesser will be condemned unless he gets a final pleading that will reverse the board."

"Why worry about the lad's body? His soul is your concern."

"Our souls, yours and mine, are of equal concern. We're responsible for that boy's death, and we're responsible for his murderer. . . ." I began.

"Like hell!" Red interrupted. "We weren't in the washroom when Krale was strangled."

"Sex-frustration did it," I insisted. "When we started these humanids going steady."

"If Nesser was frustrated, then he should have been writing dirty words on the washroom walls, like any normal lad. Jack, look at it this way: We both need that hanging to teach law and order, and it's a rare opportunity for you. Once Nesser's condemned, he's going to be receptive to salvation as he never was before. And a fine star it will be in your crown that the first criminal on Harlech was also the planet's first convert. Tell him about the angels in heaven if he's sex-frustrated, but don't go into details. Think what an example he'll make for your movement, showing that even unto the least of these divine grace is not denied."

His enthusiasm was catching, but there was a hitch.

"I don't fancy that boy as the first Christian martyr," I said. "He's a publicity hound without any remorse for his deed. He even asked to have you direct his execution on television."

Red picked up the cards again and began a slow shuffle. "Now, that's not such a bad idea. Throw it in as an inducement to conversion. 'Death Live on Television,' there's our title. It would make a very dramatic scene: Nesser mounting slowly to the gallows and you walking beside him, Bible in hand, gowned in black, slowly chanting a 'Te Deum.' . . ."

"I don't chant 'Te Deums.'"

Red palmed the deck and stroked his chin thoughtfully. "So Jesus had a red beard. . . . Say, Jack, how are the shoulders on the lad?"

"Red, you aren't crucifying that boy."

"It would give the play a touch of O'Hara realism," he grinned.

"Be serious," I said. "I'm not interested in dramatics, and I don't want that boy to die. I want you to enter the pleading, for you're the only con artist on the planet who can get the boy off."

"Wasn't Nesser one of my students in Religions 1?"

"Yes, he had a superficial interest in religion. He was altarboy at the wedding."

"Oh, I remember him. Is he insane?"

"Not legally. He ran away from the scene of the crime."

"I taught him the Commandments," Red said. "No, Jack, I can't defend the lad."

"I'm not asking you to defend him. He admits to the crime. . . . I'm asking you to convince Reno he should not be hanged."

Red thought for a moment. "I'll defend the lad for a fee."

"What fee?"

"You play Jesus and let Cara play Mary Magdalene."

"Red, it's against my principles to impersonate Jesus."

"It's against my principles to defend a boy who has broken my Commandments. I'll swap you principles for principles."

"I'm not in the business of swapping gold for lead," I said, standing up. "Get back to your cheating."

As I turned and stalked through the door, Red called out, "Think about it, Jack, and talk it over with Cara."

Cara was preparing a soufflé in the kitchen when I got home. Hearing the door open, she ran to meet me in the library, and I embraced her until the soles of her feet began to caress my ankles. Only then did I release her.

"You are troubled, my husband."

"It's Red again, Cara." I took her hand and walked her back to the kitchen. "That guy confuses me."

Cara placed my chair at the table and poured me a beer. "Talk to me, Jack. It is the duty of a wife to comfort her beloved husband."

"When Red and I were roommates back in Mandan, our personalities were matched by computers," I told her. "We're supposed to have separate-but-equal personalities that differ but interlock. The matching is supposed to keep us from getting on each other's nerves during a long space flight when we're cooped up together. Otherwise one of us

might develop stalker's fever, a form of space madness
where a man hunts his shipmate down and kills him. In a
sense, Red and I were mated by a computer, but at times
I think he's a computer error."

"Don't you like Red?" Astonishment was in her voice.

"Certainly I like him, but sometimes it takes an effort. I
went over and asked him to take over as Nesser's lawyer.
Mine was a humanitarian request for humanitarian reasons,
don't you agree?"

"Yes, Jack. You are noble."

"What does Red do? He's casting for the Easter play. He
wants someone to play Jesus who can carry a cross and
grow a beard. So, he tries to trap me. He knows I need
him for Nesser's defense, so he softtalks me into playing
Jesus. . . . He even threw in a nice juicy role for you. He
knew I liked you as the angel in the Christmas Play. Anyway, he pretended to be smitten by my resemblance to
Jesus. Of course, no one knows what Jesus looked like."

"What did he want me to play?"

"A blond Mary Magdalene. Imagine that! She's supposed
to be a dancing girl who's so smitten at her first sight of
Jesus she jumps into a shimmy. But listen to this, Cara. He
wants to play the Crucifixion scene on the surface. I'm supposed to lug a cross all the way to the top of the knob during the season of equinoctial storms."

"The fire storms are not constant in the skies of spring,"
Cara said, "and as Mary Magdalene I would be beside you
to warn you if one approached. Even you could reach shel-
ter in time. I think you should play the hero."

"Cara, I'm not worthy enough for the role."

"You are certainly worthy enough to play the role, Jack,
and I am unworthy enough to play Mary Magdalene. Watch
me shimmy!"

She shimmied.

"Cara, don't! It's indecent."

She stopped, bent forward at a ninety-degree angle,
rested her elbow on the table, chin in her palm, and asked,
"But is it interesting?"

"Yes," I had to admit.

"You would make a wonderful Jesus," she said. "And
if you can make the same face you did when I shimmied,
you could carry the agony scenes very well."

"Cara, I will not impersonate Jesus in Red's Easter extravaganza. The man was born with a sense of irreverence.

And I will not have you playing Mary Magdalene as a lewd dance-hall girl. Red would have me cakewalking to Calvary."

"What's 'cakewalking'?"

"A slow shimmy—and quit moving your hips."

"My dear husband Jack, you have told me not to take these plays too seriously. Now you are taking a play very seriously."

"It's a spiritual matter, my dear."

Cara snapped upright, her green eyes sparkling with anger. "Whenever you can't explain a matter, you croak 'spiritual'! Until you explain to me why you won't play Jesus and will not let me play Mary Magdalene—with a shimmy—I will not lift my little toe to do a thing for you."

Suddenly I had insight into Red's jaundiced view of blondes, but I held my anger. "My concept of Christ is sacred."

"Then project that concept to the planet and gain converts. Red will have his play regardless. Will you leave the task to some heathen on Harlech because you lack a Christian's courage? Or do you fear the fire storms more than your forebears feared the lions of Nero?"

She had several points there, I had to admit. "I will meditate on the problem after supper."

"Be sure that you do. And be sure that you come up with the right answer—yes."

Cara spoke to me only once during the meal, and her silence was more gruesome than the overspiced soup, flat soufflé and watery coffee. Grown hypocritical in my loneliness, I remarked cheerfully, "How do you prepare such light soufflés, Cara, dear?"

"Spiritually," she snapped.

I fled to the study for my shortest period of meditation on record. Red's remark that Nesser might serve the movement well as a criminal redeemed had attractive implications from a policy standpoint, and unless Red put forth his best effort Nesser was condemned anyway. The more I weighed the problem, the more I grew convinced Nesser had to hang.

Validly, then, there was no reason for me to play the role of Christ other than those given by Cara and by Cara's own pique. But Cara's pique was reason enough.

I went to the door of my study and called Cara. She came, moving rigidly. "I'm calling Red," I said, "and I want you to listen."

She stood in silence as I lifted the phone. "Red, I've talked the matter over with Cara and we've decided to play the roles you offered in exchange for your services as a lawyer."

"Good," Red said. "Thank Cara for me."

"Thank her yourself," I said, "she's in my lap."

And she was, leaping and twisting in the air to make a perfect two-point landing.

After a flurry of conversation between the two, I returned to the phone. "Red, if I'm going to star in your opus, I want final script approval."

"Nothing doing, Jack. I'm not starting a star system on this planet. I can't have everybody's finger in the pie."

"Red, I'm willing to give you something in return for a few minor concessions."

"What do you want?"

"No additions or deletions from the dialogue of Jesus as printed in red in the King James Version of the Bible."

"That's reasonable."

"No dancing girls at the Last Supper."

"I'll take that one under advisement."

"Cara shall be costumed in the dress of the period."

"Even for the shimmy scene?"

"Especially for the shimmy scene."

"What else?"

"No nails in my hands. I hang myself from the cross."

He chuckled. "That would give it the O'Hara touch. . . . But what are you conceding?"

"Nesser," I said. "Forget him."

CHAPTER
TWELVE

Nesser was not forgotten.
   Bardo, Marti and Fisk had been delaying the trial in order to assemble a bombshell they exploded under the prosecution.

On the day the trial reconvened, there were nine witnesses in the courtroom and not one was a character witness. They came from the three continents and the remote polar cap. None had ever heard of Nesser before the trial, but all were intimately linked with Nesser's victim, Krale.

A ranch hand, from University 10, where he was being retrained to herd gazelles, had suffered brain damage when caught in a lightning storm; he was functioning again with Krale's cerebral cortex. A sawmill worker was using Krale's left arm and right hand. Krale's genito-urinary tract had brought happiness to a young lady named Jan who had suffered a hormone imbalance and was now enjoying life as a young man named Jon. Krale's heart still beat in an aged scholar on this very campus. Krale's thalamus had restored the emotional capacity, atrophied from disuse, of a theoretical mathematician, and his lungs still breathed in the body of a lichenologist who had suffered lobar frostbite at South Polar Station 12.

After all witnesses had been interviewed, Bardo stood and read from an affidavit certified by the school's Department of Biocryogenics. It reminded me of a shopping list for a housewife in a butcher's shop:

Liver:	Bea the Student, University 27, South Continent.
Pancreas:	Fork the Seiner Captain, Shrimping Station 6.
Kidney, left:	Han the Pupil, Grammar School 2876, Middle Continent.
Kidney, right:	Et cetera . . .

Every item of Krale's corpus was either present or accounted for, down to his toenails.

Now I understood the reason for the long delay. Bardo, Marti and Fisk had been stalling for time until the parts of Krale could be grafted onto other living bodies. I also understood their references to the "alleged murder" and its "alleged victim." Krale was alive and well on three continents, the polar icecap, and on and under the high seas.

"May it please the court," Bardo stated, "since the heart of Krale beats here" (pointing), "the lungs of Krale breathe here, the progeny of Krale will spring from there . . . since it has been amply demonstrated that Krale is, in fact, not dead, may it please the court to rule that no murder has been committed, that a mistrial has occurred and that the prisoner be released on the cognizance of these witnesses, who represent, in fact, the living alleged victim of the alleged strangler, Nesser. We move that this case be dismissed."

Suddenly the spectators were on their feet, cheering. For weeks, Bardo, Marti and Fisk had been led, shoved and pushed into an untenable position. All Harlech had alternately jeered and moaned over the lawyers in their struggle against formidable odds in defense of a client who had aided the cause of the prosecution. My own judgment in appointing the trio had been covertly questioned. Now my judgment was redeemed by the cheers that the steady bang of Reno's gavel was subduing.

Reno's voice, flat, authoritative, rang out: "Attention in court. Motion of the defense counsel will be considered in chambers. Court is recessed until Law Class, one week from today, when the final decision will be rendered."

I left the courtroom for rehearsal feeling pride in my students not unmixed with chagrin for having let myself be outpaced. Frick stopped me briefly outside to comment, "Commissioner, if those slickers get that hoodlum off the hook, murder will become the fashion on Harlech. We must preserve order, despite the law!"

Word of the legal coup had easily outlegged me to the soccer gym, where my entry into Jerusalem was scheduled for rehearsal, and the cast was agog. Consensus was unanimous that if law followed logic, Nesser would be freed.

Cara had no part in the entry scene and was absent. I missed her, for I was truly troubled, legally and theologically, over the outcome of the case, and Cara's presence comforted me. Red sensed my preoccupation and cut short the rehearsals so that I might hurry home to my wife and the evening news summary.

When I entered my den, I could hear Cara bustling in the kitchen, and I called a greeting back to her because the television set was beginning to glow. As I stood in the center of the room, watching, she crept up behind me and embraced me, nestling her head against my spine. Although I was flattered by her devotion, I might have wished for a little more sense of civic interest in my wife, an interest she would have to cultivate once I had returned as Procurator of the North Continent.

But my own interest drowned out my passing concern. "And now the planet awaits the decision of Reno," the announcer finished. "Next week will bring the most important precedent in the short history of Harlechian jurisprudence. It is rumored that Reno will request an audience with Jack the Teacher."

That rumor came from Reno, I knew, and Reno was coming to the goat's house for wool. As the glow died on the television set, I turned and embraced my wife. She lifted her lips to mine, with uncharacteristic demureness and there was no hanky-panky around the ankles. Surprised, I held her at arm's length, and looked into her green depths to see if she was ill. What I saw was the indrawn rapture of a religious ecstatic, or that of a pregnant woman. Knowing Cara, I knew that it was not the former. "My dearest, you'll soon be big with child."

"Jack my Beloved," she said, disappointed, "I wanted to be the first to tell you."

"You did, dearest, with your saintly aura."

My remark pleased her and she glowed. "I shall be big with your child, Jack. As big as a beached whale, I hope, for I want our son to be the giant among males that his father is."

"No, dearest, I want a daughter as petite and as lovely as her mother."

"Well," she moued, "I can't satisfy everyone. But I insist, I'll have no bandy-legged female such as Kiki's. I'll settle for your blue eyes but I want our child to have my legs, hair and brains."

At that moment my cup should have been running over, but it was punctured by one sudden concern. "When is the blessed event?"

"Late in the Fourth month or early in the Fifth."

Her indecisiveness sprang from an absence of a lunar cycle on Harlech, and I calculated rapidly in my mind. "Cara, it *must* be early in the Fifth, at the earliest."

"Tell that to the foetus," she laughed.

I did not laugh but held her close to guard my expression from her. "Sweetest girl," I murmured, "this news calls for meditation. Leave me with my happiness until supper's ready."

She flitted lightly back to the kitchen and I sat at my desk, head bowed. Basing her gestation period on our first encounter, an early Fifth-month pregnancy would barely clear the seven-month barrier that would qualify our child as a human being. Any date in the Fourth month would disqualify the infant and annul our marriage.

Birth less than seven months after conception would not

only brand our issue as subhuman, our child would be evidence that I had engaged in bestiality. Actually, the connotations frightened me more than the legal penalties. Among procurators, rank has its privileges, but our child would be ranked somewhere higher than a dog and a little lower than the gibbons, for gibbons are Earth anthropoids.

Then there was Nesser. Christianity was on the verge of losing its first Barabbas on Harlech. An unrepentant sinner would be granted manumission of his sins through legal shenanigans rather than grace. Legalities were threatening my home, my offspring and my ministry.

How could I advise Reno? Earth's only precedent in this area had been set two centuries before and it was not favorable to my cause. It had been ruled that the organs of a dying man were up for grabs and the decision to remove such organs did not constitute murder. Besides, medical science on Earth had not reached the stage where the very follicles of a corpse's hair were preserved for transplant.

I was meditating rapidly when Hal the Assistant announced that Reno wanted an audience. "Show him in," I said, affecting an air of composure.

Reno entered and stood rigidly at attention until I said, "At ease, Reno, and be seated. Bardo, Marti and Fisk have kicked you a curving ball, so I take it you want my legal opinion?"

"No, Jack the Teacher. I need some spiritual advice."

Although my gaze did not flicker, I was amazed. It was as if Napoleon had come to the Pope.

"Logically," he continued, "dismemberment does not constitute murder, but in the matter of Nesser versus University 36, I feel it strategically necessary to make a tactical error and depart from logic. If I free Nesser on the facts of this case, justice wins the battle but society loses the war."

"Reno," I said, "you sound more like a lawyer than a general."

Reno ignored my quip.

"In Religions 2, you spoke often of the soul. Legally, what is the soul? Is it something apart from the body?"

"It is not something apart from the body; it is something above and beyond the body." Then I remembered that I was speaking to a soldier, and so I asked, "Has Red the Teacher spoken to you of *esprit de corps* in a military unit?"

"Often, Jack. He speaks highly of Earth's Harrier Corps, which he says has never yielded to the enemy."

"He's right," I nodded. "They are the combat troops of the United Space Navy, descendants of the old United States Marines. Their *esprit de corps* is an essential part of the unit and is nondivisible among its members. Once, in a surface war on the planet Marlon, units of the Harrier Corps were dispersed among divisions of the United Space Army that lost three battles in succession. The Harrier Corps was re-formed into a single unit under its own command and attacked successfully to swing the tide of battle. Their spirit was a part of their unit as the soul is a part of the unified man, and that spirit could not be divided. The soul is the spirit. It is the same with individual soldiers."

He looked at me studiously and asked, "Does your religion offer a fighting spirit?"

"Indeed," I answered. "Mine is a church militant. It has war songs—'Onward Christian Soldiers,' for instance. The 'Battle Hymn of the Republic' is a rousing marching song."

"Thank you, Jack," he said, rising.

"One request, Reno. If you find a way to hang Nesser, give me two months to redeem his soul in the hereafter."

After supper, Cara and I called Red to announce the coming event.

"Wonderful," he said. "When's Cara expecting?"

"Early in the Fifth month," I answered.

"That should clear her as human," Red said, "but it may put the quietus on your return as a colonizer if Harlech qualifies for World Brotherhood."

"There's still the planetary-defense clause," I said.

"Don't count on it. Fifth month! That means a casting problem. We can't have a pregnant Mary cavorting on the stage. We can't risk the bairn for a shimmy, can we?"

"Not on your life," I agreed. "Cara wouldn't think of playing the part in her condition." Suddenly I was caught by a sudden fear, and turning to Cara I asked, "Would you, dear?"

"Of course not, Jack. Motherhood is the first duty of the devoted wife. You must carry on the family's dramatic tradition alone."

One week later, in a courtroom charged with tension, Reno ruled that, though no *de facto* murder had occurred, Nesser had destroyed the personal integrity of Krale and should be punished under provisions of the Mosaic Code. "An eye for an eye, a tooth for a tooth and a soul for a soul," Reno intoned. "It is therefore decreed that the defendant,

Nesser, two months from this date, shall be hanged by the
neck until temporarily dead, at which time his body shall
be remanded to the organ banks and his soul into the custody of Jack the Teacher."

It was a decision worthy of Solomon. Bardo, Marti and
Fisk were complimented for their logical victory by the prosecutor, who was in turn complimented by the defense for
his legal victory. There was an air of gaiety in the chambers
shared by all but Nesser, who had been deprived of his
role as the first condemned criminal in the modern history
of Harlech.

Looking at the dejected Nesser, I felt Christian compassion. I promised myself that, if he cooperated with me, he
would not be denied a mention in the annals of the church.
And he should be willing to cooperate, I reasoned. Now that
his physical demise was ordained, his only choice left was
the direction his soul should take.

At peace with the world, I hurried to rehearsal with a
certain eagerness. Red's enthusiasm for the Passion Play was
proving contagious, and frankly I felt that I was not only
preserving the sanctity of the Word by my participation but
that I was giving the role of Jesus a dimension no other
actor could have brought to the part. Humility, reverence
and strength of character were not traits I had to simulate
anymore than the beard I was growing. Besides, as Red
pointed out, I could become the only actor to influence
history since John Wilkes Booth shot Abraham Lincoln.

At rehearsal, Red announced that Cara had withdrawn
from the role of Mary Magdalene and that she was being
replaced by Tamar. This news did not disturb me. Cara had
her daily reports from Frick attesting to my fidelity, so she
would not be jealous, and Tamar had the hips for the role.
When it came to the shimmy, Tamar was a method actress.

When I arrived home that evening, a little too late for
the news broadcast, Cara was hardly interested in Tamar
as her substitute. She was fretting over Reno's decision.

"I have no sympathy for Nesser," she snapped, "but
Bardo, Marti and Fisk proved that no murder had occurred.
Since there was no murder, where is the logic in dismem-
bering a functioning entity?"

"It's not a matter of logic," I explained. "It's more a
matter of justice. Under the Mosaic Code—"

"Vengeance, you mean! Not justice," she snapped. With
the petulance of the pregnant, she turned sullen on me.

"Moses says 'an eye for an eye.' Red, in Religions 1, says, 'Thou shalt not kill—except in defense of thy home planet.' Then you say, 'Turn the other cheek.' Who's in charge of that Bible of yours? You, Moses, or Red?"

"Red has nothing to do with the Commandments," I said, "except for a slight addition that he will have to answer to to me. Those Commandments were given to Moses by God."

"Now you bring God into it. Why don't you all get together and establish policy? Talk about Bubo! I'm sorry, Jack. I suppose I'm disappointed over Reno's illogic. . . . Would you call the commissary and ask the steward to defreeze a watermelon for me? All I wish for supper is a crisp, juicy, red-ripe watermelon heart. And don't forget to tell him I want to cut the watermelon myself. All day I've dreamed of watermelon."

"That's because you're pregnant with an Alabama child," I told her.

While on the phone, I decided to take the microfilms of *Battles and Leaders of the Civil War* to blow up, print and bind to give her a sedentary interest during her pregnancy. She read English with fluency, and I would underline the names of the Confederate generals who were my ancestors to let her know what brave genes our offspring would inherit.

Walking hand-in-hand with her to the refectory, I was sure that Cara was tranquil beyond upsetting, but three minutes after we arrived, she was storming again. A notice in large type was on the bulletin board.

> In accordance with counsel given by Jack the Teacher, my legal advisor, Nesser the Student was this day condemned to be hanged and dismembered for a murder he did not commit.
>
> *Bubo the Dean*

"That man's out to get you, Jack!" Cara's eyes flashed. "He's crediting you with Nesser's hanging by delegating the wrong authority."

So Bubo thought! Actually, he was hanging himself. Once I returned as Procurator of the Northern Continent, Bubo would not be Executive Vice-President in Charge of Testing Earth Toilet Commodes. He had demoted himself to Chief of the Janitorial Staff, Washroom Division.

"Hush, honey," I said. "Bubo can't harm me."

"Can't he? He knows that Harlech is split down the middle over Reno's decision. With that announcement, he has prepared half of Harlech to hate you. Illogic is a greater crime here than murder."

"It doesn't matter, darling. I have plans for Bubo."

"Jack, you have only the bravery of the stupid. You are no match for Bubo."

For a wild moment I was tempted to tell her of the I.C.A., but logic stopped me. It would be senseless to calm her fears with an injection of terror, and she was angry enough already at Bubo.

"Calm yourself, dear, and cut your watermelon."

"I will not," she said. "I don't want any watermelon. Go get me some pork chops."

Cara was correct about the division on Harlech. That night my attendance at chapel was cut from twelve to six, and the next afternoon, before rehearsals commenced, I mentioned the incident to Red and questioned his addition to the First Commandment. Red flatly refused to delete the phrase "except in defense of thy home planet."

"These students are too literal-minded and too logical to accept flat statements. If Reno had not had the good sense to use the phrase 'temporary death' in passing the sentence, he would have been violating the Commandment himself. But don't worry about attendance. Something you said to Reno the other night about militancy and the Christian spirit struck his fancy. He's ordering a squad of centurions to attend tonight's meeting."

I knew what I had told Reno, and on the spot I resolved that tonight's sermon would take as its text "Not Peace but a Sword."

Thereafter followed my best rehearsal for some time. After rehearsal, as I slipped into my tunic and strap and deposited my robe in my dressing-room wardrobe, I paused for a moment's meditation over the blessings I had received and the blessings I was soon to deliver.

That evening a large gathering, not merely of cadets but of Frick's secret police assigned to the cadets plus their camp followers, joined me at the close in a rousing rendition of "Battle Hymn of the Republic." Cara glowed with pride after the service and planted a chaste kiss on my forehead (all we could risk in her condition) and said, "Jack my

Husband, you are very good when you're playing to a receptive audience. As I listened to you preach, my toes itched to grasp a spear and hurl it at the infidels."

After the cadets came, word was spread on the campus that a happening was taking place in Jack's chapel and uniformed policemen joined the cadets in growing numbers along with camp-followers and stationhouse hangers-on. I toyed with the idea of expanding my schedules, but I did not wish to overburden Cara, and Nesser stood as adamant against the Word as Lee had stood before Richmond.

Nesser was a key strongpoint in the battle I waged. If he stood fast on the eve of his dismemberment, then my winter campaign might be bogged down. Once Nesser was taken, I could begin to roll back the line of paganism.

Nesser was not to be taken.

His eyes glowed at my word pictures of heaven. He fidgeted when I spoke of angels and he quailed before the image of hell. With his instinctive dread of fire storms, it was little wonder that he feared hell, but I was offering him an alternative, heaven, and Harlechian logic should have jumped at the fifty-fifty odds. On the other hand, logic might be restraining him from total commitment. The boy knew he was a sinner, morally and by court edict, and he might have figured his chances at heaven were less than even.

Following Red's suggestion, I began to speak on the glory of angels, and Nesser's eyes glowed with an interest not unmixed by sadness, which I took as foreshadowing repentance. Cara's delicate condition added fervor to my theme, but to my credit I never attempted to tamper with the anatomy of the ethereal bodies. What Nesser chose to read into my words was Nesser's concern.

Tamar's dancing was another matter. It took will power to drag my eyes from her shimmy, and the harlot sensed my discomfort. She added new bumps and grinds to her dance that would never have been permitted in old Jerusalem. Red the Satyr complimented her performance with such gusto that Kiki always escorted him from the scene after rehearsals.

At once I had another problem. Now entering her sixth month, Earth time, of pregnancy, Cara was knitting away optimistically at a set of long booties and reading *Battles and Leaders*. Judging from her appearance, I began to fear that Red's theory was wrong and that cross-breeding with an alien species was not slowing her foetal development.

Once I was shaken from my worry.

A month before presentation of the Passion Play, four days before Nesser's scheduled hanging, with only a week remaining before Cara was past the seven-month barrier, I was attending a morning rehearsal on a weekend run-through of all but the final two scenes of the play. By then my beard was flourishing, my hair had grown long and I had gained enough confidence in my acting ability to argue a point of interpretation with the producer-director.

This morning, Red was edgy. Judas was giving him trouble by underplaying the sneers and sidelong leerings that had become *de trop* for O'Hara villains. Kiki was playing the Mother woodenly and from the frostiness between the two I suspected a domestic tiff. We struggled through my entry in Jerusalem, the tavern scene, and slogged toward the climactic Last Supper scene, in which Tamar expresses her love through her dance.

Possibly to flaunt her charms before Kiki, Tamar danced with a sensuality that left me aghast. Vexed, Red shouted from the seats, "Hold it, Tamar! Run through that third movement, again, but tone down the grind. I don't want the audience climbing over the footlights. And you, J.C.! Quit ogling the dancing girl. You're supposed to be tempted but you're not supposed to succumb."

Angered partly at Red's rebuke and partly at myself for letting my interest show, I settled down behind the table, determined to look on Tamar's dance with tolerance and compassion, nothing more.

Salome, in all her degeneracy, never danced with the abandon that Tamar evinced in the run-through. My poker face must have spurred her, for her body strummed with the insistence of tom-toms. My body responded to her vibrations but not a flicker of movement showed on my face. As she sank in a final bow of exhaustion before me, Red called, "Judas, look at J.C.'s face. That's the expression I want from you, lust winning over righteousness, when you're offered the thirty pieces of silver. . . . All right, Tamar, you can knock off. Go home and take a cold shower."

Contritely the girl left, and I was concerned by the skills she had put into the dance and its effects on the audience. It was a gourmet bit for dance fans and a hard act to follow, even with the Last Supper. However, I was composed and ready when the Roman soldiers entered and led me away.

As I had no part in Pilate's hand-washing scene, which followed, I left for my dressing room with a feeling of relief. Tamar would not dance again until final dress rehearsal and by then, lest all signs erred, I would have Cara by my side.

Once in my dressing room, I closed the door, slipped out of my robe and washed the greasepaint from my face and neck. When bent over the washbowl, I closed my eyes against the sudsy water and a vision of Tamar dancing—so vivid it was dimensional—flashed on my mind. I tried to force the vixen's image behind me with thoughts of Cara's gentle face, but my antidote was not entirely successful.

I dried my beard and neck, combed my hair and carried my robe toward the closet. But the ways of flesh are devious. Though I had come from portraying holiness, symbolically I stood before the wardrobe on a satyr's cloven hooves and sprouting horns. So I lowered my head and closed my eyes, seeking to exorcise my demon with prayer. Thus I did not see the toes snaking from behind my wardrobe curtain wherein the harlot had hidden.

Sodom and Gomorrah!

Momentarily, I went rigid from the shock of the wench's touch. Then she struck, with the deftness and aim of long practice. I staggered back, ensheathed and entwined in the peculiar embrace of the women of Harlech. Her legs encircled me lightly but with a python's strength.

Tamar was hoist on my petard!

No arms on Earth could have broken the grip of those thighs. "Tamar," I ejaculated, "why me?"

"For art," she breathed. "It would never do to have a lewd Lord in a Passion Play."

"Whore of Babylon!" I cried.

"Never been there, Jack. Never want to go there."

"Unleg me, strumpet!" I ejaculated again, but my plea fell on unheeding ears. Tamar was growing rigid.

Though outwardly motionless and stiff as a board, Tamar was dancing, to an unseeing audience of one, a fantastic shimmy which combined aspects of the can-can, the tango, the rhumba and the cha-cha. In desperation, I grasped the promontories on her chest intending to flail her head against the deck and render her senseless, but prudence stayed my hands where they fell, my fingers kneading nervously. As rigid as the girl was, a tap might have broken her neck, and where would I have been had *rigor mortis* locked me in her embrace? Full well I knew, I would have been scurrying buck naked through the tunnels of Harlech with my burden cantilevered ahead of me. Then I would stand in the subzero temperatures of the cryogenic morgue, unclothed, while attendants hacked Tamar into removable pieces. If I survived the cold, the courts would claim me, for no judge would accept my plea that I was resisting rape. I would be condemned permanently to death, for no Harlechian could use aught of me in an organ graft.

So caution stayed my hands until Tamar had her will of me and slid to the floor, where she lay whimpering at my feet. I laid her in the cloak room, hung my robe, donned my tunic and strap and closed the curtain to shield her from the gaze of wandering charwomen. She was sobbing quietly, and if my limited experience on Harlech was any gauge, I knew she would be limp and sobbing for a long, long time.

Fully clothed, I stepped into the corridor, closing the door behind me. No one was in sight, but a musk lingered in the air. A male had stood outside the door.

Then I remembered that Frick was having me shadowed, that daily reports on my activities were read by Cara. In matters of this nature, my wife was a woman of little faith. Breaking into a cold sweat and a fast run, I sprinted down the tunnel for the police station. If I could not head off today's report before Cara read it, within four days I would be envying the soul of Nesser for its quiet winter resort in Hell.

CHAPTER THIRTEEN

Frick was reading the report when I rushed in, and his face was whiter than mine. "Frick, as your Commissioner, I don't wish to use undue influence, but that report must be squelched."

"Jack, this report was squelched before it was written,

not as a favor to you but to protect the department. We need you as Commissioner. But it's not the report that bothers me. We've got to prepare you an iron-clad alibi. . . . Listen, you came here half-an-hour ago and went to Nesser. He's asking for you, anyway. You've been giving him spiritual consolation, ever since. I'll doctor the sergeant's log to make the record jibe."

"But why the alibi if you squelch the report?"

"Tamar. This one was a whammeroo and she's bound to talk. Not to Cara. Tamar's got better sense. But gossip starts among the girls. We'll have to give you a cover story to brand the gossip a lie."

"Frick, I'll go along with the scheme, but don't get the wrong idea. I'm innocent. I even thought of bringing rape charges against the girl."

"I'll buy that, Jack, but no judge would. Rape is one *delicti* no female can indulge in without a *corpus*. . . . Call Cara. Tell her you've got Nesser on the ropes, and I honestly believe you have. Keep your voice calm, natural, then go back to Nesser."

Cara's even tones assured me all was well, and I was reassured when she snorted at the reason for my delayed return home. "Are you Alabamans *always* fighting for lost causes?"

"But, dear, I'm the boy's spiritual advisor."

"That boy doesn't need spiritual advice," she said. "He needs a hacksaw and a one-way trip to another continent."

Nesser was pacing his cell when I went back to him. His face was haggard but his eyes were determined. "Jack the Preacher, I've been reviewing Christianity in my mind. Since the Dean of Deans died for my sins, I don't want Him putting in the time without me cashing in the benefits. But there's one item you haven't made clear. Those angels you were talking about. Are they good at hip flow?"

After Tamar, I was in a better position to drive a bargain. Gently but firmly I told him, "There is no giving or taking of hip flow in Heaven."

"Good," he said. "Then baptize me."

"Are you implying, Nesser, that you will not want hip flow in Heaven?"

"Most certainly, Jack. I'm leaving my body here. Otherwise, I'd rather be in Hell."

Using his tin mug as a chalice, I sprinkled the lad and

proclaimed him the first convert on Harlech. In a daze, I left him still on his knees and went back to the station-house. To the sergeant on duty, I said, "Call the telecaster and tell him this day Nesser, the Harlech Strangler, was anointed into the Christian faith by Jack the Teacher and that his soul is now ready for Paradise. . . . And take his cup back."

If I had hurried, I would have been but a few minutes late arriving home, but I merely rode the belt to get a few minutes alone with my thoughts. My telecast would help disperse the odium Bubo had given my name because of Nesser's sentence, and the conversion would also be a military victory over the forces of evil. It would serve as the inspiration for tomorrow's sermon, "Counter-Attacking Evil."

By the time I got home, the first newscast had been made and Cara complimented me. "Now, I can have more of your time, and Bubo has been given the back of your hand."

"Yes," I said, seating myself beside her on the sofa. "And how do you feel?"

"A little bloated," she said, "but otherwise all right."

"Can you hold on for another week?" I asked.

"I can hold on for eighty years."

Cara had not understood the gist of my question. On Harlech, the responsible male was seldom aware of a woman's condition and it was a new experience for Cara to find a man responsive to her condition to the point of even sharing her morning sickness. Child-bearing on Harlech, translated "hip-flow output," was treated as lightly as conception itself, called "hip-flow input."

"Mother, can you feel the child kick?" I asked.

At times she was pleased and at other times piqued by my solicitousness. Tonight she was piqued. "If this child ever kicks, mother will have a new navel."

"Let me know if you need me," I said, "I'm going to prepare tomorrow's sermon."

"I certainly won't need you tonight," she smiled, patting her stomach.

When I crawled in beside her that night, reviewing in my mind the sermon I had written, it suddenly dawned on me that I had completely forgotten Tamar. Truly, I had forgiven the girl.

I awakened in the morning to the subdued ringing of my telephone. Gently, I rolled off the bed and took the call in the library, noticing that it was eight o'clock on the surface. "Jack the Teacher," I said.

"Jack, this is Frick. Nesser hanged himself ten minutes ago from a crossbar in his cell. He left a note for you saying he was leaving ahead of schedule because there was no point in delaying the trip. . . ."

"Where was he going?"

"To Heaven. He wove a rope from his tunic cloth. . . . Jack, this Paradise concept might be ill-advised from a law-enforcement angle."

"Stow the theology, Frick. Where's the body?"

"Being taken to cryogenics for salvage."

"Call the morgue and tell the chief dissectionist to hold the body intact until I get there. Then call the infirmary and have them drive a litter to my quarters in twenty minutes and deliver my wife to the morgue."

"Is she dead, Jack?"

"No, she's quick. Detail eight patrolmen, one sergeant and yourself to the morgue in dress uniform. Wear your epaulets."

"What's up, Jack?"

"Nesser died a Christian and I'm giving the boy a Christian funeral. I want you to attend."

"Yes, Jack."

Red was still in quarters when I reached him. He immediately approved of the funeral as a show of student solidarity and as an example of Earth sympathy. "I'll be there with Reno and a squad of centurions."

I hung up the phone and re-entered the bedroom. My stirring had aroused Cara, who asked sleepily, "Is something wrong, dear?"

"Yes, Nesser has hanged himself."

"Oh! Do you want me to get breakfast or do you want to eat in the refectory?"

"Neither at the moment, dear. I must go preach at the boy's funeral."

"Why?"

"I'm the boy's pastor. As my wife, I wish you to attend."

"What about me as a person?"

"As a person, I'd rather you didn't in your condition. But as the wife of the preacher, it's a ritual you must observe."

"Of course, Jack. I love Earth rituals."

"This is a sad rite, beloved. Do you have a black tunic and a veil?"

"Veil?"

"Yes. A netting."

"I have none here, Jack. I have hundreds at the salmon hatchery."

"Then we must make do with the black tunic. I must leave now to make arrangements, but I'm sending a litter for you. It will be here in twenty minutes to carry you to the morgue."

"I much prefer walking to the morgue."

"This is for your health, dear."

"All right, my beloved husband. But see that they stop me outside the vaults."

"I shall, dear."

I went directly to the morgue and set up a lectern before the viewing window to be used as a pulpit. Briefly I explained to the chief dissectionist the purpose of my visit. He entered the vaults and directed that the body of Nesser be wheeled before the observation window on an operating table. At my suggestion, he had four of his assistants line up behind the body in the manner of pallbearers. In their black thermal suits, they were a ghoulish lot but ritually effective.

Through the speaking tube the director told me, "I can give you twenty minutes for the funeral, Jack the Teacher."

"That should be sufficient," I said.

Hastily I scribbled out a few comments to make on the dead, asking human forgiveness for his frailties and divine mercy at the Judgment Seat. As I worked up the sermon, the police filed in followed shortly by Red and his centurions. Now all had arrived but Cara, who was probably having trouble getting into her tunic.

Cara was needed only as a symbolic touch, and I knew the director was anxious for me to begin, so I turned and waved to him that I was ready to commence the funeral. Placing my watch on the lectern to gauge my time, I briefly outlined the life of Nesser as it was known to me, and I spoke of his genuine contributions to the legal and clerical annals of the planet.

Intent as I was on the eulogy, I still noticed that a Dean's messenger had entered and spoken to Red. Red left immediately but the Dean's messenger remained. He was appropriately dressed for the occasion, but his presence marred my composure. If Bubo was up to another trick, he had certainly chosen an inopportune time for harassment.

To drive temporal concerns from my mind, I spoke at length on the happiness Nesser had gained from his conversion. Actually, I spent a little more time on the eulogy than I had planned, for I was stalling until Cara arrived. But now she was definitely late, so I had to commence my prayer.

For the sake of Frick, I dwelled at some length in my prayer on the sin of self-slaughter. It was my purpose to reveal to the Police Chief that a condemned criminal could not "beat the rap" by committing suicide. On the other hand, for General Reno's edification, I extolled the dead boy for the reckless militancy of spirit that had led to a frontal assault on the citadel of Heaven. For potential converts present, I prayed loud and long that boundless mercy extend to the soul of Nesser.

To walk a political tightrope in the course of a prayer demands careful weighing of each plea beforehand, so the prayer took longer than its allotted time. Yet, when I raised my eyes after the "Amen," Cara still had not arrived.

Then I turned to bless the remains of Nesser and discovered a breakdown in communications between the chief dissectionist and me. He had given me twenty minutes, apparently not from the commencement of the sermon but from the time of my arrival on the premises. When I had turned to signal him that the funeral was beginning, evidently he assumed that my signal was to start the dissection. Unknown to me, as I delivered the sermon the dissection had been in process behind my back. So when I turned to bless the mortal remains of Nesser, all that remained for my blessing was something—it looked like a liver—being hurried to the banks by a morgue technician. I blessed that.

With gravity becoming the occasion, I paced slowly out of the room leading the procession of mourners. Inwardly I was vexed. On this, the most solemn ceremony of his ministry, the helpmeet of the parson had not been in attendance.

Outside, Reno complimented my synchronization of sermon with the dissection, and Frick was a vastly relieved young man. "Your sermon cleared up a few points that were bothering me, Jack. Do you think Nesser's soul will make it through the gates?"

"There are two schools of thought regarding suicides," I answered. "Red's school holds that Nesser will be suspended in limbo, forever outside the gate. . . . Where is Red?"

"He talked to the Dean's messenger and left."

I turned. The messenger still stood by the door, waiting and forgotten. "You got a message for me, boy?"

"Yes, Jack the Teacher, if the ceremony is over. Red the Teacher told me to wait until you had finished."

"I'm through."

"Red said to tell you that he had gone ahead to explain to Cara why you were late."

"Explain to Cara? Where is Cara?"

"At the infirmary, Jack. The office directed me to tell you that Cara was delivered of a four-pound baby girl while borne on the litter to the morgue. It was an easy birth."

For a long moment, I stood upright in shock and horror. It was yet three days before the end of the Fourth month. Cara had failed to meet the deadline. Our child was not a child. What was it then; a fawn, a cub, a lamb, a leveret? What was the diminutive for kangaroo?

I turned and sprinted toward the infirmary at breakneck speed for an aging Harlechian.

The nurse at the reception desk greeted me with the expressionless face of older Harlechians. "I must check Cara's room number, Jack the Teacher, for I have just come on duty."

As she turned to her files, my attention was drawn to a huge, black-bordered poster on the board behind her. In type large enough for a billboard, it read:

> This day Nesser the Student hanged himself following the advice of Jack the Teacher, his spiritual advisor.
>
> *Bubo the Dean*

The nurse looked up. "Six doors down, to your left."

All my dramatic ability was needed for me to unclench my fists and teeth and replace my anger with an expression of happiness as I strode to Cara's room.

Cara looked up at me and smiled weakly as I entered. "Jack my Beloved, I littered on the litter."

I chuckled as I looked down at the infant in her arms, and my chuckle broke into a low, mirthless laugh that rolled from my throat in rising waves of near-hysteria, and then subsided into silence. One glance at the bright red fuzz atop the little girl's head and the cleft in her chin and I knew

how the animal should be classified. That girl was a kid—
the offspring of a goat.

Cara had been reading the wrong history books during
her pregnancy. For an understanding of the infant's genealogy, she should have read *Annals of the Irish Rebellion*.
Legally, I was the father of Red O'Hara's child.

It is axiomatic that the greatest menace to astronauts is
other astronauts. Gazing down on Red's child in the arms of
my wife, I felt love for the innocent one (who can blame a
child for its genes?) and bitterness toward the wanton in
whose arms the baby rested, but beyond those emotions I
felt the beginning glow of that obsession feared by those
who have never felt it, a scourge more dreaded than the
raptures of space, stalker's fever.

With this act of infamy, Red the Adulterer had furnished
me with the cue and passion for his murder.

"Isn't our child lovely, Jack my Beloved?"

"It is a lovely infant," I agreed, "but if it's mine, it is not
a child."

She looked at me in sudden alarm. "Why is that so, Jack?"

"To qualify as a member of my species, the child must
be the product of a seven-month pregnancy at a minimum,
eleven at a maximum. You fell short of qualifying by three
days. Legally, my marriage to you is annulled and the
infant itself becomes *prima facie* evidence of bestiality."

"What is bestiality?"

"It is a legal charge, punishable by not less than six
months' confinement and not more than two years, brought
against one who copulates with a lower order of animal."

"Then I will take my punishment gladly, for your
sake, Jack my Beloved, if I can keep the child with me in
jail."

Her wide-eyed innocence and charm of naïveté deceived
me no longer. "Such charges cannot be brought on the basis
of present evidence, for the child is not of my issue, wanton," I said.

At that she sat up, her eyes flashing. "How can you say
such a thing, my bandy-legged husband? I have loved no
one but you. When I reached the age of lik flik. there
were no boys at the hatchery fit for spawning. You were
my first teacher and my only love, for you were a watcher
and I am a watcher. These toes have never touched a Harlechian. And don't call me wanton, squinty-eyed Jack, or I'll
hug you like you've never been hugged before."

Her fury and genuine indignation carried the force of belief if not of truth, but I rallied to the facts. "That red hair, that cleft chin, are those of Red O'Hara, not mine."

"If this child is Red the Teacher's," she said, "then it is a nine-month baby and it is an accident."

"Such things don't happen by accident," I said curtly. "Either you do or you don't."

"I didn't," she screamed, flinging herself face-down on the pillow and sobbing and pounding her fists into the mattress. To guard the child from harm, I lifted it from the bed and held it in my arms. Even though its mother was a liar and a wanton, the infant in my arms was indeed beautiful.

Cradling the baby, I rocked it slowly back and forth, singing down to it:

> Bye, baby bunting,
> Daddy's gone a-hunting
> To get a freckled Irish skin
> To wrap his baby bunting in.

As I crooned, the little girl opened her jade-green eyes and smiled at me, an Earth smile, warm and radiant, and her tiny feet reached up and patted my face. Her touch captured my heart as her mother's touch had done. I cooed to her and she gurgled back. Not yet a day old, she had conned me into loving her—and why not? Except for her hair and dimpled chin, this child was Cara's, whom I had taken for better or worse. Now I would take the baby and rear it in my own image and never a word of Gaelic would sully those tiny lips.

When I finally tore my eyes away and looked up, Cara had propped herself on an elbow and was looking at me with pleasure and amazement. "You are cooing to my child better than you did to Kiki's."

"Our child, Cara. What matters the sperm in contrast to such ova? By the laws of God and man, you're my wife, and I claim this girl as my own despite the intransigence of its mother."

"Your eyes sing to me, Jack."

"Yours are singing, too," I said.

"They would sing louder if you would tell me what 'intransigence' means."

"In this instance," I said, "it means a premarital inability to control desire."

"But I never knew desire until I found you," she insisted.

"Cara," I said, "I wouldn't let Red marry my sister, but I can't believe he's a rapist. This child is his issue."

"Then it's a false issue," Cara snapped. "Red the Adulterer has no claim on our baby and I deny him. You are my beloved. With Red I did not even grow rigid."

"Then you admit to the liaison?"

"I can't admit to the liaison because I don't know what a liaison is, but if it means that I participated in a class experiment conducted by a teacher, then I'll admit it."

"What form of experiment?"

"During my first semester," she explained, "I studied Love, Courtship and Marriage on Earth. Red asked for volunteers to demonstrate the marriage part of the course." Suddenly her eyes glowed with memory. "You know me, Jack. I love play-acting. Red chose me because he said a blonde could stay limp, and Red the Producer said that I was very natural in the role, just like an Earth blonde."

Fury gripped me at her words. O'Hara, despoiler of the innocent, had seduced a virgin for a classroom experiment. The beast must die and I would authorize myself as his executioner. Bubo's next message on the bulletin board would be a warning to all future philanderers on Harlech:

This day, Red the Adulterer was executed by Jack the Avenger as morally noxious to the climate of Heaven.

"You felt no ardor at all, Cara?"

"I have felt more from a doctor with a gynescope. . . . But I will say this for Red the Producer, he puts a little touch of realism in all that he does." She gazed down on the child in confirmation. "But the baby isn't blue-eyed."

"Our next will be blue-eyed," I promised her.

"Won't it be lovely, Jack? A red-haired girl and a blue-eyed boy!" Suddenly her eyes clouded over. "But you will not be beside me when our son is born, for you are returning soon to Earth."

"No, Cara," I said flatly. "I'm staying on Harlech."

"You will let Red return without you?"

"No, dearest. If Red returns without me, soon your planet would be overrun by Earth warriors seeking me as a defector, and the warriors are conditioned to kill all who do not wear their uniform."

"How could they find you here?"

"By retracing Red's course on the ship's flight recorder."

"Then demolish the ship."

"I can't. It's self-guarded against lasers or any explosive known on Harlech."

"You must not destroy Red the Teacher. You would be hanged because it is not lawful."

"There's an unwritten law on Earth that says a man can kill another for seducing his wife."

"But I was not your wife when Red conducted the experiment. It happened two months before we were married. Why can't you return with Red and come back as you planned?"

I fidgeted, partly from my anxiety to be out hunting and partly from embarrassment. Stalker's fever is a mental ailment. I could not bring my wife to face the fact that she had married a lunatic. "Then I would come only as a conqueror, my dear, under the direction of a Proconsul from Imperial Earth. It is better that one man die than that your people become the slave workers of the Interplanetary Colonial Administration."

It was out! The name of the I.C.A. had been given to an alien, but it no longer mattered, for I, too, was an alien. With my words, I cast my lot with Harlech.

Cara sensed my gravity, for her voice was suddenly very gentle. "What is the Interplanetary Colonial Administration, Jack?"

"The investment department of Earth General Insurance Company," I blurted, "which owns all the assets on the planet. Once there were many nations on Earth, and wars between them threatened the company's profits. So the company began to assume the costs of governments, for a monopoly of the insurance business, and discontinued taxes for a slight increase in premiums."

Swiftly I explained to her how the amalgamation of Earth governments brought peace to the planet. "But the company still had the problem of expanding its investments," I told her, "so the company branched out into the space field. My country's old C.I.A. was elevated to cabinet status and put in charge of extraplanetary investments as the I.C.A. Red and I are officers in the United Space Navy, which is a department under the I.C.A."

Then I explained to her the function of the I.C.A. to acquire and exploit new planets. As she listened, the old lack of expression settled over her face. "You would have turned a planet of scholars into laborers."

"For you, I would have turned the angels of Heaven into demons in Hell. . . . But it's not that bad. As a civilized planet, nonwarlike, your people would have been given reduced insurance rates."

"That is an honor not entirely without dilution," she said. "As much as I love you, I would not sacrifice your planet to scholarship. Could Harlech not qualify for the Brotherhood of Worlds?"

"No," I said, "because you have no military defenses. Earth would have to place you under a mandate and spend large sums to protect you from marauders."

She thought for a moment, then asked, "And from where would these marauders come?"

With the clarity of revealed knowledge the answer came simultaneously to my heart and lips. "From Earth," I answered.

She smiled weakly, reached over and took my hand. "Be with me, always, Jack, but don't assassinate Red until you have talked to me later. Right now, let me sleep. I have had a difficult birth and I am tired."

"Bubo's messenger told me the birth was easy."

"It was not the baby, but the baby's fathers."

Her eyes were drooping, and I kissed her forehead and left.

Her last request only steeled my resolution. Always on Earth, I knew, the donors in artificial insemination were kept secret from the mother from fear she might fall in love with her child's father. But Red O'Hara would never claim a piece of this action. My temperature was soaring with his terminal ailment.

Stalker's fever is not unpleasant for the feverish. I thrilled with the ardor of rage as I strode toward the subway station, my muscles loose and springy, my senses alert. I was a high-school boy again, heading for the tennis courts and singles with the prettiest girl in class. Once on the train for the soccer field, my sense of well-being animated the faces of the adults aboard. When I walked to the surface, sniffing air moist from evaporating snow and checking the sky to find it clear, I broke into a dog trot toward the ship, and the activity brought elation.

At last Red had presented me with the gift I most desired, moral justification for his murder. Our lives had been building to this climax from the moment he conned me out of the lower bunk at Mandan. Tension had stepped up a

notch when he ran out on me in my fight with the M.P.s.
Then the fish-eater had desecrated Brother Ben's temple
with his Gaelic jabber, and only he was capable of rewriting
the Commandments, putting whores in Bethlehem and setting a harlot dancing at the Last Supper.

Sacrifice and blood atonement!

Now the dam was broken, Selah, and my soul would be
cleansed in the waters of the flood. Carnality had been his
tragic flaw. His permissiveness had permitted my rape by
Tamar in the cloakroom, and now he had fathered my
child. Until this Antichrist from Meath was consumed by
the Conquering Lion of Alabama, the lion could not lie
down with his lambs at peace in their folds of Heaven.

In my exultation, I was almost nipped by a rolling barrage of lightning as I skipped up the ramp of the space
ship and clambered up the ladder to the armory on the
fourth deck. There I collected all the weapons aboard, two
rifles and two pistols, and tossed them into a duffelbag.
Then I set the ship's security system for a lethal purge to
be activated by remote control on the alarm transponder in
the buckle of a belt I strapped around my tunic. To prevent
the slaughter of an innocent, I set the lethal purge to respond to a body temperature of 98.6 and the color red.

When I reached the ramp again, the lightning was gone,
the sky was a milk-hued blue and the passing storm had left
a tracery of wet snow clinging to the tree limbs that gave
a Christmas-card sparkle to the woodland. Waddling
through the snow with my bag over my back, I felt so much
like Santa Claus I broke into a Christmas carol:

> Jingle bell, jingle bell,
>   Jingle, jingle bell.
> Oh, what fun it is to gun
>   O'Hara plumb to Hell.

Madman? Perhaps. But never had I known such joy.
Only one small regret marred my happiness: I wished
O'Hara could be with me to share my merriment over his
coming demise.

CHAPTER
FOURTEEN

Back in my quarters, I put the weapons in my wall safe—with the exception of a pistol I tucked in my jockstrap—and walked across the tunnel to Red's quarters. He was out, as I expected, but he had left me a note with his secretary. I took it, settled myself on his sofa and read:

Dear Jack,

By the time you read this, I'll be far away. Mind you, I'm not running. I want to give your forgiveness time to take root and grow, for nothing must happen between us that only one of us will live to regret.

Cara is blameless. Her face bothered me at the time you introduced us, but I could not place her in my memory. Sight of the babe recalled her to me and I can assure you there is naught between us. Cara loves you and thinks you're the child's father. Let her continue to think so. My own relation with her was clinical, and, if I recall correctly, extremely one-sided.

Truly I hope when the storm has passed we can return to Earth next summer as friends and leave this planet to peace. But now I cannot risk the length of a peacepipe between us.

As ever,
Red

P.S.: You would have starred as J.C. May you find in your heart the strength to continue the Passion Play. It will be forever. You and I will pass away.

I folded the note, placed it in my tunic and rose. Speaking to his secretary, I said casually, "I would like to leave a message for Jack if he calls in. Tell him that he suffers a misconception. My grandfather was red-haired."

From Red's office, I went to Bubo's. The black-uniformed

centurion at the gate snapped to attention when I strolled up. I braced the boy: "Draw in that stomach, soldier!"

He drew in his stomach.

"You're a sloppy excuse for a praetorian guard," I snapped. "Let's see your drill maneuvers. Right-face! More snap into it, soldier! Forward, march!"

He marched off. Walking behind him a short ways, I yelled, "In cadence, count step!"

"Hut-two, hut-two," he chanted. As his voice dwindled down the tunnel, I turned back and entered the work area, heading for Bubo's office. Bubo's student manager rose to bar my way. "Jack the Teacher, it is forbidden to enter the Dean's office without permission."

"Son," I said, "I'm here as representative of Imperial Earth. Your rules don't apply."

Like a boxer, I kept my eyes on his feet as I shouldered past him and kicked open the door of the Dean. Inside, Bubo sat at a desk scribbling on a piece of paper. Hastily he slid it into his desk drawer as I entered, but not before I saw he was playing tic-tac-toe with himself. Without the star on his tunic, he could have been another teacher, so similar was his office to mine, and there was a nonauthoritarion whine in his voice as he spoke: "You're not supposed to walk in like that! You're wrecking the mystique. Where's my centurion?"

"You can stow the mystique," I barked. "And by now your guard's past the subway station. . . . Bubo, I'm ordering you to send out an all-points bulletin to every campus and work station on the planet denying access to all refectories to one red-haired, squinty-eyed, bandy-legged Earthman."

"Red the Teacher?"

"Who else? I want him apprehended and brought back to University 36, to face trial, before me, his commanding officer, for violation of Navy Regulations."

"Will you hang him?" There was avidity in Bubo's eyes and voice.

"Hanging's too good for the bastard," I said. Then I made the legal blooper of the century. "I want to nail him to a cross."

"By all means, Jack the Teacher. The bulletin will be sent at once."

The bulletin was sent at once. By the time I reached the police station, Frick, his sergeant and two policemen were standing at the teletype machine. "Commissioner, this APB will shake the planet. Red's an international figure."

"Which makes it all the more easy to pick him up," I said. "Get your off-duty men on duty. Prepare search and seizure warrants and cover every nook and cranny on this campus. Pay particular attention to the girls' dormitories and washrooms. But don't send any uniformed officer into Cara's room at the infirmary. Put a policewoman into a nurse's uniform and station her in the room."

"We'll find him, Commissioner."

"Remember, he's not armed but he's dangerous. He fights with his fists and not his feet, and he's clever."

"I'll put a stake-out on Reno's quarters," Frick said. "He might try to contact his own brasshats."

"Good," I said. "Once he's apprehended, jail him and call me."

"Jack, my dragnet will have him by morning. Once the station is covered, his only escape will be by space ship."

"He'll not try the space ship," I told Frick.

"We'll get him," Frick said, "and this will be the trial of the century."

Frick was a student. As his teacher, I couldn't bring myself to dull the edge of his enthusiasm by telling him there would be no trial for Red O'Hara.

From the police station, I went to the registrar's office and canceled Red's classes. Since the Passion Play was not on the curriculum, I could not cancel it, nor would I have, but I withdrew from any personal participation in the O'Hara production by a definitive act—after supper with Cara at the infirmary, I went home and shaved.

Cara came home in the morning, bringing baby Janet, and there was genuine happiness again in my quarters. Janet lighted us with her beauty and charmed us with her coos and gurgles. After all, a baby is a baby, and this mite was not responsible for her male progenitor. By the time she understood such matters Red O'Hara would have long been only a memory on Harlech.

But Frick had not found Red by morning.

He reported to me at noon. "Commissioner, the suspect must have left town the first hour. But we've got the APB out on him and he's too conspicuous to stay hidden for long."

"It might be a good idea to put a stake-out on Kiki," I suggested.

He seemed aggrieved. "Jack, I've had a stake-out on Kiki since the hunt began, and Tamar and . . ." He rattled off the names of twelve females, all holders of the Order of Saint George.

I complimented Frick on his efficiency.

Later that afternoon, Red's student assistant director for the Passion Play called me. "Jack the Teacher, Red the Teacher is absent and you're absent. I can carry on rehearsals without Red but I need you."

"You'll have to carry on without both of us," I told him. "Red will not be returning, and I have a high fever that will continue for a long time. I suggest you get a replacement for me. Reno has the gravity of appearance that would fit him for the role."

Even in my hectic flush, I realized that long-range goals were more important now than ever. Red's death would commit me to Harlech, even had I not come to my own decision in the matter, and atheism would remain to be purged from the planet. Besides, with Reno occupied, there would be less danger of a military junta seizing the reins of student government, which I wanted securely in the hands of Frick.

Red disappeared, swallowed by the immense tunnel complex of the planet. I was amazed. Frick was confused and embarrassed. He had tails on everyone who was even remotely friendly toward Red, and by the end of the first week, he had tails on the tails. The edict had gone forth from Dean Bubo not to feed Red. His face was known on the planet, and his figure would have drawn attention a mile down-tunnel, yet he was never reported.

Frick finally decided that Red had fled to the surface and had been killed by a fire storm. Logically this was the only deduction we could make. I was on the point of accepting the hypothesis when I received a letter through the air tube, ten days after Red's disappearance.

> I know that neither of your grandfathers were red-haired because your mother showed me the family album.

In the manner of Harlech, the letter bore no postmark. It might have come from any continent, or next door, and it showed me only that Red was alive and had been in contact with his secretary.

I read in the letter a base attempt to reaffirm the ties of our common origin, Earth, and to use my own mother in a play for sympathy. My fever went up a degree. I patted the pistol in my jock holster and bided my time.

At home, Red was no longer mentioned. Cara had Janet and her books, and I had my class lectures and my sermons. Twice I even dropped by rehearsals at the gym to give Reno a few pointers on how to project spiritual serenity. The stage manager, I found, had devised a system of wires strung from the standards of the centurions to assist Reno in carrying the cross to the summit of the soccer knob.

Often during that period, I would awaken in the early hours restless with the fever and slip from Cara's side. I would go to the wall safe, take out the laser rifle, and stalk the tunnels of the sleeping campus in search of bandy-legged prey. The cold metal barrel of the rifle abated my fever and I grew to love the sensuality in the curve of its stock. Pistols are for women. A rifle is a man's best friend.

Consciously I knew there was only a remote chance that I would spot Red, although it was the ideal time for him to scavenge food from garbage pails or the lockless refectories. But the activity gave vent to my urge to stalk and kept my fever at a killing pitch. I continued the drill until I blasted a hole in the solarium window one night when I fired on my own reflection.

If Cara knew of my nocturnal sorties, she kept the knowledge to herself. Good wife that she was, she restricted herself to domestic matters, which engrossed her more since the arrival of Janet. She had the baby and I had Red, and we were very happy. Even my ministry was doing well. My impassioned sermon at Nesser's funeral had counteracted the effects of Bubo's snide bulletin, and Reno had assigned centurions as lay ministers to spread the Word to other campuses. Frequently, my own Eighth-day sermons in the chapel were conducted by lay preachers since I was pre-occupied with temporal affairs.

Meanwhile, the time of the Passion Play drew nearer. Harlech tilted toward the equinox. Snow melted from the surface. The stage manager had completed his flats, the final dress rehearsal was conducted successfully and the area atop the knob was littered with plastic skulls. A planet which had thrilled to the Nativity Play now waited the climactic

drama with the same avidity that children of Earth might
have awaited another serial in "The Green Archer" or "The
Perils of Pauline."

By a happy accident, which I felt was not entirely coin-
cidental, the day of the vernal equinox fell on the Sixth
day, the Harlechian equivalent of Good Friday, in the
period between academic quarters. Cara, Janet and I decided on a family outing in the solarium, taking a portable
TV set with us. I would not allow my family on the surface,
but from our vantage point, only a quarter of a mile from
the knob, we would be able to view the final Crucifixion
scene live from the balcony.

Little Janet was hopping by then and she was delighted
more by the blue skies and the distant prospect of the sea
than she was by the television tube. Since the play was
scheduled for late afternoon to give the dramatic effect of
shadows in the last act, Janet grew tired and was asleep in
her mother's arms halfway through the play.

In all honesty it was a stirring drama. Draki gave just the
right touch of villainy to his portrait of Judas. Once out
from under the influence of Red, his sidelong leers were
diminished and instead of twirling his mustache he stroked
his beard nervously. Kiki was divine as Mary. Strangely,
Tamar's shimmy at the beginning of the Last Supper seemed
to accentuate rather than diminish the solemnity of the
scene, although Cara snorted at what she considered inept
dancing. Reno stuck to the script, as written in red ink, and
there was only one false note in the entire underground
version of the drama. When Pilate delivered Jesus to the
rabble, the centurions guarding Him wore the black helmets
of Bubo's praetorian guards, whereas the arresting soldiers
had been Reno's cadets.

It was a minor error. I had seen worse in movies on
Earth, but such technicalities disturb my sense of proportion. Conceivably it had been planned by Red as a sop to
the Dean's vanity. As I recalled there had been no praetorian guard in the dress rehearsal.

Suddenly I remembered Red's remark that the Dean's
soldiers took orders only from the Dean. Red, with his
sense of realism, would not have permitted black uniforms
to mix with the cadets' green. The only way that Bubo's
praetorians could have gotten into the act would be through
Bubo's orders, and Bubo was not that interested in dramatics.

I was mulling over the problem as the audience transferred from the underground auditorium to surface bleachers near the knob. To maintain continuity for the television viewers, Draki had written in a scene between Barabbas and the warders when Barabbas learns that he is to be freed on the day that Christ is executed. It was a vignette scene, but it had pathos, and I was intent on it when the camera shifted to the Pharisaic rabble on the surface and I turned my gaze to the live portion visible from the observatory.

Cara and I decided to take the sleeping child and walk out on the open balcony better to view the scene.

Outside, the weather was holding beautifully. Not a cloud marred the late afternoon sky and the temperature was in a comfortable high sixties. In a peculiar way, I had faith that the weather would hold for the fifteen minutes demanded by the final scene when the sky darkened and the rabble fled in terror from Calvary.

By now, on the surface beneath us, the rabble, held back by centurions, were lining the way of the cross and the cross itself was bobbing along through the mob, held aloft by the red-bearded Reno, aided by the wires suspended from the standards of the soldiers escorting him.

Then the cowled figure of Christ emerged from the throng, staggering realistically under his burden. Once he fell and a form of paralysis struck my heart, causing me to gasp. When Christ fell and rose again, the standards of the praetorians did not dip under the weight of the cross.

The cowled figure climbing the hill was carrying the cross unassisted, and there were only two men on this planet who could carry that massive weight. I was the other one.

Now I understood the meaning of the praetorian guard. They were there under orders from Bubo, orders they would obey explicitly, and I had advised the Dean that Red should be nailed to the cross.

Red O'Hara was going to be crucified, and my fever had vanished in my great loneliness for the sight of another human face.

"Cara, that's Red out there doped with lemming DNA. Bubo's going to kill him if I don't get to him first!"

I turned and raced for the down ramp, cursing myself for not obeying my hunches. It was a mile underground to the top of the knob. They would have driven the nails by the time I arrived, and the praetorians had, no doubt, been instructed to form a hollow square to fend me off. But the praetorians did not know of my laser pistol.

The weapon I had planned to use on Red would be used in his defense. I would have to face murder charges, but my comrade would be saved. And if I chose to play out the game according to my own rules, I would have the best defense lawyer on Harlech in my corner.

I ran, cursing the literal minds of Harlech, but even as I cursed the grim irony of the situation struck me. Red had wanted realism in this scene. He would get it in a way he had never planned. The very praetorian guard he had appointed to Bubo, operating under the discipline Red had imposed, would drive the nails into Red's own hands.

No wonder I had not found Red. He had been held within the sacrosanct chambers of the Dean, fed, watered and given strong doses of Cara's "powder of docility" to prepare him for this ritual sacrifice. No one had thought of searching those chambers, for they were taboo to the minds of Harlechians.

Never had the tunnels of Harlech seemed so long. After an eternity of lung-searing effort, I reached the now-empty soccer gym and raced its length toward the long up-ramp above the playing field. Before I reached the ramp, an alluvial flood of Harlechians, mouth-breathing in their panic, poured from the entrance to the ramp. It was a ghastly river pouring down that ramp impelled by ancestral terror—a fire storm was threatening the surface.

Lowering my shoulders, I plowed into them, splitting the incoming tide with the force of my charge, flinging the light-bodied beings to right and to left and straight up. "Fire storm!" they screamed, but I was heedless.

The sheer weight of their numbers slowed me until their acute perception marked my progress and they began to leap over me. Then I moved faster under the arch of whizzing bodies that lifted for my passage.

My canopy thinned and changed character. Shorts and panties of the fast-running students gave way to the crotches of older citizens, the flying robes of the costumed players and, finally, the black jockstraps of the praetorians, fleeing without the weapons they had dropped.

"Cowards," I screamed at Bubo's passing and overleaping guardsmen, "you have abandoned your arms."

But they ran shameless in their panic, and I remembered

their spears were tipped with metal, and that metal drew lightning.

Suddenly the burrow was empty of all save me. Ahead another fifty yards the exit framed the garish flickerings from the lightning. Remembering the praetorians, I slowed slightly to tug the metal pistol from its holster and fling it aside as I stumbled on toward the exit. Still running, I unhooked my activator belt and threw its metal buckle aside.

I am an Earthman, bravest of God's thinking creatures, and I had no eons of terror conditioning me against lightning, but let me assure you, Doctor, it took an act of will to hurl myself from that tunnel into the sizzling light of the storm. But when I stumbled from the cavern's mouth, into the ankle-deep mud from the rain, I found I was plunging at the tail-end of a southbound express train. The line of lightning had passed.

Slithering, staggering, breathing prayers and ozone, I turned in the darkness toward the knob. As I stumbled up the beginning slope, the blackness grew opaque as the jet stream swept the clouds into tatters. Slowly, the aura of sunset returned to the scene, the lightning flicked and died to the southwest. Now in the growing light from the sun, I lifted my eyes to Calvary. The cross was gone from the hilltop.

I knew what had happened. The crucifix had been built from seasoned timber, and its dry wood had been veined with ferrous oxide. Red had been nailed to a lightning rod, crucified and cremated. All that remained of O'Hara and his cross would be a pile of ashes sunk to the bottom of a waterlogged posthole.

I continued my progress toward the crest with the mud squishing between my toes. There was one honor left for me to accord my comrade—I would give the lad a Christian burial.

As I reached the brow of the hill, the cloud mass rolled beneath the western horizon, and the sun, balanced now on the distant line of the sea, cast parallel rays over the summit. By its light I found the posthole. On either side of it glinted two huge nails, rain-cleansed of his blood, which had pierced O'Hara's hands. Before the hole lay Red's rosary.

In the curl of my toes, I lifted the nails and dropped them into the hole with its broth of ashes, and with the side of my foot I shoved the mound of dirt from the excava-

tion on top of Red's remains and tamped firm the burial
mound with my heel and shaped with my instep. Then I
lifted the rosary with my big toe and coiled it atop the
mound.

"*Ecce homo*," I said.

Here was a man somewhat higher than the angels and,
yes, the father of my child, whose soul and mine were
linked forever, not by a Mandan computer but by a deeper
brotherhood—of shared joys, shared perils, shared dreams
and shared loves. So noble a friend done in by so foul a deed!

Anguish wrenched words from me and I cried aloud,
"Mary, Mother of God, be with him now in the hour of his
death. Amen."

Then I made the sign of the cross over his grave. A good
old Methodist had preached a Catholic's funeral.

I turned and walked from the crest, out of the sunlight
into the shadow of Red's Calvary, and the shadow lay as a
pall around me. A few yards down, the ball of my foot
struck a plastic skull, which had washed downhill and im-
bedded itself in the mud. Looking down on the grin of
that death's head, I gazed on the face of Truth: Through
the arc of space I had come with Red but a little way on
his temporal journey. Now O'Hara had made full the in-
finite circle, closing it at the beginnings of our spirit, at a
Place of Plastic Skulls, the technological Golgotha.

Unknowingly, I had whored with a god in the Mandan
houses of lust, fought against that god in the drunk tank of
Mandan jail; I had stalked the Lord's anointed through the
tunnels of Harlech and, unwittingly, I had been used by the
ultimate Judas as an instrument of Saint O'Hara's betrayal.
My sins were grievous, but I was not done with sinning.

Judas would never spend his silver. Walking into the
tunnel, I swore by Imperial Earth that Bubo the Dean
would die.

On my way home, I stopped by the tavern and ordered a
boilermaker to do homage in a ritual an Irishman would
appreciate and to steady my shaken nerves. For once the
place was crowded, but I would let no one take the stool
where Red sat when we had planned the overthrow of
Bubo. I was on my fourth drink when the television screen
lighted and the news came on. Drawn-faced, the student
announcer spoke of Red's death, paying a tender tribute to
"this far-wanderer who came to us from a remote galaxy
and a planet he called Earth, bringing us the art of drama

and giving us the gift of laughter. But there is something of a mystery shrouding his death. Reno, Cadet General of Centurions, has promised an investigation. Even the short legs of Red the Teacher should have borne him to the safety of the burrow. Just a minute—we pause now for a special bulletin from the office of Bubo the Dean. . . ."

There was a moment of silence as the face of the announcer faded from the screen and was replaced by a printed form that announced:

> On the advice of my legal advisor, Jack the Teacher, this day Red the Teacher was nailed to the cross atop the soccer knob for the Earth crime of adultery.
>
> *Bubo the Dean*

Again the announcer appeared. and for a moment he looked shaken. "Adultery, Harlechians, is a moment's dalliance with someone else's steady, no more reprehensible than sharing a cup with a friend. For that crime, a light was extinguished which lit all Harlech."

"I'll drink to that, Mac," I told the bartender.

"You've had your limit at this bar, Jack," he said.

I looked around me and saw, for the first time, the stare of Harlechians. The eyes were huge, expressionless—and below the eyes were mouths opening and closing on the silent "*ma-ma-ma*" by which they expressed strong passion. I felt like a lone specimen in a bowl of air surrounded by an aquarium of fish, and I rose and walked out, not in fear but in embarrassment.

So it was no longer "us" against "them." It was "them" against "me." Only Cara, on the whole of Harlech, knew I was innocent, and Cara could not guard me against such hostility. I had one last errand to accomplish and I was leaving Harlech forever, but first I must say good-bye to my wife and child.

Before I entered my office, I heard the sibilance of prayer arising from the chapel, and when I opened the door the area was filled with worshipers. My Good Friday sermon had been taken over by a lay preacher, Bardo the Lawyer, who was finishing a prayer for the dead. Standing behind the kneeling worshipers, I heard him finish: "And we ask this blessing in the name of Red. There is no Lord but the Lord of Moses and Red was His prophet."

"Wait, Bardo," I cried. "Red was not a prophet. Jesus Christ was the Prophet."

"By law," Bardo answered, "we cannot accept hearsay evidence, and we all know that Red died on the cross and he spoke only of Moses. So we are of the Hebrew faith. . . . But go, Jack. Your Cara awaits."

My brain spinning, I entered my office. There was more to be done on Harlech now than kill a Judas. Slick lawyers were using the rules of evidence on my Scriptures, and jurisprudence was converting my Christianity to Judaism. I had to get the Word straight before I left Harlech, and my time was short. It was one Holy mess!

In my heart I knew what had to be done, but how? I was willing to grant O'Hara sainthood, but I could not grant him co-equality with the Holy Trinity, particularly now that these pagans had pared the Trio to a Duo.

Bubo had destroyed Red's body through my inadvertency. Now Red's spirit must be destroyed on Harlech. I alone would bear the responsibility for that second death, but Cara would have to become the instrument of my purpose.

Cara awaited me behind the closed door of the library, pacing the floor in her anxiety. In fact, she had removed Janet's crib to the bedroom to increase her pacing room. She wheeled to face me when I entered.

"So, Judas, you are back!"

"Judas? You know I tried to save Red."

"You rushed to get him before Bubo's men could get him."

"I rushed to get him *from* Bubo's men," I protested, alarmed by the slow opening and closing of her mouth as she gulped oxygen. "Red's blood is on Bubo's hands, not mine."

"You authorized the administrative decision."

"For that I'm no more responsible than Red, who trained the praetorians to obey and put them under Bubo's command. Believe me, darling—"

"Believe you, you pious fraud! By your acts you are known, and your acts led to his death."

None of my sermons had summoned such passion as that which contorted the face of my wife. She was crouched and leaning forward like an animal ready to pounce, her mouth scooping oxygen to feed her wildly beating heart. And this force had been summoned by the memory of a man who was essentially a confidence man who had been tricked by a

slicker operator than he, and who had been, in fact, an
adulterer. It was imperative that I execute Red's spirit on
the spot.

"Darling Cara," I said, "surely you do not kneel at the
feet of a conniver, an adulterer—"

"Who are you to call Red names, you sermonizing hypo-
crite, cloakroom conniver, breast-bouncing philanderer,
adulterer! I have the report on you and that hip-twitching
Tamar here," she said, tapping a document on my desk.

So it was not spirituality that had triggered her passion
but a misconception gained from a report that had been
officially quashed.

"Darling," I said, "I was taken against my will."

"Liar," she hissed. "Now you're breaking Red's Commandments right and left, and he died for breaking one.
So you die, cuckold!"

I had lowered my hands, palms outward, in expostulation,
when she leaped, whipping her legs around me and pinning
my arms to my sides. Her legs, the handles of the chalice of
my only true love, were crushing me now in a python's
coils as her once-lovely voice shrieked, "Try fondling my
breasts, you scum of Earth, you beast from a planet of
apes."

Slowly her thighs were constricting me. I could feel my
elbows dig into my ribcage. My legs were growing numb
from the tourniquet she was applying to my main aorta.
Soon my arms would be welded to my body.

But she reckoned not with the lethal ingenuity of my
species. "Unleg me, Lilith," I gasped, "or I will make an
orphan of Red's child."

"Liar again," she hissed. "Now there are two of us on
Harlech who know you are helpless in the legs of a woman."

Behind her was my desk. I stepped forward a pace, bent
quickly and rapped her head against the edge of the desk
with a quick, dipping butt of my head. "Unleg me now," I
said, "or on the next tap you die."

In one last spasm of anger, she broke my lower ribs, but
she unlegged me and fell crumpled against the desk. "Get
out," she said. "Quit desecrating the house of Red."

"I'm going," I told her, "but before I leave this planet,
I'm setting two records straight, and the first is for you
alone."

I walked over to the phone, lifted it and dialed Frick's

number, 1313. A sergeant answered. "Let me speak to Frick
the Police Captain," I said.

"Frick the Snooper has been relieved of duty," the voice
answered, "and assigned to Pottery Station 21, South
Continent, by order of General Reno."

"Who's speaking?"

"Beck," the voice answered. "First Centurion, Third Phalanx, Laser Battery 8, Harlechian Planetary Defense Artil-
lery."

Stunned, I hung up, knowing there was one record, mine,
that would never be set straight. In the space of two hours,
there had been a military coup, Frick ousted and a cadre
established for a planetary-defense force. While I had fid-
dled with misdemeanors, Red had burned Earth General's
investment department with a felony. He had taught these
pagans military science in his gym classes.

Without a downward glance at Cara, I turned and staggered out. My legs were lead and my heart was ice as I
stumbled through my chapel, their synagogue now, empty
of all save the icon of Jesus hanging beyond my still-lighted
altar. I cast one farewell look around and found they had
painted the beard on the icon red.

Rebuked, scorned and rejected!

Lost forever, my girl with the jade-green eyes. Strayed,
my lambs to the pipings of a wayward shepherd. Before me
the tunnel pinpointed infinity while the walls compressed
me into a clanging echo chamber of despair. Now I knew
what must be done, and how, and only the righteousness
of my purpose sustained me after the shock of Cara's last
embrace.

Strangely, there was no sentry present outside Bubo's
office. Perhaps after this day's work, he had given them a
rest, or perhaps he had released them permanently in the
knowledge that they would never be needed again. In one
way or the other, Bubo was right, and as a precaution I
reached for my laser. My jockstrap was empty. In my grief,
I had forgotten to retrieve both pistol and belt at the
tunnel's mouth. But no matter. I could choke the beast after
he had served my purpose.

Bubo was not in his inner office, so I shoved open the door
and entered his library. He sat on a high stool at a work-
bench in a library without books. Around the walls were
shelves with brooms, mops, oil cans, wrenches, screwdriv-
ers and wiping rags. In the center of the room was a tran-

sistorized computer attached to a console. He wore a greasy pair of coveralls and was playing solitaire with a deck of Earth cards.

Bubo the Janitor merely looked up from his cards when I entered. "You Earthmen keep kicking my mystique around. Don't you know when it's time to quit?"

"One of us learned the hard way," I said, glancing over his shoulder. A nine of diamonds lay below a ten of hearts. "You made good use of Red while you had him," I added. "You even learned to cheat at solitaire."

"With me it's not cheating," he said. "As the Chief of Administration, I merely change policy to meet new situations."

"As chief maintenance man, you mean, for a self-maintaining computer, which makes you as useless as . . ." I struggled for the words to express my contempt.

"Teats on a boar," Bubo said, "which is the end-result in the evolution of an administrator."

"I haven't evolved that far," I said. "I still do a little typing." Keeping my eyes on his indifferent back, I eased onto the stool before the console.

"You aren't supposed to touch those keys," he said. "That's taboo."

"Dead men don't fear taboos," I said. "I'm sending a message on that machine, with your image, saying that Red and I were military scouts carrying out an Intelligence and Reconnaissance Patrol on Harlech for the military forces of Imperial Earth."

"You'll destroy Red's mystique," he said. "I hear the students are building him up into something of a demigod. But the centurions will kill you in obedience to the First Commandment. They couldn't let you leave here with what you know. . . . I don't follow your logic."

"That is the logic. They'll know by my death that I spoke the truth."

"You're making it easier for me," he said, reshuffling the cards. "You Earthmen are no challenge."

Then I knew I had been manipulated to this point by the man who had destroyed O'Hara. No doubt he had fed my profile to this very machine and plotted my moves in advance. Only one point disturbed me as I bent to the keyboard: How could he have known that I would leave my laser pistol in the tunnel?

Bubo was shuffling with the riffle of a riverboat gambler as I bent to the keyboard.

"Attention, all Harlech," I typed onto the compensating tape. "Be it known to all who worship at the shrine of Red the Prophet that this day I received a full and voluntary confession from Jack the Teacher, which follows: I, Jack the Teacher, did come to the planet known by its inhabitants as Harlech in the company of Red the Teacher bringing not peace but a sword. . . ."

That was the last I remember. The heel of a Harlechian who had hidden in Bubo's bedroom whipped down on the back of my skull.

CHAPTER
FIFTEEN

I awakened to a throbbing in my head of such intensity that my whole body seemed to shake. What a clout, I thought, and when I opened my eyes I was still seeing stars. I tried to raise my hand to rub my eyes and found my arms were paralyzed.

It took a full minute for me to recognize the configuration of the stars and realize they were real. When I saw the hairline of a marker creeping toward the Milky Way, I knew that my body quivered from the spinning of a gyro-stabilizer. It followed that my arms were not paralyzed but strapped to the control seat of a starship by a gravity lock.

I was about to be launched.

To confirm my impressions, I rolled my eyes downward and found an instrument panel. According to the timer, I was in the final twenty seconds of an automatic countdown. Tilting my eyes above the viewing port, I saw dangling the green leprechaun of Red O'Hara. Pinned to the leprechaun's belly was a pink slip. In the faint glow from the panel, I could decipher the message:

This day, Jack the Teacher was expelled from Harlech for violating the Dean's Sanctum.

Bubo the Dean

prayer and apologize to Red for failing him. He wouldn't have failed me. That old boy would have known when to start his retros by instinct, and he would have button-hooked the sun, not some nebula in Orion.

Red O'Hara! Now, there was a laser jockey.

As I watched the gaunt-faced man with the bloated ankles bowed in prayer, I knew he was too far gone for analytical therapy, particularly from a Platonist. Perhaps a frontal lobotomy might help, or DNA dust inhalation—about three barrels full. I felt sympathy for John Adams, but no empathy since I did not fully understand what he had done.

He said he had flipped his reference frame and I had to take his word for it. I wasn't qualified to question his mathematics. I could question his logic, but I had no desire to point out his errors in deduction, since I was sure he had flipped something.

"We sent out a space sailor and got back a blithering divine," a voice said beside me, and I turned to a colonel in the black uniform of the Harrier Corps. In the light from the decontamination chamber, the death's heads on his lapels seemed to glow with a ritual significance, as Adams would say.

"Doctor," the Colonel continued, "there's something radically wrong with the personality-testing program here when such misfits are given command of a forty-million-dollar star-ship."

"Colonel, I suggest you complain to Space Surgeon Commander Harkness. He's in charge of the Mandan program."

Adams finished his prayer, looked up and saw the Colonel. "Colonel," he blurted, "I recommend you decode my flight recorder and get a bunch of your boys to Heaven in one hell of a hurry. It'll take no time at all to convert those trylons into laser batteries."

"You're a little late, mister." The Colonel's voice almost cracked the glass. "The flight recorder was unshipped and removed from the vessel. It would take us a thousand years to relocate that planet, with or without green polka-dot drawers."

"Now, who could have done that?" Adams's mouth opened wide in an exaggerated gesture of astonishment.

"I don't know who did it, but I know who's responsible, the probe commander. Get back into your miniskirt and jockstrap, Adams. You're under arrest, for five felony and seventeen misdemeanor violations of Navy Regulations."

He slapped a riding crop against his thigh and a squad of Harriers double-quicked from an antechamber into the decontamination room.

"Thank you, Doctor," the Colonel said. "At least your debriefing was a success. The culprit will be punished."

As I watched the squad parade out at lock step with Adams in the center of their square, I knew John Adams could not be punished. He had guilt feelings as wide as the Powder River with a martyr complex to match. The more he suffered for the death of O'Hara, the happier he would be.

And the irony of it was that O'Hara, who could have been a true martyr, was not dead. There had been a crucifixion, but there had been a resurrection, probably three days later. The heel of the Harlechian that had knocked Adams senseless was more likely a shillelagh.

My certainty was not entirely from logic. There was a singing in my blood, an intuition, if you will, which was more than a hunch. I was gripped with the noncognitive awareness of truth which every psychiatrist learns to recognize, and it was telling me that O'Hara was still King Con, the king of confidence men.

Apparently the Colonel agreed with me.

"This case doesn't close with Adams," he said. "O'Hara's an Irishman. We'll have to station a picket ship in the Lynx window to keep a lookout, probably for a kelly-green ship. The wrong man came back."

Again my instincts spoke to me, telling me that if O'Hara came back, it would not be to this world. I could almost pinpoint the place and time of his return: Phoenix Park, Dublin, in 1882.

"Doctor, would you be kind enough to introduce me to your Surgeon Harkness?" the Colonel said, turning to me. "My name is Evans, Colonel Neil Ewart Evans."

Behind Evans, I could see Harkness descending from the gallery.

"Gladly, Colonel," I said as we shook hands. "My name is O'Sullivan, Doctor Michael Timothy O'Sullivan."